TEL AVIV NOIR

EDITED BY
ETGAR KERET AND ASSAF GAVRON

translated by Yardenne Greenspan

D1051248

This collection is comprised of works of fiction. All names, characters, places, and incidents are the product of the authors' imaginations. Any resemblance to real events or persons, living or dead, is entirely coincidental.

Published by Akashic Books
©2014 Akashic Books

Series concept by Tim McLoughlin and Johnny Temple
Tel Aviv map by Aaron Petrovich

Hardcover ISBN: 978-1-61775-315-2
Paperback ISBN: 978-1-61775-154-7
Library of Congress Control Number: 2014938702

Grateful acknowledgment to Israel's Office of Cultural Affairs, Consulate General of Israel in New York, for supporting the publication of *Tel Aviv Noir*.

Akashic Books
Twitter: @AkashicBooks
Facebook: AkashicBooks
E-mail: info@akashicbooks.com
Website: www.akashicbooks.com

ALSO IN THE AKASHIC NOIR SERIES

PHILADELPHIA NOIR, edited by CARLIN ROMANO
PHOENIX NOIR, edited by PATRICK MILLIKIN
PITTSBURGH NOIR, edited by KATHLEEN GEORGE
PORTLAND NOIR, edited by KEVIN SAMPSELL
PRISON NOIR, edited by JOYCE CAROL OATES
QUEENS NOIR, edited by ROBERT KNIGHTLY
RICHMOND NOIR, edited by ANDREW BLOSSOM, BRIAN CASTLEBERRY & TOM DE HAVEN
ROME NOIR (ITALY), edited by CHIARA STANGALINO & MAXIM JAKUBOWSKI
SAN DIEGO NOIR, edited by MARYELIZABETH HART
SAN FRANCISCO NOIR, edited by PETER MARAVELIS
SAN FRANCISCO NOIR 2: THE CLASSICS, edited by PETER MARAVELIS
SEATTLE NOIR, edited by CURT COLBERT
SINGAPORE NOIR, edited by CHERYL LU-LIEN TAN
STATEN ISLAND NOIR, edited by PATRICIA SMITH
ST. PETERSBURG NOIR (RUSSIA), edited by NATALIA SMIRNOVA & JULIA GOUMEN
TEHRAN NOIR (IRAN), edited by SALAR ABDOH
TORONTO NOIR (CANADA), edited by JANINE ARMIN & NATHANIEL G. MOORE
TRINIDAD NOIR (TRINIDAD & TOBAGO), edited by LISA ALLEN-AGOSTINI & JEANNE MASON
TWIN CITIES NOIR, edited by JULIE SCHAPER & STEVEN HORWITZ
USA NOIR: BEST OF THE AKASHIC NOIR SERIES, edited by JOHNNY TEMPLE
VENICE NOIR (ITALY), edited by MAXIM JAKUBOWSKI
WALL STREET NOIR, edited by PETER SPIEGELMAN

FORTHCOMING

ADDIS ABABA NOIR (ETHIOPIA), edited by MAAZA MENGISTE
BAGHDAD NOIR (IRAQ), edited by SAMUEL SHIMON
BEIRUT NOIR (LEBANON), edited by IMAN HUMAYDAN
BOGOTÁ NOIR (COLOMBIA), edited by ANDREA MONTEJO
CHICAGO NOIR 2: THE CLASSICS, edited by JOE MENO
JERUSALEM NOIR, edited by DROR MISHANI
LAGOS NOIR (NIGERIA), edited by CHRIS ABANI
MARSEILLE NOIR (FRANCE), edited by CÉDRIC FABRE
MEMPHIS NOIR, edited by LAUREEN P. CANTWELL & LEONARD GILL
MISSISSIPPI NOIR, edited by TOM FRANKLIN
MONTREAL NOIR (CANADA), edited by JOHN McFETRIDGE & JACQUES FILIPPI
NEW ORLEANS NOIR 2: THE CLASSICS, edited by JULIE SMITH
PROVIDENCE NOIR, edited by ANN HOOD
RIO NOIR (BRAZIL), edited by TONY BELLOTTO
SAN JUAN NOIR (PUERTO RICO), edited by MAYRA SANTOS-FEBRES
SEOUL NOIR (SOUTH KOREA), edited by BS PUBLISHING CO.
ST. LOUIS NOIR, edited by SCOTT PHILLIPS
STOCKHOLM NOIR (SWEDEN), edited by CARL-MICHAEL EDENBORG & NATHAN LARSON
TRINIDAD NOIR 2: THE CLASSICS, edited by EARL LOVELACE & ROBERT ANTONI
ZAGREB NOIR (CROATIA), edited by IVAN SRŠEN

TEL AVIV

HaYarkon Park

Yarkon River

Gan HaAtsmaut

Basel Street

Mediterranean Sea

TEL AVIV

Rabin Square

Beach Hotels Strip

Masarik Square

Dizengoff Center

The Opera Tower

Ben Zion Boulevard

Magen David Square

Rothschild Boulevard

Charles Clore Garden

②

Neve Sha'anan

Levinsky Park

Florentin

⑳

Tel Kabir

JAFFA

Ajami

①

TABLE OF CONTENTS

PART III: CORPSES

INTRODUCTION
THE DARK SIDE OF THE BUBBLE

When I was a kid we didn't have a car. My dad and I didn't like taking the bus, and preferred to walk. I liked the peace and quiet of walking. Dad liked being able to smoke. Sometimes, when we walked down the neighborhood's main street together, Y's car drove by. Y was one of the most famous criminals in the country in those days. He'd pull up and greet my father. He'd ask how he was and how my mother was and offer us a ride. Usually we said no, but once or twice he gave my dad a ride to a meeting on the other side of town.

One night, when I was already in high school, the evening news reported that Y had been arrested as a murder suspect. Dad, who was watching with me, lit a cigarette and shook his head. "This has to be a mistake," he said. "You know Y. How could they accuse someone so warm and kind of murder?"

Almost thirty years later I found myself sitting with Johnny Temple of Akashic Books at a coffee shop in SoHo. When he asked me to edit the anthology *Tel Aviv Noir*, I felt a little like my father in front of the television. I wanted to say, "*Tel Aviv Noir*? This has to be a mistake." Tel Aviv is one of the happiest, friendliest, most liberal cities in the world. What could possibly be dark about our sunny city, a city nicknamed "The Bubble" due to its sense of complete separation from the violent, conflicted country in which it is situated? Compared to

Jerusalem—torn apart, exploding with nationalism, xenophobia, and religious zeal—Tel Aviv has always been an island of sanity and serenity. If you don't believe me, you can ask my eight-year-old son, who walks to school by himself every day, fearlessly. Stories of crime and sleaziness taking place in my beloved city sounded about as unbelievable to me as the accusations against Y had sounded to my father.

By the way, Y is no longer with us. A bomb attached to the bottom of his car took care of that. But Tel Aviv is still around, and considering and reconsidering the question, I realize that in spite of its outwardly warm and polite exterior, Tel Aviv has quite a bit to hide. At any club, most of the people dancing around you to the sounds of a deep-house hit dedicated to peace and love have undergone extensive automatic-weapons training and a hand-grenade tutorial. This isn't a conspiracy, my friends, just one of the fringe benefits of a country that institutes mandatory military service.

The workers washing the dishes in the fluorescent-lit kitchen of that same club are Eritrean refugees who have crossed the Egyptian border illegally, along with a group of bedouins smuggling some high-quality hash, which the deejay will soon be smoking on his little podium, right by the busy dance floor filled with drunks, coked-up lawyers, and Ukrainian call girls whose pimp keeps their passports in a safe two streets away.

Don't get me wrong—Tel Aviv is a lovely, safe city. Most of the time, for most of its inhabitants. But the stories in this collection describe what happens the rest of the time, to the rest of its inhabitants. From one last cup of coffee at a café targeted by a suicide bomber, through repeat visits from a Yiddish-speaking ghost, to an organized tour of mythological crime scenes that goes terribly wrong, the stories of *Tel*

Aviv Noir, edited by Assaf Gavron and myself, reveal the concealed, scarred face of this city that we love so much.

Etgar Keret
Tel Aviv, Israel
July 2014

PART I

ENCOUNTERS

SLEEPING MASK

BY GADI TAUB

Beach Hotels Strip

It was I who came up with that name, Nicky. It seemed cool at the time. I don't know another escort named Nicky. They always either have too-Israeli names—Chen, Mor, Nofar—or names that are like neon signs saying, *Russia*. Natasha, Nastia, Ilona, Katia. But I've never heard of a Nicky before. So I said Nicky. I told her, You're not like the others. And you shouldn't charge like the others. You won't charge six hundred shekels per hour, you'll charge 1,500 per hour.

She didn't understand why I thought she'd make more money than other girls. She had almost no boobs, she wasn't blond, no hair extensions. Not a Barbie doll. She had short, brown tomboyish hair, big brown eyes. She was skinny. But she had a really pretty face. Really pretty. Those eyes. Clean. Like a model from an American magazine. Except she wasn't tall. If you saw her on the street, even dressed for work, you'd never guess. And on her days off, she dressed like she knew whatever she happened to put on would look good. There's no way she didn't know. But that's not the point. The point is, she was smart. And it's the smarts that count. In the big league, it's your mind, not your body. So I knew she'd make good money. I knew it from the get-go.

I met her at the cell phone store where I buy my girls' untraceable phones. The way it works is, you get a SIM card and a restricted number. Then you just buy minutes. I noticed her in the store. I liked her. We talked a little. She was pretty young. I thought she was an employee, but then she told me she owned the place. I wasn't sure she was telling the truth—all our conversations were half-joking. But it turned out she was. The store was hers. She laughed at me for buying so many phones. I said I was a lawyer. Maybe she also thought I was just kidding. Said only criminals bought that many anonymous phones. I told her the difference between criminal lawyers and criminals is not that great. When you work with them, you sort of work *for* them, so you're partially on the side of the law and partially on the side of crime.

So you're *half* a criminal, she said.

I told her that wasn't true either. I'd stopped working as a defense attorney. I was sick of the clients' mind games. You always had to act tough or you'd get abused. It took a lot of energy, all this honor-and-toughness shit. You couldn't call them back right away or else they sensed your weakness. You couldn't get scared when they dropped veiled threats. You couldn't accept when they offered you favors. You had to sit back, not bend forward, when they offered you a light. You had to look them in the eye when you said no. It was exhausting, being alert all the time, planning every move. So I still had the lawyer title, but I didn't work at it anymore. I became a publisher. Or half a publisher, anyway. I published one paper.

I could tell she didn't believe me, but I let it slide. Then one day I showed her my paper. It wasn't exactly a paper. It was all ads for prostitutes and call girls and transvestites and dominatrices and other sex services. But it did look like a glossy magazine—chrome paper, quality printing. It was called *Nightlife*, and you could get it for free at any kiosk or hotel or in stacks on the sidewalk here and there. Almost anyone who worked independently advertised with me.

It was a good business. I got between five hundred and two thousand shekels per ad, depending on the size. You could buy a quarter page, a half page, or a full page. I published about 120 ads in each issue, which meant 110,000 shekels a month, all with invoices and receipts, totally legal. Well, it used to be legal, anyway, until this new law was passed, forbidding the advertising of prostitution.

I thought she'd look at me funny if I showed her the paper, which is why I did it. Flirting is nice, but I like a girl to know what's what right up front, not discover it later. I wasn't thinking of dating her or anything. She's almost half my age. But even if this was just flirting, I like a girl to know. If it grossed her out, that was her problem. I wasn't hiding anything.

But she was interested. So I told her stuff. I didn't think anything would come of those conversations. I don't think she did either. She was just curious. I didn't think she'd be getting a phone and a number from me one day. It was a phone she herself had sold me a month earlier.

Her real name was Shiri. One day she walked into my office. Denim cutoffs and a tank top, her short hair the way it always looked, as if she just got out of bed. But sexy. She was upbeat and appeared fine. Or maybe she was just acting, I don't know. Her mood didn't seem in tune with what she said. She said she wanted to start working with me. It took me by surprise. What did she know about prostitution?

She said it was none of my business. She just smiled. Said she needed the money.

Okay. I told her what I always tell new girls: This is a step. She should think hard before she takes it. Once you go there, you can't take it back. And this time I actually meant it. Part of me didn't want her to get into it. A girl like her—what, let any idiot have her for six hundred shekels? On the other hand, she turned me on too. Any girl who starts advertising with me, almost any girl, unless she's especially ugly, I take her for an hour to get the ball rolling. I always pay the girl's advertised price. I don't ask for favors. If I have a good time I take her again once in a while.

I told her to charge 1,500 an hour. It was a compromise between the part of me that didn't want her to start working and the part that wanted to have her. I told her no one had advertised that kind of price with me before, but that she'd still be a hit. She thought it was funny. I told her I wasn't kidding, she'd be a star. She looked me over. I tried to just act cool and gave her my regular spiel: You pay four hundred now, you get a phone and a number and graphic design for your ad. You can choose the wording yourself, or we can do it for you. Whatever you prefer. For that price we use a stock photo. If you want a real photo of you—no face, the face is blurred—that's another three hundred. One-time payment. It helps sales, because I put in a caption guaranteeing the photo is real.

She smiled.

Once the ad is up, it's a thousand a month for half a page, five hundred for a quarter page. I don't recommend anything smaller than half a page, but if you want, you can share the half page with another girl. That's it. That's the deal. You can get back what you spend on a monthly ad in half a shift. No one splits the money with you. It's all yours. No middleman, no agency, no pimps. You're independent. Then I ended with my usual offer, except for ugly girls or transvestites: And I'm your first client. What are you doing tonight?

She smiled at me again. What if I bring my own phone? she said.

No way, I replied. The phones come through me. I smiled too.

I asked if she was free at ten p.m. I told her I'd deduct the amount she owed for the entire package—ad, photo, design, phone—from tonight's price. She didn't need to pay anything in cash. I told her I'd take two hours. Three thousand minus 1,700 was 1,300 shekels. She'd more than break even by midnight. I told her that if a girl charges six hundred shekels an hour, I can take her for three hours without hardly paying anything. And it comes out of my gross income too. Can you believe it? I told her. I can claim at least some of the sex as a business expense.

Pssshhh, she said. You have yourself a direct financing plan, huh? What about leasing? Can you lease a girl?

I laughed. Yeah, I can. Try the Chief Rabbinate, the marriage department.

She laughed too. I never took my eyes off her. She seemed to reassess me, as if she hadn't really realized who I was until that moment.

But I usually only like short-term rentals, I told her.

Why is your office so freezing? she asked, hugging herself.

I told her when she came over tonight I'd set the temperature to whatever she wanted.

I never paid as much as I did that night. The sex was great. We laughed a lot. She wanted to know how I got into this business, why I only liked prostitutes. She thought I was funny. She had this joy in her eyes, the kind of light that wouldn't survive in this line of work for long. But in the meantime, that light was worth lots of money. Fifteen hundred an hour, easy. I knew I was right about that.

After we finished fucking, we snorted some coke. We

smoked my cigarettes. We drank beer. Then she pulled out a chunk of MDMA. That came as a surprise. It was huge. Twenty-five hundred shekels, probably more. Light brown, totally clean. Good stuff.

That makes another hour of your time worth it for me, I told her. If we start feeling it before the hour is over, that is. I'll time it from the moment we drink the stuff. I counted another 1,500 and put it on the dresser. I brought out a small bottle of mineral water. She cut some crumbs into it. We drank slowly. Then everything opened up. It's harder to watch what you say when you're on MD, and it's her favorite drug. She used to be one of those nature rave girls, dropping ecstasy from age thirteen.

I asked her again how come she needed so much money. And then she told me. That's what happens on MD. It was like I was her best friend. She spoke with this passion, but I was only barely listening. Each time she ran her hand over my chest I felt ripples of heat below my skin, followed by cool blue waves, as if she had run her hand through water. Each time she touched my dick I couldn't even hear her words. It felt like blinding light. But I sort of caught on, or I managed to remember enough to figure it out later. If I'd known how things would turn out, I might have paid more attention.

Her father was a gambler. Gambling is the shittiest addiction. Her family lost their apartment when she was a kid. He lost her mother's family's savings before her mother even died. Her mother made him go to some rehab center run by a guy who learned it in India. Her father tried it, and for a few years it looked like things were going to be all right. He reopened his business, a rubber stamp shop that sold cell phones in the back room. No, it was the other way around. They had a cell phone store that she and her older brother opened at the front of his rubber stamp store. Two businesses, one name, one location. Her brother lived abroad and everything was under her name so that her father didn't get tempted to touch the money. Just in case. Then her mother died and it was her, her brother, and her little sister alone with him, and things got bad again.

Her head was on my stomach, her hand gripping the base of my dick. I couldn't see what she was looking at. Probably my dick. I imagined her dreamy gaze, but I could only hear her. I took her hand in mine and moved it up and down, slowly. After she got the pace I let her do it herself.

When she figured out what was happening with her father, she canceled his paycheck and only gave him enough pocket money for a day at a time. Her sister had just been enlisted into the military. The store, or the two stores, the stamp and phone stores, were the only source of income for the three of them—her dad, her sister, and herself. Her brother gave up his share of the business and didn't want any financial connections with them. He went back abroad. The business was doing all right, but they had lots of expenses. They paid mortgage for the part they expanded for the cell phones, they had to pay for goods, taxes, accounting. Not a lot of wiggle room.

Then one day her father didn't come home. It was a Friday. She cooked dinner. Her sister was home from the army. They sat down to dinner, and he still didn't show up. He didn't answer his phone, nothing. Gone. She tried not to let her sister see how worried she was. She said the kiddush prayer instead of him, doing an accurate impression. That cracked her sister up. She tried to keep things light, as if everything was fine. But it wasn't.

On Sunday morning her sister went back to the army, but there was still no word. At nine a.m. she got a call from the bank—one of her checks bounced, they said. A check for 100,000 shekels. She never wrote checks like that. She asked if other checks had been withdrawn. All the cash in the store's business account was gone. She asked who it was paid to and they gave her the name of a furniture store in Bnei Brak. You didn't have to be a genius to figure it out. An entire checkbook was missing. Before she could even make a plan, two gorillas showed up at the store at noon. Her father owed 750,000 shekels to loan sharks. The checks bounced and he wasn't picking up his phone. He'd gone underground. The checks belonged to the store, so it was up to her now to pay back his debt. It was her problem now, and interest was piling up. She told them she'd meet their boss, she'd fix it, it'll be okay.

That night her father came home. One of his hands was in a cast. Two broken fingers. He had tried to reason with the guy, but there was no one to reason with. So the guy broke his fingers. Her father was crying. Sitting there like some kid being punished by a teacher. She went mad. She screamed. She cried too. Then she hugged him.

I felt myself about to come and I stopped her hand. I didn't want it to be over. Even her voice felt good inside this high. I asked, Well, and then what?

She said they didn't tell her sister anything. Poor girl, she was a soldier, she didn't need this drama. That sister, she said, was something special. She learned how to play the piano from a young age. One day, when her sister was in the sixth grade, Shiri came home and heard music. The door was unlocked. She walked in and couldn't believe her eyes. Her sister was wearing one of her mom's sleeping masks, the kind they give out on flights. She was blindfolded, playing some classical music on the piano, swaying from side to side, immersed in the music. I yelled at her, she said. I told her she was wearing a mask while the door was unlocked, that someone could come in and take everything and she wouldn't even notice. But the truth is, she said, I yelled because I envied her. I was always so involved in my parents' shit, I knew everything. But that little girl had an escape. She's a good soul, my sister, she said. Clean. She herself was never clean. She was a wild girl who hung with wild people. She started doing drugs in seventh grade. Things only changed when her mother died and she took over the business and became the responsible adult.

So she went to Bnei Brak to meet with the gorillas' boss. Loan sharks put on a friendly face until you owe them money. This Orthodox guy, about forty years old, long brown beard, big smile, was sitting in the gallery of a furniture store. The gallery held the office, and overlooked the showroom on the ground floor. This was the person who loaned her father the money. He preached to her about responsibility. When a man takes someone else's money, he should have a plan for how to pay it back. Her father told him the money was intended for expanding the business, but then he played the money away and was left with nothing. So what's the collateral? The business. She told him the property that held their business was mortgaged, and that the business itself was worth about 400,000, which didn't cover the debt, certainly not with interest. The rest, he said, she should have her father pay back, or find a way to pay it back herself, he didn't care. She told him she would, she just needed a few days to get it together. She cried a little. He let her cry and then pretended to soften up and offered a solution. She's a pretty girl, he said. He could connect her with an escort agency his friend owned. They'd treat her well, make sure no one tried to give her any trouble. She told him to forget about it, she'd deal with it herself. He gave her a week to think things over. She told him she didn't need to—she'd transfer the business over to him, and then pay an additional fifty per month. It was her business how, not his. He did the math on the piece of paper. With interest, it would take her a year and a half to pay everything back. So that's that, she said. She really needed the money. She paid the first couple months using a bank loan, but now she had nothing left.

I felt myself falling in love with her, but I didn't take it seriously—that's how you feel on MD, you could fall in love with anything. She was high too. She sucked me off, this time like she was hungry for it. Come in my mouth, she said. I came in her mouth. Unbelievable.

The truth is, I wasn't totally sure it was only the MD, so I kept my distance, just in case. Falling in love wasn't part of my plan. I didn't need any trouble. I didn't invite her over again, not because I didn't enjoy it, but because I did. It wasn't about money. I didn't care about the money. But I kept thinking about her. Her thighs in those cutoffs. Her smile. Her voice. And that sister, playing the piano with a mask on, I even thought about her sometimes too. I never saw her in the store after that, she had some guy working there instead.

I had other things to think about, like that dumb law about advertising prostitution. It was almost specifically directed against me. I mean, against *Nightlife*. And the people who put escort service business cards under windshield wipers. Smart-asses, the self-righteous nuts who came up with this law. They try to protect the prostitutes, but who do they end up hurting? The prostitutes. If there's any method to lawmaking where prostitution is concerned, this is it: the prostitutes get fucked over.

It's not like I started *Nightlife* to help anybody out. I started it because it gave me the kind of standing no one else had with these girls. I knew them, I hung out with them, I learned their secrets, I heard all about their lives. They turned to me before they turned to each other. It's an isolating profession. How were these girls supposed to explain their experiences or problems to their friends from school or from home? They couldn't even begin to describe the kinds of things they've seen and the people they've met. We all walk inside the grid of normal life. But they walk under it, crossing all the lines diagonally. The world doesn't just look different from that angle, it looks upside down. I'm not trying to say that's where you see the truth. It's a half-truth, the half most people don't want to see. That doesn't mean most people live a lie—they just live one half of the truth. And those girls, they see the other half. It's not more true, even if they think it is, it's just the other side of it. But it's *also* true. So they have each other, and they have other people here and there who understand it: drivers, brothel owners, some clients. But the clients are on the opposite side of the fence, and I spend part of my time on that side and the rest on the girls' side. That's how I like it. I may not be their true friend, but I'm someone they can talk to. I spend a lot of time with them. They're a collection of wild-child types and crazies like you've never seen, and that's what I like about it. I don't know why. It's like they've given up on being normal, which is like jumping off a cliff. Like trying to fly. You can't fly. But I still like people who have the guts to try. Normal life always seemed like walking death to me anyway.

At any rate, I didn't start the paper to help anyone. I started it for me. For money, for status. But at the same time, I cut out what the law calls "pimps." Escort service owners. I never advertised services, only girls. Which meant I cut the middlemen. Services get you clients but take half the money for each appointment. Girls who advertised through me got clients through the paper and kept the entire sum. They didn't work for the driver; the driver worked for them. It's like I short-circuited the entire market. Lots of service owners found themselves with much less work. And they didn't like me for it. But by the time they figured out what was happening, they were so busy fighting each other for whatever work was left that they couldn't afford to take me on. So I got some threats. I even went to the police once when it seemed like more than just talk. But mostly these guys aren't serious criminals. They're amateurs. And those they pay protection money to, the real criminals, they didn't care enough to start a war. Why would they? They knew me. I hooked them up with the best girls. I knew the face behind each ad. Who else would they call to ask about new girls and find somebody who's their type?

So when this law was passed, I replaced the word *Escort* with the word *Massage* in all my ads, and put a red caption that read *No Sex* on each one. I read the law carefully on the Knesset website. It says you can't advertise escort services under the pretense of massage. So it says. So what? To verify that you're actually advertising sex services, they would have to check out each provider, and the police weren't dumb enough to create more work for themselves. They'd be turning a whole market sector into more work. Why would they?

But you can't be sure until you try. Two months passed, and I published two issues, and nothing happened. That didn't confirm anything, but it was a good start. I was about to print the third issue. I was on the phone in my office when Shiri walked in, pale. No light in her eyes, nothing. Scared. She was holding this big brown envelope. She put it down on the table and paced around the office. She lit a cigarette. She looked terrific. Made up, in her work clothes. Tight jeans, thin button-down blouse, kind of vintage-looking and almost see-through. A nice black bra under it.

I don't know if I can even say anything, she said. She kept pacing, wouldn't sit down. Maybe I should keep quiet.

I told her she could tell me. She had no one else to talk to, and it was clear she couldn't keep this to herself, whatever it was.

Finally she sat down and pulled a wad of cash from the envelope. Fifteen thousand shekels. Six hours. That's 9,000 charged and an extra 6,000 in tips. She stared at me as if I could solve a riddle for her. But there was no riddle. I could tell she already knew this. That kind of money was no tip. It was violence. She was wound up like a spring from all the coke they did. She'd been at his place since eleven that morning. Her nose was running. She kept sniffing.

It wasn't her first time with this client. The first time was about a week before. A two-hour booking. Three people, all loaded, and all clearly criminals. It was all right. There were other girls there, but the guy who asked for her acted like a real king. At first she enjoyed it. It was the penthouse at the Carlton Hotel. Guards at the door. These were powerful people and she thought they might one day even help her with her little Orthodox loan shark. Who knows? They liked her. They could tell she was no sucker, because she didn't act scared. She stood her ground, asked for more money the minute their time was up, and definitely didn't give them the feeling that coke would buy them more time. It amused her to see them fighting over her, until the one who acted like the boss didn't let anybody else touch her. She went home with all sorts of plans on how to leverage this relationship.

But this time it was different. Stressful. His driver called her up. He sounded Russian, said his boss wanted her to come for an hour. He told her to wait on the street, he'd pick her up. She didn't realize it was one of the three guys she met last time. Anyway, two black Lexus sedans came by. Darkened windows. This gorilla steps out of one car and opens the door for her. There's another one already in the car. She couldn't see who was in the second car. The driver was the one with the Russian accent. He tried to act smart. He congratulated her on her high price. He wanted to know why it was so expensive. Fifteen hundred an hour, he said, your pussy must be made of velvet and gold. A comedian. She didn't laugh. Told him to watch his mouth. He did. She knew how to handle herself, and he probably didn't want his boss to hear that he misbehaved. They drove like that, in silence, until they reached the Yoo Towers. They drove into the underground parking lot and pulled over at an elevator. The driver and the other guy walked with her, and another gorilla stayed to watch the cars. Sunglasses, suits. Big showoff. She walked inside.

Two armed men with security company logos on their T-shirts sat in the apartment lobby. At first she thought she'd been brought to entertain some politician or something. But it was that same guy from last time. He'd prepared. He dressed up, poured about a gallon of aftershave on himself. She felt things were getting out of hand. This wasn't how you treated a call girl. It's how you treated your date. She decided to act as if nothing was wrong, as if everything was under control. She asked him if he had taken a shower and he said he had. She said she needed one herself. It kills about ten minutes from the appointment. She took her time, because she knew she couldn't show weakness around power. She came out wearing a bathrobe he left there for her. It was an enormous apartment, but not for a family. It was his bachelor pad. She sat down on a chair and put her feet up on the coffee table. She studied her French pedicure, as if this was what concerned her now.

He liked that she wasn't scared. He asked if she knew who he was. She said she didn't. He asked if she read the papers. She said, Probably not the pages you read. He laughed. He introduced himself: Victor Simianof. She watched me carefully when she said that name. But I kept my cool. She was silent for a bit, then asked if I knew who he was. I told her I did. I didn't have any personal acquaintance with people of his caliber, but yes, I knew of him. He was pretty big in the Bukharan community in the '90s, but when the Russian immigration began he climbed over all the old Bukharan mobsters and the new Russian mobsters and took a seat at the very top. He was a name you didn't see very often in papers, but he was one of the biggest five or six mobsters in Israel. This was no laughing matter. She said nothing. Maybe she was wondering how she dared put her feet up on his table. Maybe she was thinking she took it too far.

She breathed deep, then continued talking. He said he wanted to book her for six hours if she was willing to give him a special price. She said she wouldn't. Six hours cost 9,000 shekels. Special prices you can get at department stores, she said, whereas she was one of a kind. She also told him it didn't seem as if he had any money problems. He liked that. He said cool. She counted the 9,000 shekels and put the money in her purse. Then he picked up her purse and opened it. She thought maybe he was only kidding about the six hours and was going to take the money back. No. Instead he pulled out her cell phone, turned it off, and took out the battery. I'm a careful man, he said. That's why I'm still around. He smiled. She said nothing, but she could tell this was serious.

When they began messing around she relaxed a little.

He gave her a few lines of coke but didn't do any himself. They fucked, drank some wine, laughed. Then he fell asleep and she watched television. His siesta cost him 3,000 shekels and a gram of coke. Then he woke up, they fucked again, he offered her more coke, and this time did some himself. He touched her a little, wanted her to touch him, and that was it. In the end, just like everyone else, he asked what a girl like her was doing, working as an escort. She told him what she told everyone else: she needed the money. But he wouldn't drop it. What does a twenty-six-year-old need this kind of money for? She said she was saving up for an apartment. She could tell he wasn't buying it. He said, Look, baby, I'm not stupid, so let's make a deal: don't lie to me, okay? It insults me. A good twenty-six-year-old girl doesn't become a prostitute because she wants her own apartment. Don't mess with me. He smiled. So are you going to tell me, he asked, or should I find out for myself?

So she told him about her dad who gambled all his money away. He thought that was funny. Maybe he lost it in my casino, he told her. Maybe he owes it to me. She said he didn't. He owed nothing to a casino, he owed it to loan sharks. He laughed again. You're naive like a little girl, he told her. The loan sharks might be working for me too. He offered to help her out. Any notions about how someone like him could save her flew right out the window. She knew this was not a guy you wanted to owe a favor to. She had brains.

She lit another cigarette and stared at me, wide-eyed. You think he could find out about me? she asked. I shrugged. I told her I wasn't sure what more there was to find out. He already knew she was an escort. I said he probably wouldn't go to the trouble of checking her out too much. He must hire lots of girls. I told her not to panic, not to try to disappear on him, not to give him a reason to chase her. Even if he liked her, he'd get over it. He didn't care that much about her debt. He wouldn't pay that kind of money just to show off. She stayed silent. Don't be rude to him, I said. Not because he'd punish you, but because it turns him on that you hold your own. Be a little more submissive, and he'll get bored. A quarter-smile flickered on her face for a second. She pushed the blinds and gazed out. Her eyes went soft. Lost in thought. She turned to face me again. Can I spend the night with you? she asked. I said sure. She sniffed. She was still all wound up from the coke.

She took a shower at my place and we watched television in the living room. She still wasn't calm. Eventually I took her to the bedroom and gave her some Bondormin to help her fall asleep. I got in bed with her. She wanted to put her head on my chest and just lie there quietly for a bit, but then suddenly, I don't know what came over her, she asked me to go down on her. I thought I misheard, but yeah, that's what she said. That's the kind of girl she was. I was glad to do it. She came, and then fell asleep. I lay there for another hour with her head on my chest and the smell of her hair in my nostrils. Then I gently pushed her off and lay her on her back. She folded over to her side again. I went to the living room, had a beer, and watched a show about Nazi U-boats. I couldn't concentrate. I turned it off. I went back to bed, even though I knew I wouldn't be able to sleep. I lay next to her on my side, my arm curled under my head. I watched her face on the pillow. Her eyebrows. She wasn't calm, even in her sleep. Who knew what was going through her mind? I don't know how much time passed, but when her phone rang, I jumped. It was her work phone. I suddenly felt enraged at her clients. I grabbed the ringing phone and went to the living room. I answered. This guy wanted to know what he'd get for so much money. Smart-ass. I told him that for so *little* money, she'd barely give him a blow job with a rubber, let alone fuck him. He sounded insulted. I said, Listen up, asshole, you'll never fuck a girl like that in your life, so 1,500 is charity for a scumbag like you. Then I hung up. I don't know why I did that. I smoked a cigarette and paced the living room. Finally I put her phone on silent and went back to bed. I watched her for another hour or two, just lying there and thinking before I finally fell asleep.

When I woke up she was still asleep. She had twenty-one missed calls. Even with that kind of price, there was demand. Or maybe it was *because* of that kind of price. She slept till ten.

And that's how things went on. First she slept over twice a week, then almost every night. It was crazy how we found a home in the middle of our messy lives. I stopped asking other girls over. I didn't feel like it. She kept working, and as strange as it may sound, it turned me on. When she came home from shifts, I'd fuck her like an animal. That was our best sex. Some girls get horny after their shifts. People don't realize it, but it can be like that. They fake orgasms at work. They try not to actually have them. That's losing control. It breaks down the barriers a girl builds so that she can live her life: I'm here for the money, you're here for me, and we never switch roles. But still—they're having sex all night. Even just the friction can get you hot. That's how she was, anyway. Maybe I didn't need anyone else not just because I liked her, but because she fit my kinky side perfectly: I was the closest person to her, the only one who wasn't a client.

It pricked a little here and there. I could feel the edge of where it could start hurting, the fact that other men were

fucking her, but I didn't let it get under my skin. Just a little
tickle, a little scratch: it spiced things up, but it didn't burn.
It gave things an edge. But other than that life was normal. A
home. She cooked, not great, but she cooked. She was like a
kid trying really hard, not like the woman you actually marry.
My cooking was better than hers. I taught her a little, and I
liked cooking for her, and later on, with her. We did that two
or three nights a week, before she had to go to work, or on her
days off, when she turned off her phone.

Our sex was like a tornado, our home was a warm slipper.
In her denim cutoffs, curled up on the sofa, watching television, eating Häagen-Dazs ice cream straight from the carton.
Until one night she said something strange. She was washing the dishes, and with her back to me she said: if I stopped
working you'd break up with me. I thought about it for a minute. Then I told her she was right and she shouldn't stop. She
left the dishes and walked over to me with her hands dripping
with soap. You're a sleazeball, she said. That's how I am, I
told her. She looked at me, her head cocked, but there was a
little smile on her lips. She didn't let it grow. Instead she sat
on me, spread her legs, grabbed the back of my neck with her
soapy hands, and French-kissed me. Okay, she said, if I'm going to be sleazy anyway, I'm better off being with a sleazeball.
I grabbed the back of her neck and kissed her back. Then I
fucked her on the sofa.

We lay there afterward, hyperventilating. Everything was
up in the air. We were playing with fire. I told her we needed to
be careful not to fall in love, because then everything would
blow up. You wouldn't be able to stand other people touching
you, and I wouldn't be able to stand other people touching you.

What are you talking about? she said. You're madly in love
with me.

You wish, I said.

She laughed. Her work phone rang. I looked at her. She reached her hand over me and grabbed it. There was a moment there, waiting to see if she'd answer it. She glanced at the screen. What a pest, she said. She silenced it. I smiled. Don't get too excited, she told me. I just don't have time for another one, I have a booking at nine thirty. He just needs to let me know where. Probably that disgusting Tal Hotel. He's cheap. But what do I care? I'll be out of there in thirty minutes, tops. She went to take a shower.

She came back wearing a little black dress and stockings. This guy liked her looking elegant. Whatever. I waited for her to leave, jerked off in bed thinking about her fucking at the Tal Hotel, and went to sleep. She came back sometime before dawn, got in bed without waking me up. She probably had at least two more appointments after that one. When we woke up we fucked, and then she stayed lying on top of me for a moment. I want to tell you something, she said. She covered my mouth with her hand and I thought a speech was coming. She stared at me for a moment and then said only: We're alike. She kept her gaze on me to make sure I got it and only then moved her hand from my mouth. I said nothing, but it stayed with me. Not because it was true, but because it wasn't. But she was right about being in love. I wouldn't be able to sleep at night while she was working if I didn't think she was in love too. No way.

It wasn't just weird having an escort girlfriend. Everything normal became weird too, in a way. Even grocery shopping. I would look at her ass as she bent down to pick up onions, put them in a bag, put the bag in the cart. I'd look at her ass, and think about where she may have been last night, where she was during the day, what she seemed like to people in the supermarket. Probably just like a girl with an older boyfriend. Her fingers. Where they had been and what they had done, looking so clean on the cart's orange handle.

But we lived well. Not with her money, with mine. All the money I used to spend on sex was now available. We bought whatever we wanted, we spent weekends out of town whenever we felt like it. We went to Greece twice; flew to Eilat for dinner just because she felt like it, and returned the same night. She also made more than the monthly fee she owed the Orthodox guy. She bought me clothes. She completely changed the way I dressed. And I let her. I examined myself in the mirror, wearing the clothes she bought me, and thought, Who is that guy? It felt nice. You spend your time with her like that, and you feel like a soldier in a special ops unit or an underground army. Like you're on top of the world. And then little things. Home. Comfort. Her hair dripping on the back of her tank top after she gets out of the shower. Her sweatpants. Her tweezers when she plucks her eyebrows. You look at a girl plucking her eyebrows and feel like you've grabbed the world by the balls. What the fuck? Where did that come from?

Only her gangster was like a shadow hanging over us. A black cloud on the horizon. He kept booking her. Once or twice a week the black cars came to pick her up. He left her thousands of shekels in tips. And there were signs. One time he slapped one of his goons right in front of her, just because he didn't like the way he looked at her. When he wanted to meet her someplace other than Yoo Towers, they led her to the meeting place blindfolded so she didn't know where they were. It reminded me of her little sister with the mask. Wherever it was, one of his apartments, or a hotel room, or an unknown location, he always took her into the bathroom. He wanted her to undress and get in the shower in front of him so he could make sure she wasn't hiding anything, recording equipment or something like that. And he always took her phone, turned it off, and removed the battery. But she got used to him. He was even nice sometimes. His stories. He wasn't a normal person. He saw things normal people never see. What drove her mad was that she just needed to say one word and he'd crush that Orthodox loan shark and make all her debt go away. But asking him for something like that meant giving up her freedom. That would be it, she'd be his. No matter how we looked at it, we were stuck with the Orthodox guy.

She didn't take my advice about acting submissive until he got tired of her. She tried, but it just wasn't her. She was all about chutzpah and it turned him on. But there was a limit to that too. When he made a romantic offer and she blew him off, he didn't like it anymore. He offered her an apartment in her name, and a monthly allowance that was higher than what she made. She would never have to work again, he told her. He'd come visit sometimes, and they would have a place to be together. She didn't just say no, she dissed him, and then, on top of that, she lectured him too. Listen, she said, I'm working here. My heart is not for sale, and if you think I'm going to be your slave, you have another thing coming. This is just a gig for me, this isn't friendship, and definitely not love. You can take lots of things by force, but not my heart.

He got up and told her their time was up. He took the money he'd left her on the dresser, gave her only what he owed for one hour, and called the driver. Wait downstairs, he said. She got dressed and left, making an angry face. But really she was happy. She thought that might be the end of it, he was finally done with her. Her heart was pounding. His honor might stop him from seeing her again. I told her his honor might make him hurt her. But she said she didn't think it was like that. Hurting a girl was beneath him, or at least that's how he presented himself.

She never lost her head, even under pressure. She had common sense and a good eye. I thought she might be right, but it still didn't seem like the end of it to me. I didn't say anything, but I thought it might be too early to exhale.

The paper was doing all right, and I thought maybe the whole legal business would never be an issue. But one day I was visited by two raging feminists. They were so angry they could barely speak. The one who did speak—her voice was shaking. They sat in my office. Maybe they were scared that I was some sort of gangster and that I'd try to hurt them. They wanted to give me a check for 2,000 shekels for a full-page ad. The ad would say: *Would you want your daughter to be a prostitute?* They even had the design ready. A black ad with yellow type. I told them to fuck off, I wouldn't do it. So they glued the ad to the wall in my stairwell and wrote my name on it with Wite-Out.

My office is one floor above my apartment. Same stairwell. My neighbors could see the ad. And they used the kind of glue you spread over the paper so you can't peel it off. So no, the answer is no. I wouldn't want my daughter to be a prostitute. But I don't have a daughter.

I only noticed the ad was there at two thirty in the afternoon, when I went downstairs to buy cigarettes. I don't know how long it had been there. Probably like three hours. Shiri was still asleep. I didn't want her to see it, but the glue was already dry. I peeled it off with a spatula and some of the paint came off the wall with it. I was on the news later. The feminists got stacks of *Nightlife* from the kiosks and sidewalks and burnt them at Rabin Square. I got a call from Channel 1, asking for my response. I said no comment. It was better to shut up in this case. Shiri read about it online, saw pictures of the bonfire and all those angry women. She thought it was funny. She also thought the picture of me they found from my days as a defense attorney was cute. You look like you're trying too hard to be serious, she said.

But we had more urgent business to attend to. Victor called. Or his Russian driver did. He booked her for Friday, three days in advance. She told him she had Fridays off. Not this Friday, he said. He gave her a time and hung up. I saw what he was doing. It was no coincidence that he booked her three days in advance. He wanted to give her time to stew. And she did. We both did. She barely worked during those three days, and we barely fucked. She barely ate. She was dressed and made up thirty minutes ahead of time. She wore jeans and a tank top, like any normal day. She sat near the window, smoking and waiting for the driver. The cars showed up right on time and she went downstairs. I watched from the window as she got in and the Lexuses drove off. Then I saw them turn onto Pinsker Street. I paced the house, rapped my knuckles on the walls. I calculated that if he just wanted to talk, it would take two hours at most, including travel time. Two hours went by. Then three. Possibilities started running through my mind. I even thought about calling the police. But what for? If something was wrong, how would they help?

She got back nearly four hours later. It was almost one a.m. She was pale as a sheet. He hired some chef and let her wait alone in the bedroom while the guy prepared their food. She watched television. He called her out after a little over an hour. They had dinner, just the two of them. The chef served them. Victor was kind of nice. Pretend nice. Polite. Long silences, while he pretended to concentrate on his food. She could hardly swallow. He answered phone calls during dinner, acting like she was a visitor that he had to be polite to. She had no idea where this was going. She tried to speak once, saying, Listen, if there's something you want, just say so. But he cut her off and went back to eating in silence. She went silent too. He only started talking after dessert. All very politely. Listen, he said, I don't like prostitutes. You know why? Because prostitutes are filthy. They're fine for fucking here and there, but nothing more. So you're a prostitute. So when I touch you, I touch filth. I don't like the idea of that.

So what do you want to do? she asked.

I'll tell you what I want to do, he said. You'll stop working. You'll come see me and get your pay, two hours a week. That comes up to 12,000 a month. That's enough for any girl. You can keep doing everything else as usual, but nobody touches you except me.

She met his eyes, took a deep breath, and said no. This is my job and I need the money. You know I need the money. I have a debt to pay. I only sell my time, and my time is yours only when I'm with you. Fifteen hundred an hour. If you think I'm filthy, no one's forcing you to call me.

He was ready for this; he's no sucker. So then, quietly, like he was just taking an interest as a friend, he asked: And how's Ruti doing? Is she coming home for the weekend?

She said nothing. She told me her heart went still when he said her sister's name. She never even told him she had a sister. He found out. On his own. Victor, she said, that's my sister, she never hurt anybody, don't bring her into this.

He ignored her. He spoke like he was her father or a concerned uncle. He raised a finger. Tell her, he said, that it's safer to lose a few hours of leave and take the bus than to hitch-hike. Even a military vehicle can be dangerous. There are Arabs out there, trying to abduct soldiers. And she's a pretty girl, God forbid somebody rapes her.

She cried. She begged. Victor, she said, what did she ever do?

He dropped the fake tone, stared at her. He let her squirm. Then he turned cold. You'll stop working right now, he said. He let her cry a little more and then walked over to her. He patted her head. Shh, he said. Enough. Everything's fine. Sergey will take you home. Then he left her alone at the table. In the car Sergey gave her an envelope with 3,000 shekels.

When she finished telling me about it, we sat quietly in the living room. We looked at each other. She saw something was bugging me. He said nothing about you, she said. Maybe he only knows about her.

I thought about it. If he knew, he'd have said something. We can keep a low profile, never leave the house together, and hope it works out. I said nothing. The overhead light was on, but it was like the light was hollow and there was darkness inside it.

How am I going pay back 50,000 a month? she said. We took some Bondormin and slept till morning.

The next morning we sat down with a pencil and a piece of paper, and did the math again. She had eleven payments of 50,000 shekels left to make. *Nightlife* brought in about 60,000 a month, after taxes, and I was willing to give whatever I could. No problem. But 60,000 was before paying rent for my apartment and office, alimony for my son and his mother in

France, living expenses. If I really tightened things up I could give her twenty a month, max. But even if Victor asked her for two hours a week, every week, for eleven months straight, paying her 3,000 shekels each time, meaning 12,000 a month, that only brought us to 32,000. We were still 18,000 short. I could borrow 200,000 against the business with a multiyear payment plan. That could work. It worked on paper, anyway. We decided we could swing it.

I started making arrangements the very next day. But things were different in real life than they looked on paper. She stopped seeing other clients, and when she went to see him, I didn't feel like I used to. There was nothing hot about it. It was like a dark shadow. I'd watch from the window as she got in a black Lexus and drove away. I'd count the minutes until she was back. I'd lie in bed, and instead of jerking off, I daydreamed about accidents happening to Victor. But I had no intention of trying to mess with a man like that. I could only pray for the police to get hold of him. People like him spend about half their lives in prison. Or maybe we'd get lucky. Maybe he'd grow tired of her. One day.

But so far that hadn't happened. On the contrary. She wasn't the cool, jokey, brash girl anymore. He got angry at her for rolling her eyes at him, for not even bothering to fake an orgasm, for behaving like he made her suffer. You turned the light out on my life, she told him, and I can't get comfortable when we fuck. Sorry. But it was exactly because of this that he didn't give up. We kept going that way. We had nine more payments to make.

Then one day I got a call from a detective at the Yarkon Precinct. A guy I knew from my days as a criminal lawyer. A corrupt piece of shit. Benny. The new law is serious, he said. You'd better shut that paper down if you know what's good for you. I told him to kiss my ass, I only advertised massage services. I have twenty-five files on you, he said. We called the numbers in the ads and the girls talked about fucking. Massage? Who are you kidding? I told him I had no idea what he was talking about. What are you going to do? I asked. If the girls tell me it's a massage and then talk about sex, how is it my problem? All I know about is massage. They aren't breaking the law by being prostitutes, so what do you want from me? See you around, I said, and hung up the phone.

I knew my argument wouldn't hold water in court. A judge would never believe that I used to advertise escorts and now didn't know the girls were escorts. But it can't hurt to play it cool. You never know how much of an effort they'd make to look into it, and I wasn't sure what the guy wanted. If he wanted to nail me for those offenses, then why would he tell me about it instead of getting an indictment? Something didn't make sense. So I played it cool for a while.

Two more days went by, then that Benny guy stopped by my office. Polite, official. Wanted to know if he was interrupting, if he was no bother, if he could have two minutes of my time. So I let him in. I made myself a cup of coffee but didn't offer him any. He pulled out a small tape recorder and played a recording of me telling Shiri's client that for 1,500 shekels she'd give him head with a condom. Then I suddenly recognized his voice in the recording. There was no more pretending after that. If he made the effort to get me on tape, this wasn't something that would just go away. I said fine. I told him his two minutes were up and asked if there was anything else he wanted. But then I shut down the paper.

Now we were stuck. I was out of ideas.

I'll have to go back to work, she said.

I couldn't say anything. We both knew there was no choice. She couldn't advertise. Victor or one of his guys would find her, it would only be a matter of time. Changing her name or number wouldn't help either.

I said we could try Silvie. With Silvie, things might stay under the radar. She'd heard about Silvie from other girls in the business. I'd known the woman for a long time, though not too intimately. She set up shop in the lobby of the Sheraton Hotel. She only served hotel guests. Like any other agency, she charged a 50 percent commission. I thought we might be able to haggle a bit. After all, you don't find girls like Shiri out on the street. Maybe she'd settle for 30 percent. Her method cut out all the familiar channels. No paper ads, no Internet, no agencies, no business cards out on the street. Autonomy. The hotel bellboys carried Silvie's business cards. They were the only ones, and they handed them out to men who stayed alone at the hotel, as they were bringing up their suitcases. They only gave cards when it seemed appropriate. They got fifty shekels for any business they brought in. The hotel's security manager got 200 a night, and made sure nobody kicked Silvie and her girls out of the lobby. The girls sat at the lobby bar each night until closing time, and then hung out in the lobby until around two a.m. That way, clients didn't have to wait any longer than five minutes. Prices were higher—tourist prices. Four hundred dollars an hour. But Shiri might be able to charge more. Four nights a week, let's say an average of two jobs a night, that's at least four hundred dollars, clean. Twelve hundred shekels times sixteen is a little over 19,000. It would be borderline, but at least that way there was a good chance Victor wouldn't find out.

We went to sleep that night without having sex. The air

in the room felt heavy. She pretended to sleep. I pretended to sleep. When I thought she was actually asleep I got up and went to the living room for a cigarette.

Two minutes later she appeared at the doorway, in underwear and a tank top. She scratched one leg with the toes of the other and looked at me, wide-eyed. What's going to happen to us? she asked. I can't stand people touching me anymore. I can only think of you. Even with Victor.

I didn't know if she really felt it or if that was her way of telling me she knew what I was going through. That I was losing sleep over it. Because *I* couldn't stand people touching her. Maybe that's what she was trying to tell me: That it was only temporary. That I shouldn't worry. That she was mine. Thoughts ran through my head, but I didn't want to tell her anything. I only said we'd get through it, it was only for a while.

I put her in touch with Silvie. What a character, that one. Sitting at the hotel like a tourist. A fifty-year-old woman, her hair blown out, in an updo, all sprayed. Nice jewelry, French accent. You'd think she was a wealthy French woman waiting for her millionaire husband to come down from their hotel suite. She lectured her girls on manners, as if you needed a degree from the Silvie Academy of Hotel Management to be a prostitute. Shiri got along with her. She got along with everyone. And the money was better than we thought. She got big tips. The tips made me itch. I had to stop myself from asking, and when I did ask, I acted nonchalant. Fake nonchalant. What were those tips for? For her personal touch. For her charm. She didn't just spread her legs, she gave them magic. She made them laugh, she surprised them, she made them feel it was different with them. She kissed them, licked their ears, drove them mad, talking about fantasies, maybe. It was part of the job. It was how you made good money. But it was like acid dripping on my skin, that money. Slowly. Maddeningly. I began taking sleeping pills before she left for work. I didn't want to lie awake and imagine her working some tourist at the Sheraton for a tip double the price she charged.

I felt we wouldn't be able to hold on much longer. It clawed inside me. One morning I went to the Yarkon Precinct, to Benny's office. I told him, Listen, forget about the paper. You win. That's over. But let me help you with something else. He half-smiled at me, like I was some loser off the street who came begging. You don't understand, I said. I can help you. There's this loan shark, and he's extorting somebody I know. I can convince her to wear a wire. I'll hand him to you. You'll bring in the case, you'll do good, and as an added bonus, you'll get this scumbag off my friend's back. I don't want anything in return. I'm just here to do my friend a favor. He sat back in his chair and said, Look, I'm glad to help a friend out if I can—yeah, right, some friend—but the loan-sharking market, he said, is not about random targets. Those operations are structured like pyramids. There might be an investigation about somebody at a higher level. He might just be a cog in a big machine and it would be better for us to go for the boss. If you want, you can go to National Headquarters, but take my advice, he said, drop it. You don't just pull these things off like a local sheriff.

It was bullshit. Who would even listen to me at National Headquarters? I kept my eyes on him as I said thank you. I lingered long enough to make him know I wasn't really thanking him.

* * *

Some nights, I couldn't sleep even with the pills. Those thoughts: Where was Shiri now, who was she laughing with, who was tickling her or licking her neck? It drove me mad. One night, when she was working, I called a girl over. Netta. She used to advertise in my paper, until she accumulated a few rich regulars and stopped buying ads. She was a Yemenite with a hoarse voice, smooth dark skin, and large, natural breasts. Her gravelly laugh was her best asset. We used to spend lots of nights together and do lots of coke. It was all right, but my head wasn't there. She could feel it, I saw she could. But she didn't ask. When she left she said, Keep in touch.

I took a shower. I could feel myself about to do what I shouldn't: go peek into the Sheraton lobby. Seeing Shiri sitting there in the cocktail dress Silvie made her wear.

My self-restraint had drained out. I was walking over to the Sheraton when I noticed a stack of *Nightlife* issues on the sidewalk not far from the hotel entrance. I thought maybe it was a mistake, maybe it was a stack of old copies. I took a look. No, it wasn't one of my old issues. It was new, from this month. I picked one up, flipped through it. Same ads, all for massage, all saying, *No Sex*. My graphic design. My ads. My girls.

I called Nataly, who'd been buying a whole page from me for the past two years. I got her voice mail. Her voice said she was busy with somebody who was having a great time, and she'll call back when she's done.

I called Naama. She was Russian, but had almost no accent and thought she'd do better with an Israeli name. She'd been buying a half-page ad for a while. She was surprised I called. I asked who she paid for this month's ad. She said she got a call from a guy who said he bought *Nightlife* and wanted to know if she wanted to keep advertising. Same price, same terms. She didn't know who he was, just a first name, an address, and a number. She paid him cash. Hold on, she said. I'll text you the contact info. We hung up.

So I didn't go into the hotel. I had other things to think about. I walked back home. When I entered the building my phone beeped. She sent me the number and address.

Shiri got back at three in the morning. I woke up when she got into bed, her hair wet from the shower. Two thousand dollars. This one guy gave her a huge tip. He wanted her to pee on him, so she gave him a high price. She thought it was funny. He lay down in the bathtub, naked, and she stood over him. Some pee drops splattered on her legs. It was gross, she said. I kissed her. I stuck my tongue in her mouth. I fucked her as if I could hurt that guy through her. She felt it. She hugged me after I came, holding my head hard against her neck. Suddenly everything just came out. I cried into her hug. I'm scared for us, she said. She held me tight.

I didn't tell her about *Nightlife*, but the next day I went to the paper's new office. It was closed, so I waited in the stairwell. An hour and a half and four cigarettes later, the guy showed up. He was just a guy, nobody I knew. Forty-something. He had a paunch that made him look not exactly fat, but big. Short, thick, straight hair, like a hedgehog. I thought of asking him how he got my paper, but I dropped it. I kept sitting on the stairs.

He looked at me. I looked back. He said nothing, walked into the office, and locked it from inside.

I couldn't figure it out. They shut me down but they let this guy keep it going?

I went to the bank, withdrew 40,000 shekels from the money we'd saved to pay back the debt, and hired a private investigator to track this new guy down. Someone I met in court. He was okay, relatively speaking. At least he was hard working. I said, Take this 40,000, all-inclusive. I don't care about expenses, overtime, equipment. This is the sum. Take it or leave it.

He delivered after two weeks. That asshole who was publishing my paper was paying Benny off. Suddenly everything made sense. The police couldn't care less about the law against prostitution ads. And all Benny cared about was hitching a ride on the law's back to get the paper out of my hands. He couldn't print it himself, so he was a silent partner. Like protection, but from the wrong side.

Long story short, the PI gave me a picture of Benny meeting the guy at a café, and the guy giving him an envelope. Judging by the size of the envelope, it was quite a wad. So the paper wasn't shut down because now it was Benny's livelihood.

And that wasn't all. I got a great return for my money. My PI still had connections in the police. He found out the entire business plan was covered through paperwork. According to the paperwork, the business wasn't shut down because the owner was an informant. I don't know what kind of information he delivered, or made up, but that was the dirt's clean exterior. That guy, as it turned out, had been an informant for a while. First he sold cathinone under the counter at a kiosk, back when it was half-legal, and the police let him do it because he was snitching for them. Now that the drug was completely illegal, he got the paper. They still called him an informant, but really he was just the front man for Benny's business.

Those pictures were worth the 40,000. I went to Benny's office again, and this time I acted the way he did when he came in to shut me down. Super polite. I put the photos on his desk. I didn't have to say a word about them. I talked like I was giving him advice. The advice was to get Shiri to wear a wire next time she went to see the Orthodox loan shark, so that they could get him out of our lives.

I liked seeing his facade break down, that smile he wore when I came in, like he was big and I was just some loser off the street. I liked seeing sweat break on his scalp through his thin hair. I left him an old business card, my defense attorney's card. I wanted him to remember I was no sucker.

Shiri still had no idea, but now I had to tell her. She was part of the plan. It was she who would have to wear the wire. There was no problem convincing her. I knew there wouldn't be. She'd take any chance she could get for an adventure. She had no fear, and no limits. But it wasn't just that. She stared at me, and something I thought we'd lost was in her eyes again. Like I was no longer just the guy who lost sleep while she fucked tourists. That look alone gave me a few nights of sound sleep. I leaned on the door frame while she put her makeup on, preparing for work. I told myself it wasn't going to be much longer, this ceremony, getting dolled up for them. She was focused on her face and I watched her. Then she paused and met my eyes through the mirror. Let's go away somewhere this Saturday, she said. I don't feel like working this weekend.

Benny called. All right, he said, I'll make it happen. He needed the guy's name and his place of business, and he wanted to know who the girl wearing the wire would be. Why not use a cop? he asked. I told him she'd been paying him for a long time, and that if they didn't want a civilian doing it, she and I were going to go ahead without their help and just deliver the tape, and it would be his responsibility if anything happened to her. I still have the pictures, I told him, so if anything happens to her, it's going to be your ass. She has nerves of steel, I said. Don't worry.

He said he'd check and get back to me.

I told him to take a couple days, but that if I didn't hear back from him after that I would do it myself.

I did an online search. You can get recording devices so small nowadays that anyone could do it. I was still sitting at my computer when the front door opened. It was eleven at night, earlier than Shiri normally came home. I went out to the hallway and saw her coming in, with another girl in tow. I said Shiri's name, but she didn't even turn her head. I followed them into the living room. Hot girl. I didn't get it until she said it: it was her sister Ruti.

I didn't need any further explanation. Yellow hot pants, shiny red high heels, a white tank top that showed off her breasts, fake nails. This was not a going-out outfit, these were work clothes. It was nothing like Shiri's elegant look. It was like a neon sign that read: *Prostitute*. But her face was that of a scared little girl.

Ruti sat there, her face blank. She peered up at Shiri, as if waiting to be slapped. Shiri paced the room in her black heels. The slap never came. Shiri was pale, her jaw was tight.

I found her in the hotel lobby, Shiri said. She was talking to me, but her words were meant for Ruti. I'm sitting there, and suddenly she comes in with a client. She turned to face Ruti. You whore! she yelled at her. I don't know what I'm going to do to you!

Ruti had tears in her eyes. She shuddered when Shiri yelled, as if she had actually hit her. Her fingers were shaking. She was still waiting for it to come.

* * *

Shiri didn't leave the house for two days. She wouldn't let Ruti return to the army, or go anywhere else.

It was their dad, that son of a bitch. He pulled the same stunt again, this time using checks from Ruti's private account. He actually talked to Ruti. He was crying. He said loan sharks were after him, that they were going to kill him. He made her promise not to tell Shiri. He said they had to do something. He kept weeping.

Two days later, when Shiri calmed down a little, she released Ruti from her house arrest. It was the same loan shark, the Orthodox guy, and he was also the one who got Ruti the gig. She came to beg for her father and he offered her work. He put her in touch with an escort service, told her the owner was his friend. My head felt hot. We were able to deal with Victor, and now this little shit was coming back to ruin our lives? I'd get him, with or without Benny's help. I told Shiri I would. She looked at me as I got dressed. Expressionless. I tied my shoelaces and left without shaving. I went to see Benny to tell him we were going to do it earlier than planned. Friday morning. He had three days to prepare.

When I got home Shiri and Ruti were gone. So were Shiri's things. There was nothing. As if she'd never even been there. No clothes in the closet, no toothbrush, no shopping bags, no gum wrappers. Nothing. I called her cell phone. Voice mail. Voice mail on her work phone too, the one only Victor called now. I went to the cell phone store. Nothing. The guy who worked there had no idea, but the store was still open. Where did she think she was going?

I climbed the walls. I texted her, left more voice mails. I said I just wanted her to tell me what happened. I wasn't angry, I just needed to know. Nothing. She never called back.

I began staking the store. Still nothing. Ten days went by.

I left a letter with the guy who worked there. He said he had no idea how to reach her. Shiri had given him an overseas number where he could reach her brother, said he'd take care of everything. Maybe she went abroad too. He wasn't sure but wouldn't give me her brother's number. I asked him to read the letter to her brother over the phone, to tell him I wanted to talk to her. Just talk. Whenever she wanted. Whenever she could. But nothing. Benny called me a few times, but I didn't pick up. He was probably relieved.

I finally gave up. I knew her. Once she made up her mind about something, that was that. I thought about her every night. Every day. Every moment. If I couldn't be with her, I at least needed to know that she was all right. At least that.

Then, three months later I got a phone call one morning at ten a.m. A blocked number. She sounded nervous. I told her I loved her. But she had no time for such things. Listen, she said, we can't talk like this. We have to meet. Not at my place, not at a hotel, not at a café, nowhere public. There's a store on HaMedina Square. A clothing store. She gave me the name. The shopgirl was Nina, who used to work with Silvie at the Sheraton. She trusted her. She'd know what I was coming for. We set a time.

The moment I introduced myself to Nina she became all business. She'd been briefed and she gave me specific instructions. She put me in a changing room and drew the curtain. She told me not to leave, no matter what.

Her face was serious. No smiles. I sat on the small bench in the changing room and watched the store window and the street through a crack in the curtain.

Twenty minutes later Shiri arrived in a white Mercedes SUV. A driver opened the door for her. She was wearing expensive clothes and her hair was cut in a way that made her look like a woman, rather than a girl. She walked into the store and rifled through the dresses. The driver waited outside in the car. I'm coming, she said loudly, so I could hear her. She talked at the dresses, never glancing in my direction. Don't come out, she said. She chose a dress and walked into the changing room. I wanted to kiss her but she pushed me back. No! she said. Her lips were trembling. I'm scared, she said. I'm sorry.

I heard a quiver in her voice. I sat back down.

My heart is pounding like you wouldn't believe, she said. She put her purse on the bench and hung the dress on the hook. She turned back to face me and unzipped her own dress. She was all business. I could tell she'd rehearsed this in her head. She was going to pull off her dress, but then she paused and the determination in her face vanished for a moment. She shuddered, then she pulled herself together. The familiar smell of her body lotion. Her perfume. She pulled the dress off over her head. My heart almost stopped when I saw her in her panties and bra.

She told me the story while she changed. The *Reader's Digest* version. She went to see Victor and told him she needed a favor. She'd take the apartment he wanted her to have and do whatever he said if he could help her out. She asked him to make sure her father had hell to pay. She wanted him beaten up. How badly beaten up? Victor asked her. She said he should stay alive. So they broke his spine and put him in a wheelchair. Now I give him a monthly allowance, she said. So that he can buy food. I don't ask what he does with it. If he wants to gamble it away, that's his business. I rented an apartment for him in Holon. Ground floor. And he can't go anywhere near my store. Wait here, she said. She left the changing room with the new dress on. She looked at herself in the mirror. It was convincing, that serious look girls get when they check themselves out in the mirror, trying on a new outfit. As sharp as a laser beam. I stayed inside, paced around the small changing room. The driver stood next to the car with his hands in his pockets, watching. She turned to him and showed him the dress, like in a fashion show. She twirled around, smiling, flipping her hair. She made faces. The whole shebang. Like how she used to get her tips. That was her act. He gave her a thumbs-up from outside the store window. The changing room still smelled of her perfume.

Then she came back, pulled off the dress, and stood there next to me in her underwear again. She was still practical. But I knew her. Her chest was heaving. I saw the pulse in her neck. That's the body that used to be in my bed, in a hundred rooms at the Sheraton, in my shower, in my hands, between my sheets.

The Orthodox guy was a bonus, she said. He got scared, you have no idea. Gave back all my money and returned the store to my name. It all worked out. She paused, watching me silently. All the words she'd rehearsed suddenly went dry. It didn't work out the way I wanted it to, she said. You know this isn't what I wanted. Her eyes were a question mark.

I said nothing.

Her voice broke. Can I smell you, one last time? she said. She put her face to my neck and breathed. She burrowed into my neck. I hugged her. She inhaled one last time and broke away. She put on the dress she wore when she came in, her face serious again. I could tell it took some effort to compose herself like that. She slipped a hand into her purse and pulled out three wads of crisp 200-shekel bills. Everything I'd paid for her debt, she said, and a little extra.

I wouldn't take it.

She put it on the bench.

I didn't touch it.

He'll get sick of me eventually, she said. You'll see.

I said nothing.

Okay, she said. A quick, embarrassed smile, without looking me in the eye. She left the changing room with the new dress draped over her arm. She paid for it, never turning back to me. And that was that. I'd have burned all that money if I thought that would bring her back. But it wouldn't.

I left the store with the money in a shopping bag. My heart was still pounding. The rush of seeing her was still there. It was like she was back. I thought I'd wait for her, no matter how long it took. Seven years. Fourteen years. Twenty. At some point, he'd have enough of her.

But at home, in the shower, it all fell into place. Any remnants of her perfume that were on me were now washed away with the soapy water. Standing there in the steam, everything was suddenly clear: I wasn't going to wait for her. It would be better that way. She was way out of my league. That was the truth. Even without that Bukharan asshole, she was too much for me. She was too much for me from the very beginning. People who are brave enough to jump off cliffs. More than I can ever handle.

A few months later I walked by the cell phone store and saw Ruti sitting behind the desk. I watched from across the street. She was busy with her phone. For a moment, an image passed through my mind: Ruti, ten years old, playing the piano with a sleeping mask on.

WOMEN

BY **Matan Hermoni**

Basel Street

A.

I first saw Nahum Tzobelplatz in January 2010 at the Kiryat Shaul Cemetery, for Abraham Sutzkever's funeral. It was raining. It was cold and it was sad. Sad for those present, those who accompanied Sutzkever to the grave, and sad for me. I felt as bitter as can be, for the dead and for the living too—meaning, for me. I was swimming in an ocean of self-pity, I'm not ashamed to say. I found some comfort in the sadness hovering over everyone there. Finally sadness was the lot of all the people around me and not just my own.

Yes, it was cold and it was sad. Before us lay the poet, wrapped in a shroud, and around him were his family and friends and acquaintances and admirers, including me. The raincoats and umbrellas and top hats and tears and scarves and boots and overshoes, all of those blended together. Yes, the deceased was gone from this world, and this world would miss the deceased.

I spotted Nahum Tzobelplatz among those attending. At the time I didn't even know his name. It would become known to me within a few weeks, maybe a month. But among the crowd that included all sorts of types, he, as they say, stood out. A guy, a man, a bit older than me, thin, with a schnoz and some wrinkles on his forehead. There was a sparkle in his eyes.

He wore a short and shabby peacoat and beneath it a suit jacket; his white shirt seemed veiled in some yellow vapor, like nicotine. He wore a scarf around his neck and his pants matched his jacket.

He was talking to Vladimir Gelmann, the secretary of Beth Sholem Aleykhem. He leaned in and whispered in his ear. Vladimir—Volodya, as we called him—tried to stifle a smile resulting from Nahum Tzobelplatz's whisper. He wasn't entirely successful. His lips remained pursed, but behind his glasses his eyes glimmered.

Nahum Tzobelplatz's eyes smiled too. As I said, they sparkled. That expression became engraved in my mind for some reason, a sort of inexpugnable first impression, a passport one man earns in another's memory.

Months passed, two seasons went by, before I asked him about it.

I said, "What were you smiling about at the funeral, Nahum?"

"What was I smiling about?" he returned my question. "I smiled about crying."

"If you don't want to tell me, don't tell me." I pretended to be insulted.

He wasn't impressed. He pulled a pack of cigarettes out of his shirt pocket, lit one, and returned the pack to his jacket pocket. We were sitting on the balcony of my apartment. It was June, and Tel Aviv was burning with the *Tammuz* sun. The fan sawed through the air above us. Nahum Tzobelplatz wore a white shirt and a jacket. I sweated and sweated.

We'll get back to June soon. But wait, we're still in January. Yes. We're at the funeral hall at Kiryat Shaul. There are no beads of sweat here, but rather tears and raindrops. The rain pleased me, as did, I already noted, the sadness. I am not a party pooper by nature. But at the time, in January 2010, and through the better part of 2009, things were, how shall I put it, very bad.

B.

Yes. Things were very bad, on every level, and especially on the main issues that I shall hereby detail:

a. The novel I wrote had been sentenced to oblivion.
b. I was penniless.
c. (a derivative of b, or perhaps b is a derivative of c) I had no source of income.
d. My wife told me to go to hell.
e. (a derivative of d) I still loved my wife.

About a month and a half before the funeral, I had moved into an apartment on Arba Aratzot Street. Yes. That morning I got up, packed two suitcases, two duffel bags, and two backpacks, and faltered down the stairs of the fine building my wife and I lived in, and which now housed only my wife. I left in haste, like the Israelites fleeing Egypt.

It was a month and a half before Nahum Tzobelplatz and I first crossed paths. Then, a month after our first encounter, he would show up in my apartment.

Not much had changed since I'd seen him at the funeral. I spent the intervening weeks holed up between the four walls of an apartment I rented for 4,500 shekels a month—1,125 silver shekels per wall. But it wasn't only my glum spirit that kept me within those walls. It was mostly my financial standing. Those who step out of their homes get holes in their pockets, and the bills and coins fall through the holes and find their way into the hands of café owners, bar owners, shop owners, and other kinds of owners operating cash registers. And I—I didn't have any money. I didn't have bills or even coins. As such, I didn't go out much.

And yet, once in a while I'd wander the streets at dusk, between the sun and the moon, a meaningless and purposeless wandering, my only objective to let some fresh air seep between my bones. On one of these rare occasions, I returned home to find a man standing naked as the day he was born, in front of my closet, rummaging among the shirts and undershirts and jackets. Some of these were mine and some belonged to the previous tenant, a lonely old man who passed away mere days before I moved in. The apartment had been cleared out with haste and prepared for a new tenant. (In Tel Aviv, only real estate moves quicker than death.) Its new owners, his inheritors, left his gabardine suits, top hats, winter jackets, belts, and cuff links. The deceased, when he was still alive, was an elegant man, to judge by his wardrobe. There were some nice items in there. I have to point out that, had his inheritors been in less of a rush, they'd have found purpose in those things. But they, all they cared about were the walls. The walls and the land registry. And what are clothes when compared to walls? What are fabrics compared to floor tiles? I had to sleep on a bed in which a man, I think his name was Katzanelbogen, had died only days before, but I inherited some damn fine suits. Yes. A man needs one good suit. Me, I had several.

Really, I couldn't complain.

The man who was found in my apartment, at dusk in February, had taken off one suit and was about to put on another. Shadows moved among the shutters. Dark was about to take charge of the room, and still it was easy to see that the suit the man had removed not only needed a good cleaning, but was ratty, the kind of cheap suit you buy at a textile shop in southern Tel Aviv. As far as I know, the main clientele in those shops is immigrants, newly arrived; those who cannot afford to buy jackets at finer stores, like those on Dizengoff Street. Like I said, neither could I, though some of the jackets in those display windows have caught my eye. I've developed quite a taste in recent months, as well as an eye for fabric and quality sewing. I can spot the good ones from miles away.

Regardless, a naked man was standing in my room.

The naked man saw me and nodded in greeting. I nodded back. He slowly reached into the closet and pulled out a pair of underwear (mine) and an undershirt (Mr. Katzanelbogen's) and put them on. Though he appeared slightly older than I was, he was very skinny. He had a narrow rib cage. The ribs themselves threatened to break through his skin. I mostly wondered what he could have trapped within such a narrow rib cage. What could possibly fit there? Maybe some of his organs remained outside of it, something from the endocrinological system or his digestive tract. I don't know, maybe the adrenal gland, or the gallbladder. There was no space for all of these. How could such a narrow, modest rib cage trap a soul?

Yes. The naked man in my apartment—there was nothing obscene about his nudity. In fact, he looked as if he'd just emerged from a *mikveh* or a Turkish bathhouse and was searching for his clothes. He was a man, I was a man; what he had, I had. A moment passed before I noticed this was the same person I saw at Abraham Sutzkever's funeral, whispering with Vladimir Gelmann. Now I also saw that the suit that lay on the chair in my bedroom was the same one that guy, that character, that man, had worn at the funeral. An inexpensive gray suit. I'm a bit ashamed to admit it—after all, I am a writer, a Hebrew writer, and therefore an intellectual, and an intellectual should not be wasting his time and mind thinking about trifles such as suits and fabrics, and pondering the quality of sewing and stitching—but I think that if one wears a suit, one should make it a proper suit. If you go out to buy a suit, make an effort and crack open your wallet. A nice suit doesn't come cheap. If you don't spend the money, it doesn't look right. But to each his own. I have my own suits.

C.

Nahum Tzobelplatz was born in Berditchev in 1870 and died in Warsaw in 1905. Those were the days of pogroms, in Kishinev and in Odessa and even in Warsaw. But Nahum Tzobelplatz, he did not die at the hands of rioters. He died in rather embarrassing circumstances. In fact, he died of a broken heart. It happened when one Warsaw lady, a whore by vocation, informed him that he must leave her be, doing so in the company of a man in charge of her livelihood. He was not a very nice guy. But Nahum couldn't let go. However, in order to keep visiting her bed, he had to pay, and he had no money. At any rate, he got drunk at a gentile restaurant. He didn't pay for his drinks—and oh, did he ever drink. He was caught and pummeled. A policeman walked by and didn't raise a finger to help. Those were the days of pogroms, as I've said. If policemen did nothing for Jews who were murdered for no reason, they certainly wouldn't do a thing for a Jew who was caught stealing. It was winter. He walked on the bridge over the Vistula River, stumbled, and fell. The water was frozen, or near frozen. Had it been fully frozen, he would have broken his bones, but he might have lived. The water was a bit over thirty degrees, and a thin crust of ice had formed on the surface. But the water hadn't frozen over fully, and Nahum Tzobelplatz drowned and died. And all for the love of a whore.

That's how he tells it, at least, if you care to believe ghosts.

I said, "I was sure you'd died of tuberculosis. I was sure you coughed so hard that your soul left your body."

He said, "You've been reading too many books."

I said, "What do books have to do with this?"

He said, "It's a famous literary rule: a Jewish writer dies of tuberculosis, not of whores."

I said, "To each his own."

He said, "Whores are for the French, not for the Jews."

I said, "Times have changed."

He said, "You know the one about Rashi and the French?"

I said, "I know it," and hoped silently that he wouldn't tell it. I blush all the way up to my earlobes whenever someone tells that joke. My prayers were answered this time. If not other prayers, at least this one.

He didn't tell it. Instead he said, "Literal meanings need not be explained."

I sighed in relief.

He continued: "The homiletic is that what's good for French writers is good for French writers, and what's good for Jewish writers is good for Jewish writers."

I said, "I didn't know you were a writer."

He was insulted. "You didn't?"

An unpleasant silence ensued. He thought I knew who he was. I found out later that he thought I'd recognized him at Abraham Sutzkever's funeral, and that this was the reason I'd stared at him. But my reasons had been different. It's happened to me more than once and can be a little uncomfortable. This staring habit of mine has caused me several embarrassing incidents, and one scandal.

I said, "No." It is a well-known rule that the truth is often the best lie.

He said, "Those in the know would realize who I am. I used to be famous in Warsaw literary circles. I thought you were in the know."

I said, "I'm in the know on some matters, and less so on others."

He said, "That guy, he knew who I was right away. He'd read my story in *Hashiloach* journal in 1904." When he said this, he mentioned the name of a man, a writer, my age. We used to be friends. Any mention of his name made my vision go dark, as they say. This particular writer was now bathing in tubs of money and respect, while I wallowed in this derelict apartment, visited by a demon.

I kept my cool in spite of this and said, "Go live in his house then."

The demon said, "I merely pointed out that he'd heard of me and my stories, and it would behoove you to read them too."

I said nothing.

The insult clung to us, not letting go. To appease him, I searched for the copy of *Hashiloach* in which he claimed that Bialik, who was the editor at the time, had published his short story. He also said Bialik had sent him a letter in which he praised the story, and so on and so forth. But I couldn't find the story, or the name of my demon, Nahum Tzobelplatz, in the index of Bialik's book of letters—he was known to have all his letters edited quite carefully, what he wrote to one man becoming the property of all. I searched by Nahum's first name and last, I searched this way and that, I even asked a man I know and cherish, an important professor, if he'd heard of this Nahum who'd taken hold of my apartment, but he hadn't.

Yes. This professor has been blessed with many qualities, but modesty, as they say, was not one of them. "If I haven't heard of someone," he told me, "there must be a good reason for it."

I couldn't argue with that. And yet, not only did this demon in my apartment claim to have existed, to have been a writer, to have published in Bialik and Klausner's journal, *Hashiloach*, but he was wearing my clothes and eating my food. He didn't ask for much—he was a ghost, after all—but even a ghost has to eat something, and today everything costs a fortune. And if all of this weren't enough, he was just sitting there, insulted.

D.

Yes. We sat and conversed. I didn't have a job, and couldn't leave the house. Even if I had a roll of money, I would have sewed it into my pocket. What could I do? If any money came in, I'd give it to my landlord. My debts were growing by the minute.

As my creditors came from all directions, their advisors devising a collection plan, I sat with Nahum. On the table was a pack of cigarettes he had stolen. Cigarettes are very expensive these days. He smoked, and I smoked. I pulled the smoke from the cigarettes into my lungs and he pulled it into the netherworld. But what difference did it make? The cigarettes were free, and me, when something is free, I take it.

He asked, "Why did your wife kick you out?"

I thought for a moment and finally said, "For loving another woman, she kicked me out." Then I corrected myself: "Not really loving, just making love." That's what I said, and then blew a jet of smoke across the room.

Nahum thought for a moment and said, "A Jew, as long as there is blood in his veins, will be plagued by lust. As long as there's blood in his veins, and even when there isn't."

I said, "Yes. She was married too, the woman I made love to."

Nahum said, "I was also caught in a woman's net. With that kind of woman, fornication is seventy-seven times sweeter."

"Seventy-seven times," I repeated.

Letters addressed to me were still sent to my wife's address. Bills came here, letters went there. Good news went there, pogroms and calamities came here. Once in a while I went to her building and checked the mailbox. My wife left my letters there for me. It had been a long time since anything came.

I sighed. Nahum sighed too. Then we sighed together.

I said, "What kind of Jew are you, Nahum? It says, *Thou shalt not commit adultery*. It says, *Thou shalt not covet*."

Nahum Tzobelplatz said, "So it says. A Jew, as long as there's blood in his veins, evil will feed on that blood." Then he pondered again and after several moments of silence said, "As long as there's blood in his veins, and even when there isn't, evil will feed on his soul."

I said, "Yes. She read chapters of the novel I wrote, the woman I made love to. Then she wrote me a letter. She wrote, *Your words are intoxicating as a drug*. That's what she wrote me."

Nahum Tzobelplatz said, "A similar thing happened to me with the chapters I published in *Hashiloach*. There was one woman, quite well-known. I was in Warsaw and she was in Odessa. Her husband was a very famous man. She told him she was going to see her sister in Lviv and instead came to see me in Warsaw. Later on, the whole thing got out. People gossiped, *Nahum Tzobelplatz, he's involved with so-and-so's wife*."

Nahum Tzobelplatz is involved with so-and-so's wife. Yes. Each time I checked the mailbox, I thought the building door would open and I myself would emerge, carrying the two suitcases, two duffle bags, and two backpacks so full that their zippers threatened to burst. I stood there on the street and called a cab. It arrived within two minutes. And Nahum Tzobelplatz is involved with so-and-so's wife.

I said, "The woman I had an affair with, her husband is also very famous. Not in the literary world, but in the business world. He's a rough person, and she's tender. The chapters she read of my novel, she told me, awoke hungry demons within her."

Nahum Tzobelplatz said, "And my lady, she wrote, *I'm possessed. A dybbuk is devouring my heart.* That's what she wrote. She told her husband, the famous man, that she was going to one place, and instead she came to me, to Warsaw."

I said, "I used to meet my married woman in one of her husband's apartments. He was so rich he forgot he owned it. Sometimes," I reminisced, "she rented a room at the Hilton instead, right over the cliff. An egret would land on our windowsill and tap the glass with its beak."

Yes. That morning a letter was waiting for me in my wife's mailbox. It was a letter from my wife herself, the owner of the mailbox. She asked that I go to the post office and give them my new address, so that any mail for me bearing her address would be forwarded to my apartment. *It would save you the trouble,* she wrote. Then she added, *The first six months are free of charge.*

A taxi stopped outside the building. A man I'd never seen before disembarked and walked inside. Judging by his jacket, he seemed to be in good financial standing. I have an eye for fabrics and everything to do with sewing and stitching. Yes,

I'm an intellectual, but even an intellectual needs one good jacket, and a jacket like the one the man wore as he got out of the cab shows taste and wealth.

I sighed. Nahum sighed too. Then we sighed together.

Nahum moved in his seat. "The rich, even the richest, they never forget a piece of property."

I said, "The rich don't, but the filthy rich do. There's rich, and then there's *rich*."

Nahum said, "Women," and sighed. I sighed too. Again we sighed together. He lit another cigarette. I took one too. As long as it's free, I'll smoke. Cigarettes are very expensive these days.

I've been sitting with my demon for four months. The demon doesn't ask for much, and I give him what I have. If someone needs to move into your home, at least let it be a demon.

Yes. Things are still tough. Especially on the following issues I shall hereby detail:

a. The novel I wrote has been sentenced to oblivion.
b. I am penniless.
c. (a derivative of b, or perhaps b is a derivative of c) I have no source of income.
d. My wife told me to go to hell.
e. (a derivative of d) I still love my wife.

THE TIME-SLIP DETECTIVE

BY LAVIE TIDHAR

Rabin Square

The Girl in the Window

I saw her first in a reflection in a shop window.

Along Ibn Gabirol, heading to the square, just before the street where Rabin was shot.

She wore a white cotton dress and sandals, her hair was auburn, our eyes met and hers opened wide in surprise. I glanced quickly away. Then I turned around to see her but no one was there. When I looked back into the shop window, even her reflection was gone.

Tidhar

It had been strange but the moment passed. I chalked it up to the heat, my mind playing tricks on me. I was in the center for an interview with a writer, a young novelist who has had some success overseas. His name was Tidhar, Lavie Tidhar, and he had won an international award, the World Fantasy Award, the week before, and so the paper wanted me to talk to him for a feature. I had spoken to him on the phone a couple of days earlier, in preparation, and he told me of his obsession with old Hebrew pulp fiction. In particular he was interested in the old stories of private detective David Tidhar, which had come out in the 1930s. The coincidence of sharing the detective's family name fascinated him. His original family name had been Heisikovitch, which his family had changed in the

1970s, just before he was born, part of a long tradition of immigrants reverting to Hebrew names. He and the detective were not related.

Though we had agreed to meet by Rabin Square, he didn't show. When I rang him he apologized and said his wife was unwell and could we reschedule, and so we did. I was still thinking about the girl I saw; there had been something so old-fashioned about her dress, it was like what my grandmother used to wear as a girl when she arrived in Israel all those years ago from Transylvania. I grabbed a shawarma from Dabush and then, wiping the grease from my face, decided to escape the heat and the noise and so went into Landwer.

Landwer is an old coffee house, perhaps the oldest still surviving in Tel Aviv. I stepped into the cool room and sat by the window and ordered an iced coffee. I flipped through a David Tidhar pamphlet that I had found at great expense to prepare for the interview, but which I hadn't yet read. The detective's photo stared at me from the cover in faded black-and-white as I opened the pamphlet and began to read.

Erzsebet and the Detective

The famous detective, David Tidhar, was in the café. He wore his trademark fedora and a long trenchcoat, despite the heat. The waitress was fawning over him, and a young boy ran up to him and asked for an autograph, which the detective gracefully signed. Are you working on a case? the boy asked, and the detective smiled and patted his head and said he was just ordering a cappuccino.

Only the month before, Tidhar had single-handedly foiled an international group of diamond smugglers operating out of Jerusalem. Dressed as a woman, he pursued them to Paris, where he revealed himself dramatically at the Moulin Rouge club in the Place Pigalle. Now the gang were safely behind bars. *Haynt* was filled with tales of his exploits, as were the Hebrew tabloids. Even now, you could see a couple of *shmekes*, working for the tabloids, milling outside with their cameras.

The detective was waiting. He kept his eyes on the doors of the café. Landwer, on Ibn Gabirol Street, named for the golden-age poet, was across the road from Kings of Israel Square. A zeppelin was parked in the sky above the square, the large Star of David visible on its side. Electric cars passed quietly in the street outside and men in hats doffed them politely as the girls passed.

Then she walked in.

She wore a light summer dress—they had been all the rage in Paris the year before. She wore sandals on her feet. Her skin was pale, not brown like some of those farmer girls from Galilee. For a moment she paused in the doorway, a little anxious, watching the people sitting inside. Soft music played—Chopin, on Landwer's electric radio. Years ago it had been the first café in Herzlberg to install an electric radio. A landmark, an institution, Landwer was. The detective, David Tidhar, half rose in his seat. The girl saw him and relief momentarily flashed on her face. She walked to him. He stood up fully and pulled over a chair for her, then waited for her to sit. She sat. They both did.

—You are the detective? In her hand she was holding a pamphlet. It was familiar. It detailed the detective's latest exploits, as published every week by his faithful biographer, Shlomo Ben-Yisrael. Like any other volume in the Hebrew Detective Library, it comprised thirty-two pages and carried the detective's likeness prominently on the cover. The last two pages contained ads for Ascot Cigarettes (*Smoke Like A Man!*), Elite instant coffee (*Quicker—Better*), and for the

King David Dirigible Company (*Comfort in the Skies!*)—one vessel of which was floating outside, above the square.

The pamphlet was priced at 200 *pruta*. Thousands of copies were rushed off the presses every week, to be sold at kiosks across the country. While the stories are frowned upon by some educational types as nothing but cheap entertainment, our youth cannot, understandably, get enough of it.

—I am he, the detective said. He looked at the girl keenly. His gaze was soft, but one had the sense it could turn cold and hard when faced with a wrongdoer. One heard stories, from the days before our country became the peaceful and civilized place it is now, when this place was not yet called Tel Aviv, the Fount of Spring, but rather Palestine. How he had killed more than forty Arab marauders with his bare hands, how he stalked a gang of murderous bedouins and assassinated each one in cold blood, all in service of the dream.

—You are Erzsebet? he said.

—Yes, the girl replied.

If the detective noticed the non-Hebrew form of her name, he withheld comment. Gravely, he signaled to the waitress to bring his new companion a hot chocolate. Then he reached into his coat and brought forth a tobacco pouch and a pipe. It was a Bruyere pipe, made by Parker of London. The detective packed the tobacco carefully into the pipe and lit it with a match. He blew out fragrant smoke and gazed at the girl, Erzsebet, through the haze. He waved the match to extinguish the flame and dropped it into the ashtray on the table.

—What did you wish to see me in regards to, Miss Erzsebet? the detective asked. His eyes seemed to twinkle. The girl still held the pamphlet, awkwardly. Its title this week was *The Time-Slip Detective*.

—Do you ever think none of this is real? she said. Her

voice was quiet, but carried a sense of desperation. The detective's eyes lost their sparkle. Had become, indeed, hard. His silence seemed to infuriate the girl. This! she said. All this! Her hand rose, swept across the table, sending cups and saucers of delicate Viennese china to the floor, where they broke with an obscene sound. The girl stood up, still shouting. All of this! She was waving the pamphlet. It was stained red. The girl must have cut herself on the glass; a thin gash had opened in her pale flesh, and she was bleeding.

—Sit down! the detective said.

The girl sat down. Her shoulders shook.

—I don't know what to do, she said. I see them, even now, I see them. Look! She pointed at the window. Pointed at her reflection.

Kfir

I turned to the window. The cold blast of air-conditioning made my hair stand on end, the pamphlet felt grimy in my hand. In the reflection I saw her, instead of myself, sitting in the same place I was occupying. I was startled, it felt to me as if I were reading a book. What is your name? I said, and at exactly the same moment I saw her lips move, forming the same question, though I could hear no sound come out. Kfir, I said, urgently—

Erzsebet

—Erzsebet, *ikh heys* Erzsebet, the girl said, *vos maynt* Kfir?—

The Wrong Door

—That's my name, I said, Kfir, and, Erzsebet, what kind of a name is Erzsebet?

It almost felt to me, trying to read her lips, like she was

speaking Yiddish. But that was madness, as mad as a zeppelin with a Star of David on its gondola hovering over Tel Aviv. Behind her I could see a man dressed in a raincoat and a fedora, like something out of an old pulp novel. He was staring at me. I pushed back my chair, it crashed to the floor. The girl's hand, I saw in the reflection, was bleeding. I turned around. It was too cold inside. I felt trapped inside the glass. Other customers backed away from me. I have to get some fresh air, I said to no one in particular. I reached into my pocket, brought out a handful of coins, left them on the table. I had to get out. I staggered away, but I must have taken the wrong door by mistake.

Trapped

The detective said, How long has this been going on?

—I keep seeing them, the girl said. The sound of desperation in her voice was real. It's like being trapped in a film reel with no escape. You have to help me. Please.

—You should not have come to me, the detective said, and there was something sad, but also cold, in his voice. Come with me, he said. He paid for the drinks though they had not yet arrived. He put away his pipe and stood up. He was a man of the law. I said come with me! He took the girl by the hand and she cried out; it was the one she had cut. The detective paid her no mind, dragged her from the table toward the door. My car is parked outside, he said. It was a Sussita, from the Autocars Company of Haifa. The girl did not resist him. The detective pushed the door open and they went outside, into the glare of the sun.

Gunshots

The sun hit me and for a moment I was blinded. I blinked

back tears. When I opened my eyes fully I saw the city, but it was not the same city. A zeppelin hovered over Rabin Square, an impossible Star of David on its gondola. The people were dressed in European fashions, men in light suits and hats, women in dresses. Their cars moved like tiny beetles along the road, not making any sound. A car whose chassis was made of fiberglass was parked nearby. I heard the door opening again behind me. I turned and caught sight of a man in a fedora and a trench coat. He saw me at the same time I saw him. Something in his demeanor troubled me. I dropped when I saw his arm rising, clutching a handgun. The shot was muffled. The gun was of a type I had never seen.

—You should not have come here, he said, and his voice was like that of a biblical prophet, promising doom. He raised his hand again to fire. At that moment a small figure emerged behind him. The girl I'd seen. Erzsebet.

—No! she said. She pushed his arm and his shot missed high. She ran to me. We have to go! she said. She took me by the hand. We ran.

Behind us I heard the man shouting. He sounded incensed. I will *shtup* you in the *tuches*, you little *feigale*! he said.

—*Kacken zee ahf deh levanah!* Erzsebet shouted back. We ran around the corner and his third gunshot hit a streetlamp and showered us with glass.

I *think* he threatened to fuck me in the ass, and I *think* Erzsebet told him to go take a shit on the moon. But I can't be sure.

—Quickly! Erzsebet said. I could half understand her, she spoke Hebrew intermingled with Yiddish, words I barely remembered from my grandparents' house. A streetcar! she said.

I gasped as a silent tram appeared from Frishman and along Ibn Gabirol. The doors opened and we jumped inside.

Herzlberg

—I'd heard stories, she told me, later. We were in a house on the Yarkon. It is not so much a river as a brook. Its water was clean, I could see fish swimming, and children were bathing across the way from us, shouting and laughing. Where I come from that same river is filthy, though there had been recent efforts to clean it. I remembered the case of a girl who had been thrown into the river—her grandfather had murdered her and put her body into a suitcase and sailed it down the river.

—What sort of stories? I asked.

—About people like you. About another place, like this one. He will find us, you know. He is the foremost detective of the era, a hero. I should not have gone to him. We do not have much time.

—It's so peaceful here, I said.

—It is wonderful, she agreed. She leaned against me. How I hate to see that other place! she said.

—You're still bleeding. Here, let me . . . Awkwardly I tried to clean her hand, to bandage it.

—Leave it be, she said, stroking my hair. Your clothes are so . . . strange, she said. She smelled of fresh milk and sweat. Her skin was so pale.

—There are many problems where I come from, I said. Now I stroked her hair too. We sat very close together. It felt unreal, the heat and the humming of bees, in the middle of the city. But this was not my city. We have wars, I said. Terrorism. We fight with the Palestinians.

—Palestinians?

—The people who used to live here, I said.

—Oh, she said. We don't have them.

Her lips were close to mine. She was warm, but she shivered in my arms. Oh, Kfir, she said. She kissed me and I kissed her back.

—What do you mean, you don't have them? I said.

—It was Herzl's dream. This. All this. *Altneuland,* he called it. Old New Land. We call it Tel Aviv.

—That's what we call the city, I said, and she laughed.

—That's silly. We call it Herzlberg.

—But what happened to the Arabs? I asked. To everyone who lived here before you came?

She shrugged. They would have ruined the dream, she said. And I remembered Herzl's book, the electric lights and the well-planned cities and the airships passing high above in their slow majestic flight, from the snowy peaks of Mount Hermon to the shores of the Red Sea. A land of happy, modern Jews.

—There was no room for them, she said. So they had to go.

She kissed me again. She was on top of me, I was lying on my back in the grass. I heard a sound then, like a distant explosion. That woke me, I think. She grew less substantial in my hands. I felt a sudden fear grasp me. A place so clean, so orderly. She kissed me again, began to pull my T-shirt off. And I thought of soldiers in green uniforms getting on a bus, of politicians shouting with spittle flying, of the sound of the siren on Memorial Day, and she grew less substantial still, and I heard car doors opening and shutting, and I thought of an El Al flight, of the long line for security, the endless questioning, the body scanners, the cramped rows and bad kosher food and black-clad Hasidim changing diapers, of the calls of the mosques in Jaffa and of Victory ice cream up on the hill, and she grew ever less substantial, and I heard footsteps coming close, not hurrying, and saw the shadow of the detective fall on the grass beside me, and I saw him raise his hand.

For a moment our eyes met. He nodded once. He was just an outline by then. Don't come back, he said. I heard the gunshot, but when I opened my eyes it was just some Filipino construction workers having an impromptu picnic by the Yarkon, next to an Arab family who were setting up a barbecue, while two young women jogged past and someone with more enthusiasm than sense was trying to row a boat on the river.

The river smelled. And I walked home.

Tel Aviv

It's getting better now. The news helps—Channel 2, Reshet Bet on the radio once an hour, CNN, the newspapers. Rockets over Gaza, an exploding bus in Tel Aviv, the deaths and mutilations anchor me, a rope to pull me back into the right place and time. The sight of a concrete apartment building blown open with mortar, a child's plastic doll on the ground, its blue eyes staring into the camera. A mass funeral, a coffin draped with a flag, men waving guns in the air, and I realize with a start that I can't even tell who they are, Muslim or Jew.

The news helps, and I immerse myself in the secondhand bookshops, the moldy, lurid paperbacks from the 1960s, with unlikely author names such as Mike Longshott and Kim Rockman and the pictures of scantily clad women, two-foot-tall Korean secret agents, monsters, ghosts, Nazis, and cowboys; and I avoid that damned Hebrew detective, David Tidhar.

I hope to never see another bloody zeppelin.

This story was originally written in English.

SLOW COOKING

by Deakla Keydar

Levinsky Park

I'm the only one who asks for a Thursday-night shift. Stella and Diana have barely worked here for two years, so no one asks them what shifts they want. But I'm a veteran, and I still ask specifically for that shift.

Thursday night is the hardest shift. It's bearable until seven or eight in the evening. Probably because customers are still busy with showers and dinners. But I guess after their kids go to bed they realize the supermarket is about to close for the Sabbath, and then our phone lines nearly overload. Thursday-night customers are the most nervous and suspicious. Any delay, any substitute product we suggest, any special offer we're obligated to tell them about before completing the order, makes them lash out at us. But we put our emotions aside. That's the first rule of working at Plenty Market. Over the years I've found it easier than I'd expected.

On Thursday night we split the workload. Except for at ten o'clock, when I usually do pickup while Stella and Diana answer the phones. That way we get more done and increase our chances of getting a promotion. After Stella once walked around for over forty minutes looking for untoasted cashew nuts, and another time when Diana almost got fired because she couldn't find nonkosher matzo meal, and dared argue with the customer, claiming it didn't exist—we decided I would do pickup. No customer can confuse me.

And I like working these hours. Diana plays classical music on the main checkout speakers, and it's dark outside but bright and colorful inside. I push the cart with one hand, hold the list of orders in the other, and imagine all the Friday-night dinners our customers are planning. Not that there are many surprises. Other than that guy from Jabotinsky Street, who orders thirteen cans of tuna and four family-packs of toilet paper every week, or that woman from Ben Yehuda Street with her seven family-size bags of jelly beans (one bag per day, her husband doesn't know, she once told Stella), most families make a standard order: salmon or frozen tilapia or Nile perch, ground beef, rice, pasta, vegetables. Very similar to my sister Shoshi's Friday-night menu.

I also load a shopping cart for myself on Thursday night: five tomatoes, five cucumbers, cheese, bread, lemon wafers to have with my coffee. That's all I get, even though I have an employee discount. That's all I need until Saturday, and on Sunday morning I'm back here anyway. Thursday is the only night shift I do since the conversation I had with Mati six months ago.

Mati had just come home from work and I immediately noticed the lunch I packed him had not been eaten. He said he didn't have an appetite, which isn't like him because he always eats, even when he's sick, especially meatballs with rice and peas in red sauce, which I had made that day.

I watched him all evening, hoping it wasn't serious. Even when the kids showered and played, and when one of them ended up in tears, as usual, and they didn't speak all through dinner, even then I noticed him looking at the omelet like there was something wrong with it. I gave him a glass of water and two painkillers. Was he trying to act like a hero? I told him to rest, but instead he read the kids a story, helped them brush their teeth, and didn't sit still all evening.

Later, when we got into bed, I picked up my book and waited for him to reach for his. But instead he leaned back and sighed. I moved closer to him and pressed my lips against his forehead like I do when I check if the children have a fever. He fidgeted.

"Do you feel all right?" I asked.

"No," he said, and sighed again. "I don't feel good."

"What hurts?"

He was silent for a moment, then said, "I think I need a change."

My knees began trembling under the covers. "What kind of change?"

"I don't think I can live here anymore. I need a break."

"Did you tuck the children in?" I asked. "They throw off their blankets at night."

He stared at me for a moment. "No," he said, and started getting up, but I beat him to it and he remained perched on the edge of the bed. I arrived at the children's room breathless, as if I'd just run a mile. I turned the light on. They were sleeping deeply. The eldest with her arms spread to her sides, legs stretched out, the youngest squeezed tight like a beetle.

I felt my pulse in my ears. Every day, ten people make the same assumption he just did: that *I'm* their problem. If a product is out of stock, if the delivery person can't find their home, if the frozen corn thaws by the time they get it—it's my fault. My job is to cordially fix the problem, or, as our manager puts it, "to remove the human factor from the equation," and compensate them accordingly. I squeezed my knees tight and returned to the bedroom, running my hand against the wall. He was sitting up in bed, looking at me.

"You need a change," I said, "but I'm not the problem."

I leaned against the door and glanced at the frame hanging over our bed, with the printed photo of Mati and me in

Palma de Mallorca from ten years earlier. We had saved for that vacation since we met and hadn't gone on another one since. The photo was almost completely faded now.

"So what are you saying?" he asked.

I took a deep breath. "You sit in your lottery booth all day, not moving. Your world is narrow. All you see every day is people losing money. What do you expect? You think you can do this for another twenty years? You said it yourself: the best moment of your day is when you prank call me—and now *I'm* what you need to change?"

My knees were still trembling. I realized I never ended up tucking in the children, and I left the light on.

"Did you always think that?" he asked.

"Yes." That was a lie. His work was steady, with good benefits and all the retirement and insurance funds. It was our future.

"So what do you suggest, that I quit?" he asked. "Who's going to hire me? At my age? I have no education, no connections. All I know how to do is sit in a booth."

"Find another job and then quit, that's how it works." I glared at him. "You don't just break up a family like that, Mati."

A few days later we heard honking outside the house. The kids and I went out to the balcony. A giant red truck was parked at our curb and behind the wheel was none other than Mati, glowing with joy, though he'd found the most dangerous job there is—delivering chemicals, driving at night on the most treacherous roads in Israel. It paid even less than his lottery job and it offered no special benefits, but I didn't say a word. I remembered that Mati was born with an excellent sense of direction. He could always explain to me, slowly and quietly, where to turn and when, and what I should be seeing on my left and right. And the kids were excited.

He drove at night and slept during the day. When I left for work he was just getting back, and when I came home he left again. He complained about the noise the kids made when he tried to sleep during the day, though sometimes he'd wake up upset from the sound of me yelling at them to be quiet. He announced that he was going to sleep at his mother's place from then on, and one day the kids told me he'd rented a one-bedroom apartment right around the corner.

I asked him over for a talk. What a waste, to rent a second apartment, and so close too. Like throwing away money—rent, food. He said it was only temporary, that his mother was getting on his nerves, that he needed his own "quiet corner" but wanted to stay close to the kids. He'd get a couple of beds, and then they could come spend the night at his place when he wasn't working, and I'd have some peace and quiet too.

But who wanted peace and quiet from the kids? On the contrary, I wanted them around me all the time, making noise. I played Monopoly and trivia with them, helped them with homework, walked to the park, went to get falafel, played music in the living room, and danced. I even liked dozing off with them in our bed, in front of the television, one of them on either side of me, and then waking up with them in the morning, warm and sleepy. My sister Shoshi kept saying, "This must be hard on you," but I said it wasn't. I had less cleaning and cooking to do. If I had any complaints, they were directed only at myself.

Then things started to change. It was as if the kids suddenly lost their patience with me. If I hogged too much of the blanket at night, if the pita I made them for school fell apart, if I didn't sign a letter from their teacher that they never even showed me, they got pissed off. And they were hungry all the time. They roamed the kitchen, opening and closing fridge and cabinet doors. I cooked and cooked and nothing satiated them. They banged their fists on the table like prisoners. Sometimes I couldn't help myself and banged their plates down on the table in response, sending the food everywhere.

When I went to work with defeat on my face, Stella and Diana suggested I try to imagine they were customers. Put your emotions aside, tell them it's temporary. The kids would ask me about twenty times a day when Daddy was coming home, as if that same question didn't drive me mad as well. And I just kept saying it was temporary.

One day Mati called to tell me he got a couple of mattresses and wanted the kids to stay with him from Thursday night to Saturday, his days off work. I wasn't going to have any of that. What was he thinking, leaving me without the kids all weekend?

"This is their home," I told him. "You want to see them on Saturday? Come home."

I didn't give up. I took them to dinner at Shoshi's on Friday night. In the kitchen, she scolded me that the kids were telling everyone I wouldn't let them see their dad. What kind of primitive behavior was this, she wanted to know, fighting him at their expense? I was going to end up with no husband and no kids.

That's how I ended up giving away my kids for the weekends. Thursday night to Saturday night. No kids.

Since last March. It's been over six months.

I immediately asked the manager for the Thursday-night shift.

And on my very first shift, I noticed Dr. Alex Michael.

It's not that this customer, from 31 Bloch Street, was anything special. But he was a pleasant surprise after so many irate, impatient, and rude customers who made me regret not heeding Stella and Diana's warnings about this particular shift. He said "please" and "thank you." I took down his order with special care, and asked, "Would you like anything else?"

He said, "Yes, to tell you that you're very nice."

I thanked him and we said goodbye. Mati didn't think I was nice. The kids didn't think I was nice. Even Shoshi didn't think I was nice, trying to avoid going to her place for Friday-night dinner. Without the kids, there was no point in going, but she kept twisting my arm. "It's important that you get out of the house," she said.

I thought maybe this was Dr. Alex Michael's first time ordering groceries and that's why he was so kind, but I checked the records and found that he was a veteran customer at Plenty Market, and that he called every Thursday at ten o'clock and almost always ordered the same thing: pitas, vegetables, fruit, yogurt, chocolate milk, frozen food, meat, chicken breast, pasta, cornflakes, cleaning supplies, low-cal bread, sugarless cookies. A normal family. Two or three children, an overweight wife, a husband who does the grocery shopping. Mati used to shop for us as well, using my employee discount.

I kept signing up for the Thursday-night shift and waiting for ten o'clock. Even when he sounded tired, Dr. Alex Michael never made me feel like he held me responsible for the shortage of organic trash bags, or for the kilo of rotting apples he got the week before. He never asked suspiciously about the price of an alternate product I offered him, as if I had anything to gain from selling him something more expensive. On the contrary, he said he trusted me completely, and that I should make the substitution without even asking.

But two months ago, in August, something changed. Dr. Alex Michael's large family order grew smaller: three apples, two pears, dental floss, cleaning supplies. I thought maybe they were going on vacation. People have many reasons for changing a standing order. We can't ask the customers personal questions, of course. But by the fourth week I got the picture. No cornflakes, no star-shaped frozen schnitzel, no Splenda.

It was the order of a family man who found himself spending a large chunk of his time alone.

I was surprised by the tear that left my eye as I typed in Dr. Alex Michael's order. Five cucumbers, butter, half a loaf of bread, half a carton of eggs, frozen chicken nuggets. He asked if I had gotten a cold in honor of winter and told me to take care of myself and drink hot tea with lemon. I couldn't help myself and asked if he was a general practitioner. He said he was an orthopedic doctor, a hand specialist. We ended the conversation.

Stella was eating canned mackerel with a plastic fork and handed me a tissue. She looked at me as if she had a right to everything I was feeling.

I waved my hand at her. That mackerel she was eating was much pricier than the five shekels worth of merchandise we were allowed to eat per shift. It could put our jobs at risk. The contracting company would have no problem replacing us with cheaper, younger hires who didn't steal mackerel. I know. Lots of employees have come and gone in the time we've been here. Diana, Stella, and I were the only ones who survived.

She said its sell-by date had passed, and that she took it from the returns cart.

I apologized.

She came closer, enveloping me with her large body, and said I had to try it because it tasted like her home. Stella's home was in Romania. She used to be a math teacher there. Diana came from some Ukrainian village. She used to be a pianist. I'm the only one who was born in Israel, and I'm the only one who didn't use to be something else.

This past Thursday night I came to my shift all dressed and made up. Stella and Diana thought I had a date after work, but actually, my date had ended two hours earlier.

Mati called at four. He finished work early and asked if he could pick up the kids within the hour. I said fine, as long as they had a chance to finish eating before he came. He agreed. Without thinking too much, I took some minced meat and chicken breast out of the freezer and placed them on the counter to thaw. Then I showered, put on makeup, and started cooking. I chopped, I stirred, working quickly, like I was a participant in some sort of contest, though my food tastes best when it's slow-cooked. Within thirty minutes, I had a pot of rice and a beef stew on the stove. I fried twenty schnitzels, charred some eggplant to make a salad, chopped vegetables, and even unfroze bread in the microwave—something I never do. The kitchen was filled with nice smells. It had been forever since I last cooked a real meal. The kids usually had lunch at school, and I spent weekends alone. There was no point in cooking for just myself. I called the children over to taste the food, and they said it was delicious, which boosted my confidence. It quickly started to look like I was cooking for the entire neighborhood.

At five o'clock Mati honked outside.

I signaled to him from the balcony to come up, but the kids had already run out and climbed into the vehicle, bouncing on the seats. I saw him tell them to wave at me, and they did, looking like they couldn't wait to get out of there. He glanced at me from his high seat, waiting for me to wave back and let them go, so I did.

When I returned inside I saw they forgot their schoolbags. I could have called Mati, but I didn't. Let him deal with it in the morning.

I examined the pots. I still had two hours before my shift. What was I going to do with so much food over the weekend, all by myself? I felt like dumping it all, but I couldn't throw away food when there are children starving in Africa.

It's not like I was unkind to the customers during the evening shift, but it took me almost ten minutes to find the family-size pack of lavender-scented laundry softener, and I quoted the wrong sale price for tofu. Diana and Stella rolled their eyes at each other as they took delivery orders. Then Stella pretended to fall asleep, and Diana pretended to throw up. They made each other laugh, but I only followed the large clock in the main register: 9:50, 9:55, 9:58, 9:59.

"Plenty Market phone orders, good evening."

"Hi," he said. "Good evening."

"How can I help you?" I asked, as if I didn't recognize his voice. Stella and Diana were watching me, their hands on their hips, as if they'd caught me. Then I realized I was smiling.

"This is Dr. Alex Michael. How are you?" he said, and then added, "From Bloch Street."

I answered that I was well. I took down his order carefully, as if I couldn't remember it by heart. I offered him seasonal winter specials: croutons, strawberries, a six-pack of Krembo. He answered, "Yes, please," to all of my offers. When you're a doctor you can afford all the specials. It doesn't end up actually saving you any money, but it's fun. The only thing he refused was the Krembo, the one thing I would have definitely bought.

"There are no kids here, nobody to eat it," he said.

"I understand." I couldn't say more than that, of course. He was silent.

"Would you like anything else?" I asked, though I didn't want to end the conversation.

"Actually, I do want a few more things," he said.

It took a moment to register. "Go ahead."

"One kilo lentils," he said.

"Yes?"

"Two kilos rice."

"Why?" I couldn't believe I said that out loud.

"Excuse me?"

"What?" My head was tingling.

"Did you just ask why?"

"I asked . . . why you wanted rice and not pasta," I stuttered, "when we have pasta on sale, three packs for ten." I signaled to Diana to pass me her juice, took a large gulp, and coughed.

Diana and Stella watched me with concern.

"Fine, I'll take some pasta as well." I could hear him chuckle. "And while we're at it, do you really want to know why I need all these things?"

"Only if you want to tell me," I said weakly, though I never wanted him to remember me making the mistake of asking why. I felt sweat stains spreading under my arms.

"Then I'll tell you," he said. "And maybe you can even help me."

"Me?"

"I've decided to join a group that brings food to Levinsky Park, maybe you've heard of it?"

"Levinsky Park? We live in the area."

"So you must know there are refugees living there," he said.

"What, those blacks? In the tents?"

"Yes, the refugees." He cleared his throat. "So you've seen them."

"I told you, I live pretty close." I couldn't figure out what he was getting at.

"Well, I wasn't fully aware of what was happening there. I haven't been to the park in years, and it turns out the group that goes there, to Levinsky, is saving those refugees' lives. These people ran away from war, but they have nothing here—no food, no home, no safety, no protection. They ran from a political war to a war of survival."

"No one is forcing them to stay here," I said.

"Without getting into that debate, the fact is they're here now. They're hungry and tired. And when people are in those circumstances, they do things they later regret. This group is giving them a hand."

"And you want to give them a hand too?"

"Yes," he said.

"Is there a shortage of starving Israelis?"

"Unfortunately, no, there isn't. But I've wanted to volunteer for a long time, and I find this to be a noble cause, and I'm not ashamed to say it's also convenient. There's no bureaucracy, no donations to some questionable foundation. All you have to do is bring a pot of food and hand it out. That's all. You cook—they eat. It's the kind of good deed that speaks to me."

"That really is kind," I said. I meant it too.

"And it's a mitzvah. Did you know the Bible warns us about how we should treat foreigners no less than thirty-six times?"

"Honestly, I didn't know that."

"Society's morality is tested mainly through its treatment of the other, those who are different."

Alex Michael didn't just think I was nice, he was actually having a conversation with me. But I didn't really have an opinion about all that stuff, so I just asked, "How can I help you?"

"I need a simple recipe. You seem to know about this stuff, and I'm the kind of person who can even mess up an omelet."

"I really am a good cook." I smiled. "In our neighborhood I'm famous for my cooking."

"Great. So I need a recipe for lentils and rice. You already added those to my order. I hear the combination of carbs and proteins is the most nourishing for the refugees."

"Don't you have anybody to help you?" I asked. "I mean, if you've never cooked before."

"I want to do this myself, precisely because I'm no cook."

I knew the real reason. Asking for help is emphasizing that you're alone. "Okay, then, write down this recipe for red rice."

"Red rice? Is it complicated?"

"Not at all. Red lentils are ready in no time, and you cook them inside the rice. Do you have any cumin?"

I could tell he was reading off labels from his spice cabinet. "Nutmeg . . . parsley . . . cinnamon? Paprika? Do any of these work?"

Stella and Diana furrowed their brows at me.

"I'll add cumin to your order. It's 9.99, okay?"

"No problem, whatever you say."

I added tomato paste as well and dictated the instructions. When he finished writing them down, he said, "Wish me luck."

"Isn't it scary, going there?"

"I went there recently with some friends of mine who go almost every day. Not only was it not scary, it was fulfilling." His voice suddenly trembled. "I don't know how to describe it. Seeing a hungry person eating something you cooked yourself, and enjoying it, and feeling satiated. You know what that's like?"

My stomach cramped.

"It's extremely satisfying," he said. "It makes you forget about everything else—whether they should or should not be here, the Minister of Interior's decision, the risks. They're here, they're hungry. They can't speak a word of Hebrew, and you can tell they're in distress. It's been raining. So why not help them if we can? They're people, just like you and me."

You and me. That excited me.

"Why don't you open today's paper?" he said. "There are pictures. See for yourself. It's absurd. In the first pages, happy farmers after the first rain. In the last pages, you see pictures of refugees hiding under plastic bags, looking for shelter. You have to look at it."

I was already pulling the newspaper from the stack and flipping through it. Their dark faces really were very sad, and their tents were little more than large plastic bags. "I see," I said quietly. "It's a crying shame."

He sighed.

"When are you going there?" I asked.

"I was planning on going tomorrow afternoon. It's Friday, so I have time."

"I have time too," I almost yelled. "And not only do I have time, but I have pots full of food I don't know what to do with. My ex-husband has the kids all weekend. I have rice and meatballs, schnitzels, eggplant salad—they'd love my food, the blacks. They won't know what hit them."

He laughed. "That would be great!" Then he lowered his voice. "But maybe . . . you should try calling them Africans or Sudanese, or refugees. It's none of my business, I know, but they might take offense."

"Fine," I said, but really I was thinking about how I had just said *my ex-husband.*

"So if you come around five," he said, "we can actually meet!"

"I'll be there," I announced happily.

"You'll easily recognize me, I wear red glasses."

"You'll recognize me by the smell of good food, doctor."

He laughed. "Please call me Alex."

"Good night, Alex," I said and hung up. I felt like jumping up and down, but I held it in. The duration of our conversation blinked on the screen: twelve minutes. In the seven years I've worked here I've never had such a long call, not with the children, not even when Mati called me from his old job, bored, yelling at me in funny voices: "Hello??? I didn't get my milk!" "I was charged for a pack of mineral water I didn't buy!" "Where are all the condoms I ordered?"

The phones were ringing off the hook now, but Stella and Diana had to know everything.

"We're meeting tomorrow," I said.

They clapped their hands, and I stood up and took a bow before I realized I was blushing.

"What are you going to wear?" Diana asked.

I used to love Fridays, just like everyone else. Errands, cooking, cleaning, no work, quiet, Sabbath candles, family, prayers. But ever since Mati messed up my life, I began hating that day. It's not that I didn't value some peace and quiet from the kids, as Mati would say. I did. But I didn't need Mati to make that call, or Shoshi's judgment at our dinners. I had stopped lighting candles, stopped saying prayers. Nothing about this day seemed sacred anymore. I sat on the balcony and watched everyone else preparing for the day of rest, while I just waited for it to be over.

But this Friday morning, I went to work in a great mood. The first thing I did was copy down Dr. Alex Michael's cell phone number. Just in case. I also took a red plastic delivery crate to carry all the food in. Diana and Stella each brought bags of clothes from home. We couldn't wait for the shift to be over. When we finally turned off the lights and computers, we locked ourselves in the bathroom like teenagers. Stella pulled out a ball gown with rhinestones and lace, and Diana began laughing. "I told you to bring her high heels. What did you bring her a dress for? You think you two are the same size?"

Stella examined me. "More or less."

"She's tiny, that one." Diana pointed at me and laughed. Then she pulled out a beautiful dress, made of sparkling purple sequins. "This is *the* dress. Made for a princess." She patted the dress adoringly and sighed. We'd heard about this dress months before when she bought it for her granddaughter's bat mitzvah. We all lent her some money so she could afford it, and in return, we got invitations to the bat mitzvah.

"Worth the money, right?" Diana said.

"Worth it." Stella felt the fabric.

"Every shekel," I agreed.

"But you can have it only if it fits easily, okay?"

I tried it on carefully. I could zip it up, no problem. I didn't have a mirror, but judging by their excitement, I could tell I looked great.

"There's a problem with your boobs," Stella said, and without hesitation pushed her cold hands down my bra and adjusted my breasts. "You grab the bra with one hand, you pull the boob up with the other, and there you go, it's up."

"Take good care of that dress," Diana said.

I told her she shouldn't lend it to me, but she insisted: "A date is a date. It's not an everyday thing for you." She clapped her hands with delight.

When I got home I stretched the dress out on the sofa so it wouldn't wrinkle. It was luminous, and even though I knew it suited me, I also wasn't sure I'd have the guts to wear it.

I put the pots back on the stove to heat them up. I brought out the Sabbath candles. I was glad I hadn't thrown them away, like how I intended whenever I saw them in the drawer. I prepared the candles, closed my eyes, and my stomach turned over with excitement. I knew I wouldn't be able to catch a bus on the Sabbath eve, and I didn't want to pay for a taxi. I decided to walk over to Mati's place and borrow the car; it was still my car too.

Standing at Mati's doorway, I was glad to be wearing Diana's dress. He looked me over. I still wasn't used to him not kissing me. I glanced inside, expecting to see the kids glued to the television, but they were drawing quietly. They jumped out of their seats when they saw me and hugged me as if it wasn't only yesterday that they left my house, hardly saying goodbye. They were bathed and the house looked tidy. I hugged and kissed them, then asked how they went to school without their backpacks, and Mati said, "They didn't go. No big deal, right?"

The kids looked at me with hesitation, but I smiled and said, "Yeah, no big deal. The most important thing is you had fun."

Yeah, they had fun. They went to the beach to watch the big wintery waves and had hot chocolate at a café. That night they were going to order a pizza, they told me with excitement. I made an effort to smile, even though I wanted to scold Mati. What kind of Sabbath dinner was this? Pizza?

"Where are the car keys?" I asked. "I need the car today."

Mati raised an eyebrow. I could tell he'd lost some weight. He'd let his hair grow out, which suited him. He was dying to ask me where I was headed, but he only said, "No problem," a couple times. Then he picked up the crate of pots and said everything smelled wonderful.

"Of course. What did you think it was, pizza? It's a stew, rice, schnitzels, salads. It's the smell of your home. Why wouldn't it smell wonderful?"

I leaned down to hug my daughter before saying goodbye. She asked if I was going to a ball and I said I was and that I would bring her back a surprise. The little one climbed on me, asking to come with me. I hugged them both. The parent who isn't around is the one they love.

Mati paused before handing me the keys. "Is it a long drive or a short one?"

"Why do you ask?"

"Because of gas," he said. "There isn't much in there."

"Only because of gas?" I smiled.

He glanced around and finally said, "No, not only because of gas."

I didn't really understand the conversation. I sat in the car and stared back at my family. If he asked me to stay right then, I would have, with the pots. But he just stood there with the kids. I started the car. A French chanson began playing. I drove away. The car was very tidy. A new air-freshener tree hung from the rearview mirror. There were no crumbs on the floor and no lottery tickets, only a dark-red fleece I once bought him on the passenger seat. I touched it and then pulled my hand away. I called Shoshi. I told her not to wait for me. I might make it on time, I might be late, I might not make it at all, and I might come with "him."

"With whom?" she asked.

"I have a date. With a doctor," I said.

I wouldn't say anything more, enjoying this lie. But then I actually began imagining myself showing up at Shoshi's with Dr. Alex Michael, an orthopedic hand specialist from Bloch Street.

* * *

I was familiar with the ugly streets that surrounded the Central Bus Station. Neve Sha'anan, Chlenov, Solomon, HaGdud Haivri, Fin. Sooty streets, in spite of all the rain. Nothing could wash away all that dust and dirt. The market was empty. Blinking lights. Whorehouses. Makeshift casinos. Rotting vegetables rolling around in the streets. Asians, Russians, Africans, walking on the sidewalks or in the middle of the road, going in and out of businesses. Nobody used the crosswalk, everybody stared at me. I locked the car doors. The 59 bus I take to work bypasses the station. God knows how I got myself in this mess.

I found a parking spot right across the street from the park. I pushed my breasts up inside my dress according to Stella's instructions and got out. I stood in front of our old car, and remembered I still looked like a princess headed to the ball. Even though I was just there to drop off some pots and say hello to Dr. Alex Michael.

I put my cell phone and car keys in my purse and stuck it under my arm so I could lift the crate. Two Africans sat on the bench, watching me. I didn't want to make eye contact, so I just picked up the pots and began walking. They followed me. I clutched my purse tighter. I was worried about my cell phone, it wasn't insured. One of them came up to me. I walked faster, and he sped up too. Then I stopped abruptly. I put the crate on the ground and hugged my bag to my chest. He stood next to me and I looked around frantically. He pointed at my pots. His clothes were ragged but his shoes, white dress shoes, looked brand new. He bent down to the crate, and though he didn't say a word, I understood from his gestures that he was offering help.

Then I saw the line.

I don't know why I imagined ten or twenty black people standing around and waiting for their food. I'd never seen such a long line of people. There were tons of them, maybe five or six hundred. The newspaper said they'd been living here for almost a year, but I saw no dwellings, only improvised plastic tents. They were all men, all in ill-fitting clothes. All standing quietly. One Israeli volunteer wearing a straw hat walked around handing out plastic spoons from a Plenty Market bag. I felt a knot in my gut. It was because of my party dress. I went back to the car and grabbed Mati's fleece. Once Dr. Alex Michael saw me, I'd put it on.

The black guys waited with my crate where I left them, and one of them pointed to the head of the line. That was where food was being handed out, and that was where the man with the red glasses waited. I could feel my heart in my ears. I proceeded gingerly.

The line moved very slowly, but the Africans didn't push or yell. Instead they said thank you. My kids could learn from them. The volunteers handing out food looked like workers in a factory. Stella and Diana could learn from *them*. The sun had set, but the scene was lit up like a garden party. A few volunteers peeked in my pots and thanked me for the food I brought. Lightning illuminated the sky, followed by strong thunder. Everybody peered up. Everybody but me.

I spotted the red glasses.

Except for a doctor's coat, which of course he wasn't wearing, and the fact that he was a bit shorter than I'd thought, he was just like I'd imagined him. He had a handsome face. Gray hair, broad shoulders. I felt myself blushing. "Doctor?" I said. My voice was hoarse.

He squinted at me, trying to figure out if he was supposed to recognize me.

"Didn't you notice the smell of amazing food?" I smiled.

He gave me a strange look, and a shudder of fear ran through me.

"It's me, from Plenty Market."

His face suddenly brightened. I exhaled. He shook my hand warmly. "We finally meet!" he beamed. "It's about time, I'd say. Listen, when you said you'd come I couldn't tell if you meant it or if you just wanted to get me off the phone!"

"Now you know I meant it." I laughed.

"So, what do you say? What do you think?"

I wasn't sure if he meant what I thought about him or the situation we were in.

"It's powerful, isn't it?" he answered for me, motioning around. "When we spoke last night, I felt like maybe I was showing off about what a good person I was before even doing anything."

"You really are a good person," I said.

"Thanks, but you can't know that." He smiled.

"You made me do a good thing. That says something about you, doesn't it?"

It began raining.

"So how did the red rice work out for you?" I asked. "Can I try it?"

His face turned red. "I didn't end up making it."

"You counted on me, huh? Look what I brought." I pointed at the pots and felt very proud of myself once again. I wasn't just a princess; I was a good cook too, just like he'd imagined.

"Actually, I counted on my wife," he said, pointing behind him. I felt my eyes widen. "I wanted to do it on my own, without her help, but I chickened out. I asked her to cook and she ended up joining me for the distribution. Look at her—she's been here for two hours, but she's already a pro."

The wife with the weight issues stood there, wearing a long black dress, ladling food from large pots into plastic bowls, handing it out to the black men standing in line. Her hair was up in a bun, and she was wearing red glasses too.

"Mika!" he called.

The woman turned around.

He pointed at me. "She came!"

She looked at him, then me, then back at him. I shifted my weight between my feet. I forced a smile.

"The woman from Plenty Market!" he called out. It was like they had a bet on whether or not I'd come.

She opened her mouth, as if saying, *Oh!* and raised a spoon in greeting.

"I'll give her your pots. This is so great," he said, bending to pick up the crate. "Thank you."

"When did you get back together?"

He stood back up and his eyes told me I was mistaken. They had never broken up.

"Sorry," I mumbled. "I apologize, forgive me."

He just stared at me.

"I got the impression that—"

"That what?" He stepped closer.

"I don't know. For some reason I thought you were divorced." I put on the fleece, which was way too big for me. I hugged my arms around my body and still felt chilly. I didn't take into account Mati's smell, which permeated my senses. It was a cologne I once bought him. I put my hands in the pockets. There was a folded twenty-shekel note in there, probably from last winter, when I was still buying him fleeces and colognes at the mall. One store after the next.

A few of the volunteers stood on the side, talking. One of them said, "Guys, who has a car?"

I raised my hand, then followed Mika with my eyes, waiting for her to see my pots and be impressed, but she hadn't gotten to them yet.

"So why did you think I was divorced?" he asked.

"It was a mistake. I'm sorry." I glanced down at my heels.

"You didn't do anything wrong," he said. "I'm just curious."

I was so tired. He was waiting for an answer.

"Your order changed in August," I admitted. "You always had a family order, and suddenly it was five tomatoes, five cucumbers, pitas. A single man's order. I thought something might have happened. Between you two, I mean. But I was wrong." I forced myself to smile again. "But it's a good mistake. How wonderful, you're married."

"You're right," he said. "We moved into a bigger place in August, because Mika got pregnant. I kept working at the clinic on 31 Bloch Street. That's why our order changed. I never thought you'd even notice."

"Please don't report me."

"Why would I?"

"It could jeopardize my job, I'm a contract worker."

"On the contrary, we'd be happy to write a recommendation letter."

The drizzle increased to large drops, like somebody spitting down on us. I covered my head with the fleece.

Somebody called out, "Car owners, wait on the side."

Volunteers began packing up the pots and getting the refugees into cars. I couldn't figure out why. I took the opportunity to grab my empty pots from under Mika's nose and hurry back to my car. I couldn't find the Plenty Market crate, so I stacked the pots on top of each other and hoped they wouldn't come crashing down. I had no choice; I couldn't leave my good pots behind.

My hands smelled of meat and garlic. Finally, I sat down behind the wheel. I saw Dr. Alex Michael and Mika cross the street in front of me and lowered my head quickly. They didn't see me. They disappeared into a white jeep with four Africans. I started pulling out of the parking space. I thought of a warm shower. Of my pink sweatpants. Of slippers and thick socks. Maybe a movie on television. Suddenly the volunteer with the straw hat stood in front of the car. He signaled something to me and came closer. I rolled down the window. He leaned in and said, "There's just one more to drive over."

"What?"

"We're driving the refugees over to the school for the night—the public school a few blocks away." A moment later he began leading an African across my headlights. "You have nothing to be afraid of." The volunteer smiled. "You'll drive between our cars, we'll make a convoy." Before I had a chance to say anything, the back door of my car was opened and the refugee sat down between the kids' booster seats. I turned to the volunteer, begging him with my eyes not to leave me alone with the guy, but he was immersed in explaining the route. "113 Meor HaGola Street. You know it? It's very close. Turn right here, then left on the second street. Keep straight at the square, then two lefts, and the school will be on your left, across from the old lot. Everybody's already there. Wait for us." Then he disappeared.

A furniture store sign blinked before me. The refugee didn't move. Neither did I. I didn't dare turn to him or speak, and he didn't say a word either. I even breathed softer. After some time I got out of the car. I searched for the volunteer, the convoy, but I didn't see anyone. The rain grew stronger. I got back into the car, not making eye contact. I turned on the engine and the heat. I thawed my fingers in the warm air. The clock showed 19:03. They were eating the first course at my sister's. Fish. The volunteer forgot about me. The school was ten minutes away.

I drove according to his directions. 113 Meor HaGola Street. Maybe I took a right where I should have taken a left. Moreh Nevuchim Street, Shivat Zion Road, Khakmei Atuna, Balaban, Maimon. This was my neighborhood, but I'd never heard of those streets in my life. I made a U-turn. I tried to drive back to where I came from, but found myself somewhere unfamiliar again. I made another U-turn, and only then noticed it was illegal. There wasn't a soul out on the street, though, so no one saw. A few times I thought I recognized a street or a corner, but I was wrong. Shvil ha-Tnufa, Shvil ha-Meretz, Ha'Amal, Bar-Yokhai. Streets I'd never set foot on.

The refugee remained silent. I could almost imagine I was alone. Maybe he was asleep, or dead.

We passed carpentry shop after carpentry shop. Plastic factories. Closed restaurants. Workshops. Everything was dark, locked up. A group of drunks crossed the street. I took a left, then a right, another right and a left, trying to remember what I could from the volunteer's directions, but I found myself back on a street of deserted buildings. I was dizzy. The rain got stronger. I kept driving aimlessly, not wanting my passenger to suspect I was lost.

I pulled out my phone and dialed Dr. Alex Michael's number. Mika picked up, and for some reason I hung up. She called back a moment later and I had to reject her call. She gave up after seven or eight tries.

At some point the refugee said something behind me. His voice was higher than I'd imagined. I murmured something back, not looking at him, as if I had understood him and didn't want to talk. He must have realized I was lost. Now he knew I had a cell phone too. A woman, alone on Friday night, in a revealing dress, high heels, makeup. What was I thinking?

I saw the yellow light of an approaching taxi. I rolled down the window quickly and signaled for it to stop. I'm sure the driver saw me, but he sped off, spraying muddy water right into my face. I lowered my head and wiped my face with my sleeve. I peeked into the mirror and suddenly caught him looking at me. I glanced away. He said something again. I zipped the fleece up all the way until Mati's smell almost suffocated me.

I saw him moving nearer through the corner of my eye. My breath quickened. Then his head was between the front seats, near my shoulder. I clutched the steering wheel with my nails. Maybe it was better for me to get into an accident and end it all. *Mom loved you, kids. Mom loved Dad.* The guy touched my shoulder.

I screamed and slammed on the breaks.

He reached his hand out further.

I bit him as hard as I could until I tasted blood. He whimpered like an animal. Only then did I release my teeth. I also unbuckled my seat belt. He pointed at the gas light that had turned on, then jumped out of the car and ran off.

I didn't even notice it turning on.

I went out after him, yelling my apologies, but he ran much faster than I could with my heels. I was out of breath. Finally I stopped in the middle of the street. I cried like you cry only when you're alone.

But when I looked up I saw I wasn't alone. The refugee was standing nearby, next to a large trash can. We stared at each other. I took a step toward him and he moved away. I pulled a first aid kit from the trunk. I pushed it to him across the sidewalk. He examined it, and me, suspiciously. I signaled to him to open it. He put a Band-Aid on his hand, watching me all the while. Once his hand was bandaged, he crossed his arms. He might have to see an orthopedic hand specialist because of me.

I stepped closer. I didn't know what to say. Then I gave him my pinkie for a truce. He didn't understand.

He pulled a picture out of his pocket. A man and a woman, a boy and a girl. He was the man in the picture. For the first time I got a clear look at his face. A big face, strong eyes. They were wearing festive outfits. It must have been a special occasion, but their expressions were serious.

I pointed at the children in the picture. "Ethiopia? Nigeria?" I asked. My voice was still hoarse and my teeth hurt.

"Sierra Leone," he said.

I didn't even know where that was. He nodded at me as if to ask about my family. I took my phone out of the fleece pocket. I flipped through the pictures on it, reliving the scenes of my broken family. Finally I found the picture of us from Diana's granddaughter's bat mitzvah and showed it to him.

He pointed at Mati and the kids. "America?" he asked.

I shook my head.

"Germany?" he asked. "England?"

"Israel," I said.

He turned from the picture back toward me, squinting. "Israel?" he asked, and pointed at the ground, verifying they were actually here.

"Israel," I said. "Tel Aviv."

He held up his arms questioningly.

Well, I didn't have an answer. Why was I here, my feet in a pool of dirt, so far from them, while they were so close. An ambulance wailed far away. I stood up and repeated, "Israel, Tel Aviv."

I walked back to the car and sat behind the wheel.

He followed me.

He slid in between the kids' boosters.

I got gas, using the twenty-shekel note I'd found in Mati's fleece. I started recognizing the streets around me.

I pulled up by Mati's apartment. I peered at the guy in the rearview mirror, killed the engine, and got out. I saw my reflection in the windshield: a princess in fleece. I said, "Israel, Tel Aviv," and pointed at Mati's apartment.

He glanced back at me. Finally he nodded.

I knocked softly. I heard the kids running excitedly behind the door, yelling that the pizza was here, and to get some money. The door opened. The little one saw me and cried out, "Mom!" The older one stood next to him, and so did Mati, the bills waving in his hand, which froze in the air. They all stared at us with gaping eyes.

I signaled to them to make way, and they did. I gestured to the African that the path was clear, and hoped he'd come in. I put the pots on top of the stove. He came in. Nobody said anything, not even Mati. They all just kept staring at me. I pulled out a chair and took a seat at the head of the table, signaling to the others to sit down. The kids sat on one side, Mati on the other, and the African across from me, holding his bandaged arm close to his body.

"Go on, say the kiddush prayer," I said to Mati.

He sat up, cleared his throat, and began: "Blessed are You, God, king of the universe, who made us holy with His commandments and favored us, and gave us His holy Shabbat, in love and favor, to be our heritage, as a reminder of the Creation."

The kids looked from me to the African, back and forth, raising their eyebrows, rolling their eyes whenever they met mine.

"It is the foremost day of the holy festivals marking the exodus from Egypt," Mati continued. "For out of all the nations You chose us and made us holy, and You gave us Your holy Shabbat, in love and favor, as our heritage. Blessed are You, God, who sanctifies Shabbat."

I turned to the kids and said, "Amen."

"Amen," they mumbled after me. They weren't even listening to the prayer. I was waiting for Mati to finish too. I did my best to ignore the looks they stuck me with, sharp like nails.

"Blessed are You, God, king of the universe, who brings forth bread from the earth."

"Amen!" I said quickly and loudly, indicating to the children to do the same.

They repeated like parrots: "Amen!"

I finally served the food. Rice, meatballs, schnitzels. So much color and aroma. I gave the African a nice portion and he nodded with gratitude. I said, "Bon appétit."

Those were the magic words. All at once, all eyes left me and focused on the food. Mouths began chewing, the room was filled with the pleasant sounds of forks against plates and spoons against bowls. Good food sounds. My food. Nothing could ruin their appetite for it. Not the little one's, not the older one's, not Mati's. They passed the challah between them, and the side dishes, peas and meat and schnitzels moving across the table. It was like they hadn't eaten all week.

They didn't even notice that I wasn't eating. The food was hot and steamy. The African's eyes met mine. He was sitting quietly, just like me, in front of a full plate of food.

PART II

Estrangements

CLEAR RECENT HISTORY

BY Gon Ben Ari

Magen David Square

Ten years on the job taught Tycher how to put away an unsolved case with the delayed pride of a prophet. A missing detail would surely flicker in the future, shedding light on the case. It was as though he and he alone understood how time worked. But the writer's case was different. The case had been closed four years ago, and still, whenever Tycher recalled it—spotting one of the writer's books in a store window or online—he was submerged in the kind of dread one felt before a high school test, or in a dream whose rules changed ceaselessly.

He couldn't even scratch the surface of the case before it had been closed. It was a combination of lack of cooperation on the writer's part and despair coupled with inflamed sinuses on Tycher's. Even after the case was closed, he never discussed it, not even with his friends. Though he himself had never read the writer's work, he was familiar with his name and knew of the writer's popularity. Regardless of their stature, Tycher was always protective of his clients' privacy. "Being a private investigator," he told them, "is 50 percent investigation and 50 percent privacy."

Usually, this mantra won him silently nodding smiles. But the writer was different. He was neither silent nor smiling. Instead he had said, "I need you to be 100 percent investigator, and 100 percent private."

* * *

When Asaf's second son was born he invited Tycher to join him on a trip to Southeast Asia. Tycher couldn't spare the money or the time. As a plan B, Asaf suggested they go to Amsterdam to eat mushrooms. He regarded it as a consolation prize, in a nonchalant manner Tycher could never afford to adopt. Tycher lost his temper during the Skype call. First he mentioned something about Mika, and then he yelled that his sinuses were so badly congested, the changes in air pressure during the flight would blow up his skull.

Asaf said: "And I was supposed to know that how, exactly?"

Later, Tycher blurted at Asaf that just because he owned his own company and could take time off whenever he pleased, it didn't mean everyone could.

"You have your own company too," Asaf replied.

"It's not the same thing," said Tycher. "Yours is an Internet company, you could leave for a week and when you got back it would be exactly the same. Mine involves *people*. If I left for a week, when I got back it wouldn't be the same. Some of them would lose money, some would flee the country, others would become religious, go vegan, start dating someone, die. They'd be completely different people."

"Just like the Internet," said Asaf. For a moment neither of them could do anything but stare at the small square at the bottom of the screen that showed their own faces.

They reached a compromise: Asaf would catch the train down from Binyamina and spend the weekend at Tycher's place on Nahalat Binyamin Street in Tel Aviv, where they would take MDMA, because Asaf had never tried it.

In the morning, Tycher woke up alone and hurried out to get breakfast in Jaffa. He ate, took in the palm trees, feeling the sinus pressure groping its way down his cheekbones toward his gums, chewing every bite for a full minute before he could get the first drops of flavor. When he was done he picked up Asaf from the train station. While they were in the car the dealer called and they asked for MDMA.

The dealer said, "What happened, was someone *born?*" And then, "Everybody has children these days. Hard times."

He didn't have MD, only LSD. It came in a sandwich bag filled with Bamba, dripped over four pieces of the snack.

"But there's a ton of Bamba in here," said Tycher. "How are we supposed to tell which pieces you dripped it on?"

"You'll be able to tell," said the dealer. The acid had drilled miniature tunnels in the four yellow peanuty squiggles. Tycher and Asaf ate it while still in the car, staring at the brake lights of the vehicles up ahead, drinking orange juice. They parked next to Tycher's building and walked straight to the beach to watch the sea.

Like every time they took something together, Asaf was gripped by a strong need to explain.

"There is this awesome group of people on the Net running experiments on themselves." The drug softened his speech and his words came out sweet and delicate. "It's called microdosing. Each day every person in the group takes a microscopic amount of LSD and then reports the effects online. They do it that way because it's illegal to experiment with these drugs on humans."

"So now you're the Explainer again?"

"Turns out it has terrific effects. Their moods are improving, their mental stability, their immune system is getting stronger. They report an increase in mnemonic activity, their relationships are better, their sex lives are better, they are capable of concentration on levels—"

"That's enough," said Tycher.

"The most interesting part," continued Asaf, "is that they report an increase in coincidences. It's as though when you're on this drug the whole world changes a little bit and you—for example—suddenly run into somebody you were just thinking about. All the time. Which is the most exciting angle of this whole thing: without planning to, they discovered that consciousness is probably—that you're like a *router* for consciousness—that it isn't limited to—"

"Look," said Tycher. He was pointing at something like a star that was vibrating over the sea. "It's like there's a war on that planet."

When they got back to his apartment, Tycher lay down on the floor and Asaf on the couch and they spoke like they hadn't since high school. As the conversation progressed Tycher felt himself growing more self-assured.

"I feel like calling Mika right now," he said. "I don't talk to her enough. Not like this. Not with courage. Not like who I really am."

"It's important to have balls when you speak to your children."

"It's the *most* important thing," said Tycher.

When the effects started wearing off they went out to look for a bar in the rippling streets. They walked into one they didn't know and stayed because the bartender was black and sang to herself. As they sat, cooling their hands on two pints of Goldstar, a song played in the background that reminded Tycher of the writer's case. The song was so ridiculously unbelievable that he was convinced he was hallucinating the lyrics ("*Someone out there has my boner picture!*" somebody screamed over the blaring of horns). He laughed with surprise, and when Asaf asked what he was laughing about, it suddenly made sense to tell the story.

He began by stressing that no matter how hard Asaf was going to nag, he had no intention of disclosing the identity of the client. But he could say this: he was a writer. "A very well-known Israeli writer. We met two years ago"—he opened with an intentional lie, instinctively covering his footprints before he even began walking—"and when I first saw him, I thought he was a relative of mine. He seemed so familiar. It took me a minute to figure out he was familiar because I'd seen him on television and in the papers. That he was a celebrity. When he came in he got his tape recorder out. He said that because he was also a journalist, he was going to record our conversations, and that if I objected, we would have a problem."

"So now I know he's also a journalist," said Asaf.

"So he presses record and starts talking. A few days earlier he got this e-mail from somebody calling himself "The Name." Under *Sender* it said only one word, in Hebrew, *Hashem*—you know, The Name. There was a video attachment. A webcam-quality AVI file showing the writer sitting in front of his computer jerking off."

Asaf raised his eyebrows.

"He wasn't aware he was being filmed, and so in the video he's looking just a little below the camera, watching something—obviously porn, you can tell by the audio. And the e-mail came with a blackmail note. Sort of. It said: *I am the Internet. Thank you for jerking off in front of me. If you do not continue to jerk off in front of me daily, I will spread this video around.*"

Asaf made an ashtray from a beer coaster, carefully folding the cardboard circle into a square. "So what did you do?"

"First I asked him if there was any chance the video was a

fake. I knew it wasn't, but I wanted to give him a chance to say it was. He said no, it was totally real. I asked: *Could you have taken the video yourself, by accident, with the laptop webcam, and it was automatically saved to your hard drive, in some temporary cache folder or something, and then someone stole it?* He said no, no, no. He had it all figured out: someone installed spyware on his computer. A spyware that uses the built-in camera on top of the screen. Whenever he went to a porn site, the spyware started streaming the input from the camera and recording it on a remote server. Whoever did it must have filmed a bunch of people, and at the end of each day he reviewed all the recordings until he found someone he recognized, someone rich and famous he could blackmail."

"Now I know he's rich too," said Asaf. "I've accumulated quite a bit of information about this writer already."

"He said the day after that he covered the camera with black duct tape. He tried to convince himself that someone was just messing with him or that he was going insane. But then, just five minutes before midnight, he realized he wasn't willing to take the risk of this video being spread, so he removed the duct tape, went into a porn site, and jerked off, just in case. He said the moment he was finished he felt like an idiot. He realized he was deteriorating toward real psychosis. But the next day he got another e-mail from the same address. *The Name.* With another video of him jerking off, wearing what he wore the day before, and another note: *Thanks. Same deal tomorrow. I am the Internet and you must fertilize me. I am the Internet and you must fuck me.*"

"Wait, how long did it take before he came to you?"

"A week."

"So for an entire week—"

"For an entire week he jerked off in front of his camera,

and it ate him up. And every day he got an e-mail with a video of himself jerking off from the previous day, along with a letter. The letters became crazier and crazier. *I am the Internet, give me Internet babies. I am the Internet and I am the omnihuman."*

"The omnihuman?"

"Fuck with the Unseen and do not cheat with the Seen."

"Hard-core," said Asaf.

Tycher closed his eyes and sipped his beer. "He said he couldn't write, couldn't work, couldn't do anything. He kept thinking about that person, out there somewhere, who had a video of him jerking off."

"How come you never came to me with this before?" Asaf asked. "What, don't you feel comfortable asking for my help? Through the company I could, like, produce a report of every spyware that was on the Net while this happened. When was this?"

"Back in 2006."

"All right then. I can already tell you that if we're talking about 2006 there's a good chance it had to do with Eden Robinov, or Kobinov. You know him?"

Tycher shook his head.

"Eden Kobinov. He was a Russian hacker from Netanya. Seventeen years old. His nickname was Trumpel-dog. He was into the whole Jewish, Zionist, nationalist thing. Against sex culture and all that. He broke into Israeli porn sites, and into all those matchmaking sites—you know, the ones with the banners saying, *Get Laid Tonight*, or, *700 Women in the Herzliya Area Want Your Cock*. That kind of thing."

"*8,000 Women from Ramat Gan Longing for Have Sexes with You*," said Tycher.

"So he took over those websites and censored them. Planted shitty fig leafs, drawn in Microsoft Paint, over all the cocks and tits. And he was phishing too. Got users' e-mail addresses and threatened to expose them if they wouldn't pay. This dude actually met people on the street and took cash from them, because in the end, when it comes to money, it's always easier to do it outside the Internet, where nothing is recorded."

"Yeah."

"I've never heard of anybody recording people on their own webcams, though." Asaf lit a cigarette. "But it's the same kind of vibe."

"Yes."

"And he was arrested a year ago. Do you think the writer jerked off daily up until a year ago?"

"I dropped the case. At first I tried to check out that e-mail address, but it wasn't an actual address. Just the words *The Name*. So I searched the usual things. Were there other similar cases? There weren't. Did anybody know a technology that made your webcam start recording without your consent? They didn't. You know what I did? I went to religious repository bins all over Tel Aviv, the ones they have next to synagogues and *chevra kadisha* branches, where religious people throw out garbage that is too sacred to be mixed with regular trash, and I rifled through them. I was thinking, if this guy calls himself Hashem, like the name of God, he might be serious about that, experimenting with practical kabbalah or something. And if so, he probably has a thing about writing the tetragrammaton, the explicit name of God. And then, if he really *believes*, he would never toss anything bearing that name in the garbage, and he would have to dump it in a religious repository. I don't know. I only had those kinds of ideas, and they led nowhere. In the end I told him he would probably be better off talking to someone who specialized in online crime. I didn't want to take too much of his time, because I knew every day I didn't solve the case was another day he was being filmed jerking off in front of the Internet."

"Was it Shimon Adaf?"

"Fuck you," said Tycher. "Don't even try to guess. And no."

"Gideon Tzuk?"

Tycher didn't have to say anything. The severe hardening of his jaw and a couple of sharp wrinkles shooting up along the corner of his brow told Asaf he'd nailed it.

"Ha-ha, it's like you're on truth serum."

"Good to know that I'm surrounded by friends who know how to abuse it," said Tycher.

"This changes everything." Asaf's face sobered. "If it's Gideon Tzuk it isn't funny at all. You know what a king that guy is? Did you read his books?"

Tycher admitted he hadn't.

"He is a king. He saved my life. *Mirror Tigers* saved me when I was in the army. In a way it was because of that book that I left the squadron."

"I thought you left because you didn't want to bomb anything."

"I didn't want to bomb anything because of *Mirror Tigers*," said Asaf.

"I thought you left because they caught you flying a plane while tripping on shrooms."

"I flew a plane while tripping on shrooms because of *Mirror Tigers*," Asaf explained. "That book is crazy. Like *religious* crazy."

"Now I really feel like helping him," said Asaf after several moments of silence. "Are you still in contact?"

"No." Tycher knew he could easily find the number, but he didn't feel like getting back into it.

More than anything, Tycher didn't want to meet the writer again. The man's presence made him uncomfortable. When he told Tycher about what had happened, the writer seemed unsure whether he had actually experienced those things in reality or whether they were a hallucination. He was struggling hard to get the words out of his mouth. But what was there to sweat over? It was as if, while he spoke, the writer had cast an ancient spell, known to few, through which he turned madness into reality, and Tycher sat there and nodded while this was happening in front of him, taking down the story, fastening it tighter to reality, and then went on an investigation, all the while feeling it, both existent and nonexistent, in the dark.

At times, when he was alone in a room with the writer, he thought, *Now reality is made up of nothing but what I say and what he says,* and understood how insanity could be contagious. When he recalled this he got that same feeling again, the feeling you have a moment before taking a test in a dream.

After the bar, they walked back to the beach to watch the sunrise. Tycher asked Asaf for a cigarette.

"Why?" asked Asaf, gesturing toward the sunrise. "Look at it. Isn't it enough?" But still he gave Tycher a cigarette, and when he leaned in for a light Asaf changed his mind and took the cigarette back and said, "I'm sorry I said that. I don't know why I said it. I'm going to get in a time machine and go back, *blu-blu-blu-blu-blu-blu,* and I'm going to give you a cigarette again, like a human being." And he gave Tycher a cigarette again, and Tycher put it in his mouth, and he lit it, and Tycher smiled.

"Rabin's dead," said Tycher. "You're in 1995."

"Too bad. I'm not even half-tired yet."

They had sandwiches at the little shop on Shenkin Street and then went for coffee at the Minzar. The drugs fed on their exhaustion, turning it not into wakefulness but rather into a persistent exposure of electrical wires. From the outside the place seemed closed, but when they went in to check, they found a few people inside, their faces still unripe with morning, wrapped in newspaper epidermis.

Right by the beer taps, sitting on a barstool, was Gideon Tzuk, alternating between coffee and beer. He looked paler and fatter than he had when Tycher last saw him, but also more focused. His eyes were fixed on a book that rested open on his knees.

"That's him, right?" Asaf whispered. "That's the kind of coincidence I was telling you about."

Before Tycher could stop him, Asaf took a seat next to the writer and said, "Excuse me, Gideon Tzuk? I'm sorry to disturb you."

The writer straightened his spine. His black overcoat made it seem like he'd been inflated from the chair up.

Tycher took a step back and watched from the pub's doorway.

"Do I know you?" When he spoke Tycher learned that the writer's voice had also changed. The smeared, alcoholic tongue was replaced with a firm, alert tone.

Asaf said, "No, but I have something important to tell you."

Gideon Tzuk closed the book.

"I was a pilot in the army," began Asaf. "At the end of 2008 I refused to bomb Gaza from a plane during operation Oferet Yetzuka, and when they made me do it anyway, I took twenty-five grams of *Psilocybe atlantis* before getting in the jet, and the whole time we were over Gaza I read *Mirror Tigers* to the other pilots over the radio. I read the gnostic parts—the parts where the guy realizes the world is the Jewish Holocaust on repeat? And it's just compressed differently each time? And it's like, God is the only one who breaks into this concentration camp to save us?"

"Did it help?" asked Gideon Tzuk.

"No, they all turned out to be whores and bombed anyway. No one was listening."

"Right," said Gideon Tzuk.

"Because of the radio. They probably muted the channel I was speaking on pretty fast."

"What kind of jet were you flying?"

"F16-D."

"So you had a navigator with you."

"Yeah, but he was cool," said Asaf. "He was on *mexicana*."

"What did they do to you?"

"Put us in military prison for eight months and kicked us out of the army. It was never reported in the media and there was no file, because it was too big of a fuck-up on their part. The fact that they even let it happen."

"So you got away with it?"

"I own an Internet security company now," Asaf said.

"They reached a settlement," Tycher finally intervened. "He was paid to shut up about it." As he stepped into the dusty light, the writer's gaze locked on him.

"Bullshit," said Asaf. "I am *so* denying that."

"I know you," Gideon Tzuk spoke through him, turning to Tycher.

"Where from?" Tycher approached them.

"Oh," said Gideon Tzuk, "you're all about the confidentiality, aren't you?" He turned to Asaf and pointed at Tycher. "You see that? That's some professional-ass private investigating. He worked with me once, but he doesn't say anything, because he is good. A good man. He crawled inside religious repository bins for me."

"Did you find any sparks?" said Asaf.

"I never talk about my clients," replied Tycher, feeling robotic. "It's a thing I have."

"Sit down," said Gideon Tzuk, looking only at Asaf. Once he sat down, Tycher could smell the writer. He smelled athletic. New. For a moment he thought: *Perhaps I really don't know this guy at all.*

"What did you say your business was? High-tech?"

"Online security," said Asaf. "Yeah, high-tech."

"Did you ever meet a guy named Derek Hammon who owns a start-up? A French Jew, he lives around here, in Neve Tzedek."

"Sure," said Asaf. "He made Turn Me Porn."

"Fucking Familiar," said Gideon Tzuk.

"Right, sure," said Asaf, "Fucking Familiar."

"Made what?" Tycher asked.

"Fucking Familiar. Initially it was called Turn Me Porn. It's a website and an app," explained Gideon Tzuk. "Let's say you want some girl from the office or school or a childhood friend, or just a friend, or a waitress, doesn't matter. You take a picture of her—you get it from Facebook or whatever—and you upload it to this website or app. It recognizes the facial features and searches the web for porn in which the main character looks like the girl in your picture. And then you can jerk off while watching her."

"Or him," said Asaf. "There's a gay version too."

"Or him," Gideon Tzuk confirmed. "And there are all kinds of special features. For example, the website asks you—*requires* you—to enter the first name of the girl in the picture you sent. At first, of course, your instinct would be to make up a name, but then you realize there's a logic to it. That it pays to tell the truth. Because the website automatically titles the videos it finds with the name you typed in. And then you get two nice little lists, one of sites that cost money and the other of free streaming sites, sorted by a percentage of how much the girl in them looks like the picture. And let's say the name you put in is . . . Give me a girl's name."

"Hey, you're the writer."

"Writers have the worst time with names."

"Dorit," said Asaf.

"Wonderful," said Tycher.

"That's Tycher's mother's name."

"So you get a list of videos," Gideon Tzuk continued. "*Dorit Sucks Niggas, Huge Cock Coming Up Dorit's Butt, Dorit's Dream Gang Bang, Dorit in Asian Lesbian Action*, and it adds something. The name adds something." He winked at Tycher.

"Do the girls actually look like the picture you upload?"

"Not often," said Gideon Tzuk. "But sometimes, let's say 30 percent of the time, it's kind of horrible how similar they look. An infinite museum, updated daily, documenting all of your exes fucking. All of the time."

"Has anyone tried uploading pictures of things other than people?" Tycher asked. "Like a picture of a volcano or of space, to see what it finds?"

The writer and Asaf didn't seem to hear him. Gideon Tzuk stared at the door by the end of the bar until one of the kitchen workers appeared there. He ordered three shots of arak. While they were being served, the writer got up and walked behind the bar, by the cash register, and found a bottle of Tabasco. He grabbed it, smiled at the worker, and returned to his seat. He uncapped the bottle with his teeth and spat the cap onto the bar, then raised it at Asaf and Tycher, inviting them to participate in a ceremony whose existence they were not aware of. They raised their glasses and lowered their heads. The writer poured two drops into each of the shot glasses. He raised his own glass again. They mimicked him as he tapped his glass on the bar twice. He then clinked his with theirs and said, "*L'chaim*. To life and not to death."

They repeated after him: "To life and not to death." And they all drank.

"Then one day," Gideon Tzuk wiped fat drops of arak from his beard and went on talking, as if he had never stopped but rather jumped over a hurdle, "I received an e-mail with a video of myself jerking off. It was right after I visited Fucking Familiar, I should mention. And the e-mail came with a threat, blackmailing me. All I was asked to do was to keep jerking off every day, or else the video would be shared over the Internet." He turned to Asaf. "And I did it every day. And every day I got a video of myself doing it the day before. And so I came to meet your friend." He pointed at Tycher. "But I didn't tell him it started at Fucking Familiar. That was too much. Because he would've asked whose picture I uploaded."

"I wouldn't have asked."

"I wouldn't have told you," said Gideon Tzuk. "And I'm not going to tell you now."

"It's none of our business," said Asaf.

"Damn straight," agreed the writer. "So then I went to see another investigator, but he didn't find anything either. In the end, you know who explained it to me? Meir Shalev."

"Oh my God," said Tycher.

"It happened to Meir Shalev too?" Asaf asked.

"No," said Gideon Tzuk. "Meir Shalev is a good friend

of mine. We are both half from Emek Yizrael and half from Jerusalem."

"Okay," said Asaf.

"A year ago I told him this story. He says, *Look, this isn't the first time I've heard this.* He wouldn't tell me who he heard it from, but I gave him permission to tell whoever it was that it happened to me too, and to ask him to contact me. The guy called the same day. A very well-known writer whose name I won't repeat. It turns out there was a support group. I didn't know about it, because I'm not really part of the inner circle. There were two musicians, two illustrators, and an actor, but mostly writers. Thirty writers, all caught up in this thing. They were investigating it together, so they had a lot more information than I did. For example: Derek Hammon never did anything illegal. Turns out we gave our consent to be filmed. It was in the user agreement you sign on the website's homepage. We clicked *Okay.*"

A cigarette butt breathed on the floor and Tycher tried to put it out with the sole of his shoe.

"The worst part is the fear. What if one day I couldn't do it, and he went public? It cripples you. What if you have reserve duty in the military, for example? Or if you're somewhere with no Internet access? Or you're sick? There's no vacation from it. It's like this, every day."

"If you know who it is, why don't you just kill him?" Asaf asked.

"We ended up talking to the police." Gideon Tzuk sipped his beer. "He was arrested a few months ago. We waited to speak to them for so long because we were really afraid it would leak. You know how it is. Police. But it didn't. They handled everything masterfully. But until that happened I spent five years in hell."

"You should write about it," Asaf said.

"No way. I don't want to think about it ever again. I can't even jerk off anymore. Just out of fear. I can't visit Google without duct-taping my webcam and the laptop mic. Not to mention being able to look other Israeli writers in the eye."

When they finished their drinks, the three headed down toward the Kerem HaTeimanim neighborhood to eat hummus at the Syrian's place. Asaf walked with his hands in his pockets, looking nervous, and finally said, "Aren't writers supposed to be able to jerk off using just their imagination?"

Tycher cringed.

"Like, I always thought writers didn't even look at porn. Because they have enough imagination."

"You've *always* thought that?" Tycher muttered.

Gideon Tzuk seemed irritated. After another minute of walking in silence he said, "Watching porn is like trying to peek beneath the hood of a car. At the engine of everything. I'm not saying sex is everything. But I am saying you can understand everything through sex. That sex is an action so close to the source, to the pure idea of interaction between two human beings, that it becomes the ultimate metaphor. Watching porn is like peering through a microscope at the movement of primary matter. Of atoms. The atoms of the relationship between giver and receiver. You're watching people—who are themselves the products of other people's orgasms—entering other people, and allowing other people to enter them." He closed his eyes for a moment. "Even between us, although we're all men, and we're all straight, and none of us really wants to fuck the others up the ass, we can still examine our relationship in pornographic terms: who wants to give what to whom, and who wants to receive what from whom."

Asaf took a deep breath and exhaled loudly. The moment they reached the hummus place, he realized he'd left his iPhone at the Minzar and went back to get it. Tycher and Gideon Tzuk sat at a corner table and lit cigarettes before ordering their food. The writer chatted with one of the owners, and when the man left he began crushing hot peppers and onions onto a paper towel. Watching him, that old sensation came over Tycher again. As if they were somehow related.

"I lied," said Gideon Tzuk. He lifted the paper towel and scattered the onion and pepper crumbs over the hummus that had just arrived.

"About what?"

"It never stopped. He was arrested, but before he was put in prison he made a deal with all the writers and artists he was blackmailing."

"What kind of deal?"

"We got an e-mail from him in which he clarified that even though the police claimed all evidence had been erased, the videos still existed on some server, probably in Slovenia. Which only supports my theory that Derek Hammon is nothing. A puppet. He said we were free of our previous engagement— being recorded jerking off every day—but we were now bound by a new arrangement. According to this new arrangement, in order to keep him from publishing the videos, we had to write a book for him." Gideon Tzuk raised his eyes from the plate of hummus. "A children's book. It would be a children's book with all our names on it. Cowritten, allegedly, by thirty writers. It would guarantee monstrous PR, because nothing like this has ever been done before. Thirty famous writers collaborating on one children's book. Not a collection of stories but a single plotline. Sixty pages. It's never been done in Israel, or anywhere, for that matter. And for good reason—because it's a shitty idea! But it's exactly the kind of shitty idea people would buy. And just to be on the safe side, all proceeds would go to a charity."

"What is this thing?" asked Tycher. He felt the sinus in his forehead pulsing.

"It's a story about a boy who speaks with the sea. He gave us some guidelines. The rough plot. A boy whose father was a sailor and died at sea before he was born, and ever since, the sea talks to him. He left basic instructions for graphic design. Lots of gold and pale blues, and other details. Everything with a round shape has to resemble an eye. He knew exactly what he wanted. The whole thing looks pretty professional. Pretty good, even. A pretty good children's book. Something no one would suspect the thirty of us didn't actually write. Because we did write most of it, following his guidelines, but also because there's some truth to it. Something I really could see myself writing, if I gave a fuck about children's literature."

"You said *we did write*. Like you already wrote it."

"It's coming out in May. All the money from it goes to autistic children. He let us pick the cause. But there's something else, you know? There's something *wrong* about this book. The words he insisted we put there—"

"Like what words?"

"Mirror, sweetness, sea, moon, wolf, abyss, brain, heart, dimension, spherical time, web, net, infinity, waves, construction, face, pipes, woods, vision."

Tycher swallowed.

"And there were other instructions. The hero had to be named Moshe. He's a boy, but in the illustrations we were told to make sure he looked a little like a girl, or wore girly clothes. He requested a scene in which someone climbs up a ladder and then goes down. A scene containing digging and unearthing glowing objects."

"Do you think it's some kind of hypnosis?" Tycher asked.

"Codes," said Gideon Tzuk. "We brainwash kids, but we have no idea what we're putting in their minds."

Tycher ignored a text from Asaf saying, *You'll never believe who I just ran into.*

They ate quietly for a few moments. Then, in a hushed voice, the writer continued: "It's not like I don't have a theory. I think there may be an event. An event in the future. An event we can't understand because we have no way of knowing it's about to happen. But there are people who are on a higher evolutionary plane—it happens with every species, some individuals just progress faster than others—and so they know this event is coming. They smell it, or I don't know what. And these people want the rest of the human race to be ready when this event finally happens. Because you need to be prepared in order to understand it. Get someone from the twelfth century to watch an episode of *Big Brother* and they won't be able to grasp it as anything even approximating concrete reality. So, because of the accelerating progression of human evolution, we won't even be able to understand the reality of our grandchildren. Maybe even the one our children are experiencing now. Because it's faster now. We don't need a thousand years to pass to be unable to make sense of reality. We need, like, fifty. And soon it'll be more like ten. And then it'll take a year before you shift into a completely different reality, and then a day, and then a second. It's going to happen any moment now. And some people are already in the next reality, and they understand better than we do what this event is going to be, and what the next generation is going to look like. And they are insanely calculating. Much more than you and I. They are on such a different level that things that appear good to them seem evil to us. They've used Derek

Hammon as their puppet. And then they took thirty writers, emptied them of every last drop of sexual drive through over-exposure, and made them sit down and write this thing for kids. So all the kids who read it will grow into *specific* people. Specific people who will then give birth to kids of their own, raising them in a way that will deepen their understanding of the ideas in this book—ideas I myself don't understand—and so on, until these ideas fully mature in a specific generation, and the event will finally happen.

"We—you and I—we don't need to be prepared for the event." Gideon Tzuk pointed at Tycher's chest with his pita. "Because by the time it comes, we'll already be dead. But our kids will have to be a quarter of this creature, this creature that can understand the event when it occurs, and their children will have to be half this creature, and their children's children will be the creature itself."

"Are there entire scenes in the book that he wrote himself?"

"No. But there was one sentence he asked—*they* asked—that a minor character repeat at three different occasions in the story. It was the easiest thing to put in, actually, because it fit the subject. The sentence was: *Here it comes from the sea.*"

"*Here it comes from the sea,*" echoed Tycher.

"They wanted this character to say, *Here it comes from the sea*. Do you understand it?"

"Sort of," said Tycher. He was shivering.

"How old are you?"

"Thirty-two."

"You're thirty-two and you *sort of* understand it. I'm over sixty years old and I understand it even less. Even less than you. You see this thing here. You were born later and so you understand it more. And your children will understand it more than you do. Do you have any children?"

"A girl," said Tycher. "She's six."

"And her children will understand it even more," said Gideon Tzuk, running a hand through his black hair. "And her children's children will understand nothing but it."

SAÏD THE GOOD

BY Antonio Ungar

Ajami, Jaffa

S aïd Katani is dead. They put two bullets in his back and another in his head, about five years ago now.

The first time I saw him was in his grandfather's garden in the Ajami neighborhood of Jaffa; he was seven years old. It was May, his father and some other men were smoking from a narghile pipe in the shade of an apple tree, the breeze from the sea was playing through the leaves. I was inside with the veiled women, watching them through a window, and Saïd was playing with two friends. He seemed intense and was very handsome, dressed with dark blue trousers and a white sweatshirt.

I never sat with the men. I'm a foreigner, I speak little Arabic, and though everyone except Saïd's father had always been polite, they never knew what to do with me, an Argentine writer who seemed to them like any other Israeli. I remember that his father stopped talking in the middle of a sentence, approached the boy while he was playing, and showed him how to use a slingshot—how to stretch out his arms, how to close one eye, how to aim. He remained with his son until my wife and I stepped outside.

His father was always a nasty piece of work. That's what my father-in-law said when I asked him about that thin, pale man with a blank stare and huge hands, who drove around the neighborhood in his brand-new BMW, always wearing shirts with horizontal stripes and white tennis shoes. I saw him on foot only on Fridays, after praying at the mosque, and then only for a few blocks before he disappeared down Ajami's narrow streets, followed by two teenagers who never spoke with anybody.

Saïd's father had always been intelligent and bad. They called him *Il Ta'lab*, the Fox. At school, he bullied his classmates and stole their money. At fourteen, he joined the emerging hashish Mafia, in spite of his father's threats. At seventeen, he left home and went to live with a little Russian capo, who adopted him as his own son and taught him everything he knew. At twenty-five, after having already killed three men, he decided to start his own business.

The area south of Jaffa, just before Bat Yam, is little more than sand dunes with a few rundown quarters for laborers, abandoned buildings, and empty lots full of garbage. Within a few years, the Fox had established a prosperous business there distributing cocaine to small-time dealers. He managed to stop killing people, instead hiring underage boys who he called his soldiers to do it for him. At twenty-eight, rich and handsome, he asked for the hand of my wife's aunt, who was then one of the most coveted single women in Jaffa.

Saïd's mother was gorgeous and shy. She married the Fox one week after finishing high school at a wedding with five hundred guests. The couple had three girls in addition to Saïd. Two of the girls got married before finishing high school, while the third graduated and became a teacher. None of them married members of the Mafia. The Fox laundered his money by buying legitimate businesses, the first of which was a store that sold kitchen equipment, which his wife ran when the children were small.

Saïd grew up between his public school, where he bullied the other children just as his father had before him, and the store, where he spent his afternoons running errands. His father beat his mother and kept another woman in Haifa, the port where he received shipments of the highest-quality cocaine from Colombia via Spain or Greece, and the best Moroccan and Egyptian hashish, always paying off, with ever-increasing sums, the port employees and the customs agents.

When Saïd's mother asked for a divorce, the Fox agreed on the condition that he would be the one to raise his son. His mother could not refuse, as she did not have enough money to even send him to school. When he was fifteen, the boy stopped playing with BB guns and received his first real one, a 9mm. After it was presented to him, there was an informal ceremony that included kisses on both his cheeks from all the members of the gang, and the privilege of sitting with the narghile smokers in the semidarkness of a café in Ajami.

As a teenager, he had only two friends. One was Arab, a classmate until he was thirteen, and the other was Boris, a Ukrainian who passed as a Jew but was just Ukrainian. His Arab friend, a member of a gang of thieves, was skinny and had sweet eyes, but soon was murdered, stabbed for revenge in an honor killing. Later the Ukrainian became his brother: he lied for him, saved his life during a chase, and proposed that they finally strike out on their own in order to maximize profits.

On his mother's side, Boris came from an educated middle-class family from Kiev, all former members of the Communist Party. The boy had seen many movies, including Mafia movies he bought, stole, or smuggled. Together, in the Fox's hideout, they watched *The Godfather*, about the Italian Mafia, four times, and *Once Upon a Time in America*, about the Jewish Mafia, three times. Inspired by such films, they developed their first business plan. While his father was taking a shower, Saïd explained the details to him.

The Fox did not offer an opinion. He just got out of the shower. That same night, when Saïd returned home, he found all of his things out on the street in black plastic garbage bags. Saïd and Boris's plan was simple and worked well. Just like the characters in the movies, they spent their time selling protection: preventing robberies they themselves would carry out if payments were not forthcoming. The Palestinian invested all the money he had earned while working for his father, but Boris contributed the bulk of the capital.

Saïd's uncle by marriage was an Israeli, about forty years old, corpulent, his head completely shaved, and a sergeant major of police headquarters in Bat Yam. Thanks to his assistance, and despite the danger of making incursions into territories belonging to much larger gangs, the business went like clockwork. Saïd and his father did not speak for years, at least that's what my wife was told by his mother, but every week she would receive from her son a roll of bills that allowed her to live comfortably.

Once their respective organizations had grown so much that it was no longer practical to keep them separate, father and son met again. The Fox had specialized in the prosperous business of methamphetamines and heroin, which had already wreaked havoc on the streets of Beersheba and Dimona. His son had continued to pillage the commercial sector, with the help of Boris and five well-chosen teenagers, as well as the assistance of the always efficient Bat Yam police force.

Their partnership resulted in a well-oiled enterprise. The Fox placed an army at the disposal of his son, and Saïd trained the teenagers to distribute the drugs on the streets. Moreover, and without charging a single shekel, Saïd and Boris brought with them the sergeant major of Bat Yam and his subordinates. From then on it was the police who took charge—in exchange for a reasonable commission for everybody involved—of guaranteeing the entrance of merchandise through the port of Haifa, and to cover up, whenever necessary, murders committed on the streets.

A year later, with business growing by leaps and bounds, the Fox and his son became, with each passing day, much too notorious. The old Mafias, as could be expected, joined together to try to get rid of the burgeoning competition. Before long, one of their soldiers was shot in the head and another soldier avenged him. Shootings from both sides became frequent. During one shootout, Saïd unknowingly killed a capo sitting in the backseat of a car.

War, like a slow, black, unpredictable snake, slithered through Jaffa's oldest streets, leaving dozens of bodies in its wake. By the time Irina appeared, five months had passed since the first shot had been fired. Tall and strong, Boris's youngest sister arrived to take care of their mother, whose health had begun to fail. Saïd saw her first from afar, standing in a doorway, and he felt that those blue eyes were shining with the sun, like in a dream.

He thought about her all day. He also dreamed about her that night, running from a fire, impossible to reach. Very early one morning, a week after he first glimpsed her, he found an excuse to go to the house, accompanied as usual by a Moldavian bodyguard, more than six feet tall and intimidating. When she saw Saïd, Irina gave him a firm handshake and a kiss on each of his cheeks.

He had never been so close to a woman other than his mother. She made coffee, and with a shy smile she talked about Ukraine, winter, the airplane. Saïd fell in love immediately. She started to feel something similar and was increasingly unable to hide it. Boris did not seem to notice. And their father, in addition to taking care of the logistical details of the business, was a man feared for his bad temper, his drunkenness, and his brother-in-law.

Soon the lovers began to meet secretly in downtown Tel Aviv. Their ritual included taking separate routes then meeting on Allenby Street, on Dizengoff Street, under the trees along Rothschild Boulevard, in neighborhoods where they felt like complete foreigners, surrounded by rich, intelligent, young Ashkenazi Jews. They spent whole afternoons holding hands, kissing on park benches, watching small clouds floating by in the sky.

They spent several months watching this life they would never have, as if peering through a shop window. They realized that they needed to be together, even if blood would have to be spilled. Sex was part of it from the very beginning. They had wonderful times in cheap hotels with names like Heaven or Costa Azul or Holidays, across from the wide beaches of Bat Yam, in claustrophobic rooms with white and red Formica, dirty windows looking out on the Mediterranean, and mirrors on the ceilings.

Eight weeks later Saïd secretly introduced his mother and Irina at a special dinner he had prepared for the occasion. My wife's aunt did not want her only son to marry a Russian, but she liked Irina right away, and the rolls of bills kept arriving every week. Saïd's mother listened to that beautiful girl and quickly gained her friendship—to Irina, she was like the mother who had left her on her own for so long back in the Ukraine.

After fifteen weeks, Boris began to suspect something. He wondered why his sister seemed so happy while going about her household chores, or whenever she went out shopping.

Much later, Saïd's mother told my wife that he decided to follow her one autumn afternoon. To his surprise, she took the 25 bus and got off on King George Street. In front of a café, she met Saïd. While they were still locked in an embrace, Boris walked directly up to them, his right hand hidden inside his jacket.

Just like in the movies they had watched together, he brought his face right up against his friend's and whispered that he would not kill him then and there because of all they had lived through together, but that from now on they would be enemies.

One week later, when the news of the romance eventually reached the ears of the Fox, Saïd made an attempt to resolve the problem, but ended up creating an even bigger one. He made contact with Irina while she was shopping at a Russian supermarket. In the canned goods and sauces aisle, wearing sunglasses and a wool beanie, he told her that he wasn't eating or drinking, that he couldn't live without her.

He then kissed her on the lips and whispered in her ear that they should go to Taibe to start a new life. Without waiting for her to answer, he gave her instructions. At two in the morning that same night, she would leave her house without anybody finding out, while he distracted the thug posted at the front door. He would wait for her in the street behind her house.

At the appointed hour everything seemed to be going smoothly, when, from the building's back staircase, a steady hand pulled out a semiautomatic. The burst that followed destroyed one of Saïd's feet, which was resting on the motorcycle. The Fox's son, though wounded, managed to flee, with only one foot on the pedal and leaving a twisting trail of blood all the way to the sea. He said goodbye to Irina under the stars, knowing that he might never see her again, then pushed the motorcycle off the cliff, and rolled down the same cliff to the beach.

He limped through the rocks, washing the blood from his wounds in the surf, suffering agonizing pain, and struggling to stay focused on Irina's sweet breath. He thought he could convince one of his father's thugs to secretly whisk him to the hospital without anybody else finding out, but that was impossible. In his paranoia, the Fox had bought three black guard dogs, and he himself opened the door when they started barking.

When he saw that bloody foot, Saïd's father offered perhaps the first kind gesture of his life. On his knees in one of the bathrooms at the back of the house, he washed and bandaged his son's wounds. After finishing he went to the living room and issued the necessary orders: A stolen lightweight motorcycle would be obtained in Holon. Two kids without police records would carry out the job without knowing where the order came from.

At eleven in the morning, just when the Ukrainian was leaving his house, a burst of gunfire shattered the windows of the first floor and grazed his right arm. Very drunk, he stood staring in disbelief at the boys on the motorcycle. One of his men died at his feet before the arrival of his brother-in-law, the policeman, who was accompanied by sirens and curses shouted over the police radio.

The response was swift. Following a quick search of the area, the two kids were located and taken to the police station. After completing the requisite paperwork, they dragged them to the cliff and tortured them until they coughed up the name of the person who had hired them. Already severely disfigured, they were thrown from a squad car into the streets of

Ajami so that the Fox's soldiers would know what to expect. The man who had transmitted his boss's order was removed from his house half-naked at gunpoint and taken to a different cliff. They shot him once in each leg, to save time.

The Fox, at home smoking his narghile under the shade of a chestnut tree, learned that the Ukrainian was not dead and prepared for the consequences. His most trusted men spent the entire morning moving everything of importance from the house to his cousin's place, which the Ukrainians had never seen and where he would have at his disposal a small jetty and a fishing boat in case he needed to escape.

When the squad cars arrived at his house the next morning, blocking the street and waking the cursing neighbors, their blue and red lights flashing through the open windows, not even the Fox's smell had been left behind. The sergeant major, trying to set a good example for his men, entered with his gun drawn. The dogs—drugged, starved, frightened by the lights—greeted him. The young policemen shot them dead before they could even yelp.

Traffic through Haifa, as could be expected, came to a standstill. The stevedores, the longshoremen, the customs agents, and the truck drivers awaited further orders. Fearing an enemy ambush, nobody showed up or even called. They heard contradictory rumors, and the last truck had not been met in Bat Yam. Wearing civilian clothes and in a foul mood, the sergeant major paid one last visit to try to set things right.

He paid what was owed, called a meeting of the employees, and announced that operations had been suspended. He ordered them to register incoming merchandise as grain and to leave it in containers in the port. One month later, when all known Arab capos seemed to have vanished and the Ukraini-

ans had started buying new weapons in Jordan, Saïd arrived in
Bat Yam in his 4x4. He unloaded a motorbike from the back
and parked it in front of the Ukrainian's front gate.

Dressed as a pizza deliveryman, he climbed the stairs with
the two guards from the entryway, then shot them dead on
the first landing. Knowing that Boris was not there, he kicked
in the door. He pulled out Irina, still in her pajamas. Outside,
a couple of his guys were shooting it out with the remaining
guards. Just like in the movies, the two lovebirds ran down the
stairs past the flying bullets. They jumped over a hedge, ran
to the 4x4 parked two blocks away, and took off at full speed.

They abandoned the vehicle a few yards from the bus
stop. Saïd wrapped Irina in a Muslim veil, embraced her in
the cold night air, and together they caught a bus to Tel Aviv.
From there they went to the Jewish city of Ashdod, where
they thought nobody would be able to find them. Saïd called
his mother a few days later, and broke down in tears when he
told her the whole story.

Two weeks later, the Fox's son arranged to have one of
his soldiers secretly pass him a gun and a roll of bills during a
Nativity procession through Jaffa. Unshaven, he waited behind a group of drunk Christians. Two children who brought
up the rear of the group of drummers said later that they saw
a white hand holding a gun emerge from among the heads of
the crowd.

The murderer shot Saïd through his temple. He fell face-
down on the pavement, like a sack of potatoes, and was shot
twice more in his back. Women screamed and people ran in
panic. The police picked up the body and canceled the procession. The telephone in my living room rang ten minutes
later. Saïd's mother told my wife that her son had been murdered by the Ukrainians.

We went to the wake. The first day, the women cried for the dead man, who was wrapped in a white sheet and laid out on the dining room table, ready to ascend to heaven. When his body was buried, his people rented a tent that covered an entire block. At least a thousand men, from Ramla, from Umm al-Fahm, from Acre, filled the tent, and there they remained for three days, in complete silence or listening to their sheiks, and smoked.

Throughout the long wait, the Fox kept his eyes trained blankly on the house across the street while receiving reports from his soldiers. Then, his face set, he whispered in the ear of the youngest among them. He had hated Boris from the start. The death sentence was handed down without further delay. He demanded the payment of old debts of honor and offered rewards. While the men, I among them, were lining up to shake his hand, the Fox's soldiers were already fanning out to search the stores and workshops of Bat Yam.

The sergeant major had to wait three days before beginning his manhunt. The worst way to insult an Arab's honor would be to interrupt his son's funeral. Even though the Fox had entered the cemetery on foot and was surrounded by soldiers and neighbors, even though he was sitting, in plain sight, in the middle of the street, there was not a policeman in the world with balls big enough to arrest him in Jaffa in the middle of that war.

At the end of the funeral, the Fox went down on his knees, grabbed a fistful of dirt in both hands, and raised it above his head. Those who could see him, including myself, cried: for him, for Saïd, for the children of Ajami, for Jaffa's fate, for that afternoon of cold wind that seemed like it would never end.

We walked home with lumps in our throats, imagining

the coming battle. The crowd of somber men took the Fox to the tent, and three days later to his next-to-last refuge in Ajami. Along the way, more joined them, many more, filling the streets, watched by policemen who clutched their radios in panic. When the cops were finally able to enter the house, they found nothing but dog shit.

The Fox had had time to escape out the back patio, sneaking through a network of gardens and alleyways and rooftops, to a house on Yefet Street, five hundred yards away, where he would hide for two months, his boys supplying him with provisions. Yet no matter how much his soldiers searched through Bat Yam, seized meeting places and distribution centers, ambushed groups of Ukrainians, the fact remained that the shootouts and resulting deaths changed nothing. Boris could not be found.

Long before all that had started, four hours after the death of his only friend and his sister's kidnapper, Boris had left Israel on a plane bound for Turkey. From Istanbul, he had entered Ukraine. His sister was found two weeks later in Ashdod. In despair at Saïd's absence, and without any money left for food, she had called her mother-in-law. Saïd's mother did not tell her what had happened, and, believing it was a way to help her, she called one of the Ukrainian bodyguards.

The following day Saïd's mother received a huge bouquet of white roses, a roll of bills that would allow her to live for a year, and a picture of a child on the ground, bleeding, without a shoe, with a caption that read, in broken Hebrew, *Your son's murderer.* Irina was taken by two large men to Bat Yam in a truck belonging to the organization. When she arrived, she found out that Saïd was dead. She wanted to return to Ukraine, but her father didn't allow this.

From then on her mother kept her secluded in an apartment and under guard twenty-four hours a day. My wife's aunt told us the entire story when we met her in the street a few days later. She didn't seem like herself: she was trembling and appeared uncertain about how or why she was still alive, as if expecting Saïd to descend from heaven and kiss her, tell her that she, too, could now rest.

We didn't want to know anything else about the whole business. All we knew was that the Fox carried on as usual in Jaffa, that the Ukrainians had expanded toward Holon and Rishon LeZion, and that they steered clear of the Arab's territory in order to avoid another useless war. Months later, emerging Arab gangs tried to take control. During those early days, the Fox was gunned down by two men who found him praying on his patio in Ajami.

Boris never returned. With Saïd's father dead and the territories reassigned, another year went by before the scandal of the Bat Yam police force blew up in the press. One sergeant, feeling cornered, decided to rat out all the others. The photo of the leader immediately showed up in the newspapers. The sergeant major was found guilty of cocaine and methamphetamine trafficking, covering up robberies, and ordering the murder of three informants, among them Saïd Katani.

Four years had passed when I ran into Saïd's sister while buying fish in the port. The only thing we had in common was his bullet-ridden corpse, and she mentioned it right away. Boris had returned. He had stayed for a short while. He had visited Irina, now living in Holon, married with two children. He had seen the grave of his only friend, his only enemy, abandoned in front of the sea.

Then, without visiting his mother or his father, he left Israel forever.

This story was translated from Spanish by Katherine Silver.

SWIRL

BY SILJE BEKENG

Rothschild Boulevard

There are many Shin Bet stories circulating in Tel Aviv's expat community. They are among our favorite conversation topics, somewhere between West Bank travel advice and anecdotes on encounters with the ultraorthodox.

Shin Bet stories—like the one about the British first secretary who came home to his Sheinkin apartment to find all the drawers in the kitchen opened. Nothing had been touched, nothing was missing. It was just the open drawers. A subtle, frosty hello.

Or like the one about the pale wife of the Swedish consul out in Herzliya, who discovered the sheets in the master bedroom had been changed one day while she was out. They were white in the morning and blue in the afternoon. And it wasn't the maid's day.

And then there's the Croatian NGO guy with the ironic mustache, who's always telling the story about the one time he found a latex glove placed neatly on a chair in his living room.

There are many stories like these—about furniture moving around, whole sets of teaspoons disappearing, clocks being turned, dead fish floating in aquariums. Stuff like that. Nothing violent, nothing harmful—except to the fish. These stories serve as warnings only, they are but a mere feeling attaching itself to the back of your neck and shoulders, sticky and thick. These are stories with one simple message: *You are not alone.*

They also serve for humor, these stories. Blaming Shin Bet is the standing joke among the expats. Every time something disappears, you can bet someone will make a joke of it. Your keys are not where you left them? Shin Bet must have taken them. Your e-mail never reached its destination? Shin Bet hacked your account. Those single socks that never return from the washing machine? Shin Bet has a storage room full of socks lifted from diplomats, lobbyists, and international aid workers. On casual Fridays the Shin Bet people wear the mismatched socks themselves, for fun.

This morning it is my husband's ID card that has gone missing again. He is late for work and from the street we can hear the driver of his armored Mercedes honking, eager to move away from the activists who have occupied most of Rothschild Boulevard for the last fortnight. My husband is hurrying about the apartment, throwing stuff around, searching for his ID.

—How is it even fucking possible? he cries.

In the kitchen I am stabbing the bloated yellow of a fried egg with a knife. The texture never seizes to fascinate me: the thin protective membrane of the yellow, how easily it's perforated, the way it bleeds itself empty in one simple, relieved sigh.

There's a roar coming from the street. The unrest is in its twentieth day and getting violent. At seven in the morning we received the first message from the corporation's expat notification service: *Demonstrations and clashes expected throughout the day in central Tel Aviv. All personnel advised to avoid the area until further notice.*

Our apartment building overlooks the section of Rothschild Boulevard where the bats live, and now the activists too.
I found them creepy at first, the bats, but they are so light, so
swift, so immaculate, like melancholic, nocturnal cousins of
the hummingbird, and I do not mind them anymore. I wonder
what it would feel like to hold them, the leathery texture of
their wings.

—I cannot believe this.

My husband is back in the kitchen, going through a pile
of *Haaretz* on the counter. It's a paradox that a man so sure of
himself is always losing his ID.

—Must be Shin Bet, he says, grinning at me, ha-ha—
stressful morning but he made a joke!—before finally locating
his ID card hiding behind the toaster. With his stuff going missing, we both know it's not Shin Bet. It's just him, his absent-
mindedness, his elsewhereness. He gathers his documents,
stuffs them into a laptop bag.

—I won't have time for breakfast. Sorry, fucking Middle
East, all these ID requirements, he says, kissing my forehead.
Hey, try to get out today, eh? See some people?

—The corporation says avoid the area.

—Hon, the corporation always says avoid the area. It's
their default advice for anything; social unrest, bomb threats,
any clustering of living organisms. I'll tell them to take us off
that stupid mailing list. Go to the beach. No one's rioting on
the beach.

I am the expat spouse. Each morning he kisses my forehead and heads out to work the politics of the Middle East.
Each morning I drink freshly squeezed orange juice, I water
the plants, I walk barefoot on cold limestone floors. I should
go to the beach, where no one is rioting.

There are more tents on Rothschild every day, popping

up between the trees, colorful and childlike, as if the activists pulled them off their parents' yards, the tents they were
playing hide-and-seek in yesterday. They have their own soup
stations, laundry service, portable toilets. There are banners
and flags, and cardboard boxes are being used for everything:
for shelter, for sitting on, for writing your message on.

The message is in Hebrew, so I can't read it. But the sound
arising from their camp is the same as in any other demonstration I have witnessed in the countries I have lived in throughout my husband's career. It's the sound of homeless desires.

*Stone-throwing reported by demonstrators in Old Jaffa. All per-
sonnel advised to avoid the area until further notice.*

I lock the heavy front doors behind him as he leaves. Two
doors, double locks on both of them. I slip the keys with the
Home Security keychain back into my pocket, and I am enveloped by the kind of echoing quiet that is only found in
too-large, underfurnished apartments.

All expat homes are like this one: tastefully decorated by
a team of professionals, yet bland and too large. Every weekend we attend dinners in apartments like these, with northern
European diplomats, journalists, associates of the corporation,
and other internationals with job titles consisting of acronyms.

When the corporation's local administrator guided us
around the apartment she excused its massiveness.

—If you want quality in this country, you have to go for
one of these new, oversized apartments, she said.

This is how you speak to northern Europeans: as if our
wealth is unfortunate, but necessary. The administrator handed
us keychains with alarm buttons, explained the different func-
tions. Activate, deactivate. Press *House* and the star at the

same time and the alarm will sound throughout the building; the security company will be notified.

This is the panic button. House and star.

I eat two eggs, some hummus. Turn the pages in *Haaretz*, do some yoga. There is a certain discomfort, boxy and sharp, in my chest. I sit on the floor and take in the room, absorbing all the details. I need to know exactly where everything is placed in case something changes, in case he leaves a sign. There have been no signs for twenty days and I know something is wrong. Nothing has been moved, rearranged, or gone missing. Everything is exactly where it should be and it leaves me restless.

Clashes reported in several locations between Old Jaffa and Florentin. All personnel advised to avoid the area and to use alternative routes.

Outside on the boulevard there is a deep howl, coming up from below, carrying aimless despair toward a clear, expansive sky. There is something embarrassing about listening in to someone else's social protest, like getting stuck at the table during someone else's family argument. All you can do is study the napkin, pretend to be deaf, mute, or stupid. I should be used to this, moving between countries in various degrees of distress. There is always someone's uprising, someone's riot or spring—and our double locks, panic alarms, automatic shutters.

We do not worry, we do not join in on the despair. We safeguard, we trust: systems, information, money. We are the kind of people they send in helicopters for.

These riots rage through Tel Aviv every summer, like a public outbreak of seasonal affective disorder. It goes back to 2011. A couple of months each year living in tents and people are able to shake away the unrest and slide back into complacency.

—Poor kids, my husband likes to say about the activists. A region of biblical fuck-ups, and they think they can fix it with crayons.

I tell him it feels real to them, probably.

And this year it is going to be different.

Clashes erupted between demonstrators, police, and IDF in the Florentin neighborhood and moving north along Nahalat Binyamin toward Rothschild Boulevard. All personnel advised to avoid gatherings, minimize their exposure, and limit their movement to the essential. More updates will be sent as received.

Things started to happen in the apartment after we had been stationed here for a couple of months. It was to be expected, perhaps, with all the stories, and the general rule for this type of living in any country: always assume that your home is wiretapped, that there might be cameras, people reading your mail, checking your laundry.

But what was happening in our Tel Aviv apartment was not quite like in the stories. These subtle hellos were not frosty, were not warnings, were not aimed at my husband or the corporation.

These messages were for me.

In the beginning it was only small things. A pearl necklace disappearing from the bathroom and reappearing on the bed. A tiny origami bird on a shelf. A vase of flowers. Objects changing places, disappearing, reappearing—things only I would notice, being the one at home. Sometimes there would not even be any visible signs, just a certain feeling upon returning to the apartment, something in the air suggesting that someone had been there.

And so I would walk through the rooms, tracing my fingers along the windowsills and baseboards, looking for uneven spots, cracks, marks. It seemed like the appropriate response of a person who believes she is being watched, however ineffectual it might be; it would of course be impossible to find whatever sophisticated equipment is being used these days.

Not wanting to seem paranoid, I refrained from mentioning any of this to my husband.

When I came home one afternoon, I found one of my dresses draped across the bed. It was the yellow dress, a pretty one, old. I glanced around, did not know what to think. I left the room, walked around the apartment restlessly, returned to the bedroom. Eventually I pulled off my top and shorts, hesitating a moment before slipping on the dress, the stiff, synthetic fabric cooling my skin. I had not worn it in years. I had been a very different person in this dress. And here she was. Once more I peered around the room, as if trying to meet someone's gaze. I sat down on the bed with a strange feeling of having finished an assignment, of awaiting further instructions. In the empty apartment even my own breath seemed to vaguely echo around the walls.

Something happens to your movements, your physiology, your entire composure the moment you realize you are being watched. The way you tuck your hair behind your ear, the way you fill a glass of water, the way you get undressed. An element of something performative. Even if you cannot see the person watching you, you can't help but feel their gaze.

And I did not know what I should do, how I should feel. I knew how I *did* feel: watched. In this apartment, I thought, nothing I did would go unnoticed, would be bereft of meaning. From somewhere within these walls, a stranger was getting to know me.

A stranger, but a gentle one, someone thoughtful. He would put out books for me to read, on subjects relating to something I had been searching for online, a conversation I'd had on the phone. He placed a blank postcard with a picture from my hometown on the refrigerator door. For all the places we have traveled, it is a town my husband has never seen.

Once he added a song to a playlist on my computer. I listened to it while running along the promenade, north to south then back along the strip between the deep blue sea and the tall white city. You know the feeling of listening to a song someone chose for you? It is a simple one, a simple feeling, sparkling and crackling.

There is a blast from the street, a heavy blast that makes the windows shudder; then the crowd breaks into a panic, all the car alarms in Tel Aviv go off. Dogs howl, glass shatters. Finally the riots are translated to a language everyone can understand.

Violent clashes throughout the central Tel Aviv area. Stone-throwing, gunfire, and teargas reported. All personnel advised to avoid gatherings, to minimize their exposure, and to stay indoors. More updates will be sent as received.

I saw him only once. It was just before the riots started. I came home in the early afternoon and there was a man standing in the hallway by the living room. I froze, keys in hand. He was taller than I had expected, dressed as an unconvincing construction worker, in large, ill-fitting overalls, his face a pale shade of sleeplessness. His eyes a peculiar green, the irises patterned with swirls, as if there were tiny storms in there.

My fingers wrapped themselves around the Home Security keychain. *House and star, house and star.* But then he was just standing there, clutching the door frame, holding onto it as if it could save his life. And he stared right at me as if I could too.

—I am sorry, he said softly in broken English.

He was so tall he had to tilt his head beneath the low door frame, making the room look small and silly around him. As if inside a doll's house. As if he had been misplaced and this universe did not suit him.

I stood before him, scriptless, knowing it was already over. He made no mistakes; I had not happened upon him by accident—he was merely saying goodbye.

—It is you, I said.

He observed me solemnly. I am no one, he said.

—Please do not forget.

His eyes rested on me for a moment. Then he let go of the dollhouse door frame, turned, and left. Later I would be baffled by the very fact that it had happened, that the whole occurrence had not shifted quietly into fiction. Later I would wonder why he had come to see me like that, only to realize he had not: he had come so that I could see him.

There is another blast, closer now and heavier, the windows won't hold much longer. I open the door to the balcony. A thick cloud of smoke chases another cloud of frightened bats out of the treetops. They never come out during the day, and now they are terrified, out of control, cutting through the sky like wild scissors, blackening the colorful tents, rising out of the heavy smoke billowing from a car on fire in the street. The flames are hurling themselves at the trees, at the sky, at crowds of people with their cell phone cameras lifted as if in an ancient ritual.

A bottle comes flying through the smoke and fire, scattering on the asphalt in a glassy splash of emerald. I step back into the apartment, pulse racing, and locate the button to close the shutters. The metal clicks slowly into place. In the dark of the glass behind the shutters I meet my own reflection.

There are stories. Everyone in the expat community knows them. Stories about furniture moving around, whole sets of teaspoons disappearing, clocks being turned, dead fish floating in aquariums. Shin Bet, we say, nodding at each other during dinner parties. These stories make for good jokes, jokes that are funny because they could be true. One day it could be you coming home to your empty apartment, finding it not quite empty. And if one day you realized that someone could see you, really see you, what would you do?

The second before the shutters fully close, a compact black object swirls into the room, slashing the dimness with its tiny frantic body, slamming itself against a wall. The creature slides down in a heap on the floor. I bend down over it and touch its dark fractured wings.

They are not leathery at all, but more like skin, like us.

And as the first stone hits the shutters, I'm weighing the bat in my hand, observing its small death. I tell myself I'm a patient one. I am waiting for a storm that belongs to me.

This story was originally written in English.

MY FATHER'S KINGDOM

BY SHIMON ADAF

Tel Kabir

1.

For many days now, I've been submerged in the work of esoteric poet Binyamin Za'afrani. The streets of Jaffa are compressed by the month of November. I can see the ugly sycamores wheezing beyond my window, quick exhalations erased by a sudden gust of air coming from the west. How is the passion for another's writing born. A little over three years ago, Za'afrani's name was uttered by every pair of lips in Tel Aviv, thanks to the last poem he ever wrote, "5767," in which he predicted the city's destruction on Rosh Hashanah of the Jewish year 5767. I read quotes from it in the newspaper, and then the entire work was uploaded to the web. I asked my doctoral advisor to change my dissertation subject. The office door was ajar behind me. I felt eyes watching us, spying from beyond the crack.

He was amused. For two years I'd suffered through articles written by him and others of his generation, on the oeuvre of one of Israel's most prominent poets: manly rhymes, rhythmic stanzas, the air of revival humming in his throat, between his teeth, mimicking the epic sound of storms and crises, the wild turmoil of the heart. Za'afrani's lines were, by comparison, dejected. Perhaps because he chose to describe the downfall of the city through fragments of the tales of residents who were already suffocating under the weight of the everyday. A woman discussing her son's hasty divorce with his brother. A girl doodling her name in the sand, having just learned how to spell it. A beggar finally locating the soup kitchen he'd crossed the city to find. And all the while, horror appears on the sidelines, chiseled onto the windows of sturdy buildings constructed for the welfare of the wealthy. Perhaps that detail caught the public's miserly attention—Za'afrani's ability to capture, even in the 1970s, Tel Aviv's race toward the future. An optimistic city: funds poured into the improvement of infrastructure; apartments purchased for a fortune; babies born into the world—but no one can guarantee they will still have a city another decade from now. Years have collapsed onto that exhausted, hysterical optimism since Za'afrani's vision was published. "5767" is the most direct of his pieces. The other poems and essays are vaguer. There is knowledge buried in them whose origin I cannot trace back to any known eschatology. Beyond them is an outside presence, threatening to permeate. Each piece is a tiny seismograph. But where would I find my earthquake, that pleasurable vibration I've been awaiting within the coarseness of sounds. My advisor laughed. I decided to get a new advisor. The Ben Gurion University in Be'er Sheva was happy to accept me. It's a fan of the marginal.

2.

I stared at the poems, perplexed, reading the same stanza over and over again, descending the short stairwell and walking into the nearby grocery store. I survived on overpriced rice, tomatoes, and canned goods. They weren't cheap either. Each time he overcharged me, the clerk's face drew into a smile. He often joked around with his friends as he operated the cash register, and their laughter grew louder as I carefully counted out the change. One evening a thought struck me. A meaning

I'd never noticed before floated over the final chapters of the Za'afrani book I was reading. And as if to enrage me, just as I decided to shake off the limpness of heat waves, I spilled my coffee on the next page. The two volumes gathering the entirety of Za'afrani's writing are held by the Rosenbaum Collection at the university library and cannot be signed out. I rose to my feet, holding the navel of the thought tightly, lest it go the way of other thoughts and crash under the weight of over-zealousness. Thirty minutes until the library closed. Darkness descended outside like a bird, carrying news of my father's kingdom. I would never make it on time from Jaffa to Ramat Aviv during rush hour, even if I took a taxi. On a whim, I ran Za'afrani's name through the library computer catalog online. I stared at the results of the query. The off-key singing of the neighbor in the apartment across from mine joined the singing of her favorite pop artists. Not only were the volumes stored at the public library in the Tel Kabir neighborhood, a twenty minute walk away, but they were available for borrowing.

3.

A bridge stretches over Heinrich Heine Street, a river of light, haste, and steel. A bridge that connects Jaffa to Tel Kabir, overtaking a row of olive trees veiled by smog and carbonated garbage. I stop at what might be the right moment, halfway across the bridge. My left calf itches. I alleviate the itch with my right foot. Light movement, a whisper through the denim. What pleasure. The air grows colder. I breathe. I'm on the bridge, wielded tighter than a knife.

4.

Was it foreseeable, the sudden change in weather, I asked the librarian. She looked at me, not understanding. A young, round woman. She smiled when I walked in. The library was deserted, save for two Ethiopian boys who were engrossed in computer screens. The librarian's eyelids were anointed with soft baby-blue eye shadow. A modest shade, if you ignore the fact that wearing makeup is, in itself, flashy. She observed me with confusion. Lightning bolts whipped the sky outside, their glow lingering for a moment in the air.

Had they mentioned a storm, I repeated the question. She said nothing. I stood by her table. I handed her the two Za'afrani volumes, which had been tucked away on the library's single poetry shelf. Oh, she said, we only got these two days ago. And you hurried up and hid them, I said. She answered drily, As you can see we don't have much space. I perused the new-additions shelf. Shiny covers, Vaseline-bright images. How, I asked, how did you get them. A contribution, she said. Yes, I said, but from whom. She didn't answer. There was a hint of ridicule in her voice when she asked for my library card. That's it, she said, we're about to close.

The building was newly renovated. Pretty columns and steps, a mass of marble, so different from the surrounding housing projects. I waited in the shadows cast by the architecture. She locked the door tiredly and turned to leave, wobbling a little, and yet erect. I blurted a weak greeting and went after her. She was taken aback. You scared me, she said. I didn't believe her. Her expression was tough, her eyes narrowed. A wind blew. The temperature dropped. There were already signs of rain, and the scent of expectation. What do you want, she asked. I didn't know what to say. I left.

5.

I checked the year of publication of the volumes I had borrowed. Signs of the storm lessened around my Jaffa apartment. The volumes were old but unused, like food rotting in its package, or formaldehyde virginity. I caressed the cover. I opened the book at the desired pages, but the paragraphs in the photocopy I had didn't match those in the books. I compared the text, sentence by sentence. Words had been changed, phrases, syntax. The courage that my earlier thought had planted in me was gone. The thought itself was trampled by the stampede of others. The same edition, the same details. Only one edition had ever been published. A distant cousin of Za'afrani's had put it together. The family objected after his body was found in the bathroom, his wrists slit, submerged in wine-colored water. I imagined the corpse, its head tilting forward, aspiring to the depths.

A snappy reporter located the cousin in the period when people were excited about Za'afrani's writing. The cousin remembered him as a boy. Back in those wonderful days, they had been true friends. He always managed to notice things she couldn't, hints and traces, aromas and sounds. Once, he found a bracelet she lost. It was springtime, an abundance of daisies. He closed his eyes and asked her to put her hand on his shoulder and walk him through the field. Her body, he told her, knows without words. He stopped without warning and pointed at the ground. She bent down and felt among the stalks, beneath the yellow burning of bloom, and pulled out the bracelet. She kissed his cheek and he was startled. Don't do that, he said. How old were they. Maybe eight. The country was young. Lots of open spaces. They grew apart. He ran away at a young age, she heard, and then came back, and ran away again. They said something was wrong with him. He lived alone, she remembered, but where, she didn't know. Now she's tired. Maybe the reporter would be willing to continue tomorrow.

I was plagued with weakness. I returned to the lines of Za'afrani that I knew well, almost by heart, to the screech that rose from them. Where is a writer when he writes, what kind of middle ground. I went outside and wandered up Yehuda HaYamit Street. Buildings threatened by the sword of refurbishing. My downstairs neighbor once shared a secret with me on the stairwell. All the young people from Tel Aviv are moving here now, she said, and prices are rising. Where will we go? It's not like we can move to the Jewish neighborhoods. All the dreams buried here, slumbering, growing moldy, natives and immigrants. Jaffa is developing into a jumble of gazes, a tangle of forces pushing away reality. I bent down to pick up a coin whose twinkle caught my eye. I looked up and the city was different. A change whose quality I couldn't judge. I was poked by the cold finger of the strange. Yehuda HaYamit Street sloped down toward the crumbling port, and I sloped down with it. I went to look at the sea in winter. Big deal, the sea in winter.

6.

The daytime librarian's motions were lumbering. Her heavy Russian accent toughened the syllables in her mouth. Who, she asked. Yes, yes, she's here in the evening, and I'm here in the morning. That's how she prefers it. Eventually she gave me the name of the evening librarian. A narrow, snaky name. Come back in an hour, she said. The library was empty. In an hour, bands of schoolchildren would flow in to do their homework. I was disgusted by the expected whispers, by the evil in their speech. I asked if she knew who contributed the Binyamin Za'afrani books to the library. Who cares, she said. All sorts of people give us all sorts of books.

The poinciana trees in the shopping center were still rain-bathed, the floor tiles mossy. Clusters of older men, elderly even, sat around stone tables, playing backgammon, checkers, cards. Loud voices and jokes in Bukhori. I looked at them. The living, what do they need. My father's kingdom is at the top of the mountains—on one side snowy prairies, on the other a cruel desert. His envoys walking the blade of the mountain range.

I examined groceries at the local supermarket, the superficial glow illuminating candy wrappers. I coveted the shapes the light scratched into their metallic sheen. On the other side of the row, a conversation took place. I couldn't see the speakers. A woman was explaining to a boy that his services would no longer be required. She emphasized each word. He answered hesitantly, in a thick, slow voice. I went outside. The daughter of the greengrocer was standing behind the counter in his shop. Her nails were tattooed with patterns and rhinestones. I stared at them until she raised her eyes to me. Yes, she said, how can I help you? I asked if I could buy an apple.

7.

She doesn't recognize me, the round evening librarian. A sort of halo of gloom surrounds her. She becomes hopefully alert, hearing her name escape my lips. She stands up to honor the sound. She stands up in my honor from her seat next to one of the children whose homework is occupying her time. The child has nut-shaped eyes, curious eyes. I was wrong about the shade of her eye shadow. It isn't baby blue, it's soft green, perhaps a shade of leek. What, she says. I wanted to ask, I say, about the Binyamin Za'afrani books. Yes, she says. Let me check the computer. She dawdles, truly dawdles. Where is last night's posture, the naked confidence of her walk. They're out, she says. I know, I borrowed them last night. Okay, so why are you bothering me, she asks. I say, How did you get them, they went out of print over twenty years ago. I see we just received them, she says. Oh yeah, I completely forgot. She tells a dull tale of the local greengrocer who won the lottery and bought a deserted building he wanted to renovate and turn into a synagogue. He found a box of books in that building, she says. I ask to see the other books from that box. She pulls out a list. I peruse it. An incredible lack of taste.

8.

I almost got run over on the way back to Jaffa. I was too nervous to climb up to the bridge. Instead I used the same trick I employed on the way there: I waited for a lull in traffic and jumped onto Heinrich Heine Street. A fast moped almost peeled the skin off my face. The door of the grocery store by my building was locked, a calm, blue metal board. When I walked into the building, my neighbor appeared before me, flushed. How terrible, she said. What, I asked. What happened to the grocery store owner, she said with a hint of pleasure. He was violently murdered last night in his apartment by the flea market. It took the police quite some time to identify the body. Her teeth appeared in all their might as she spoke, grinding against the world. There was an animal quality about her I'd never seen before, a horsey merriment. The police have started investigating, she continued before her mouth locked. The determined motion, the bulging muscles of her jaw, explained her off-key singing. She liked talking to me. She'd been waiting for the opportunity for a while now, she said.

I expected to see her standing outside my apartment when the doorbell rang late at night, but beyond the fish-eye peephole I saw the librarian. I thought about how her name matched her curvy shape. Her eyes were puffy. I didn't ask what she wanted, but let her enter silently. I don't remember when I bought the tea bags which were reeking in the kitchen. I quickly offered her coffee, before she could come to her senses, but she remained stunned, on the verge of tears.

I'm not staying, she said in a low, anxious voice. I barely got away. I said nothing. I need those books, she said, I made a horrible, horrible mistake. What, I said, what are you talking about? We just spoke about them this afternoon, and you seemed totally indifferent. She said, You wouldn't understand. Give them back to me, we shouldn't have . . . She was silent.

No, I said, no way, I still need to look at them. Please, she whispered. In spite of her general murky appearance, there was still some majesty about her, perhaps dignity, a steel thread, anyway. I'm sorry, but I need them for research, they're different from the ones . . . Exactly, she said. They shouldn't have come to us, they shouldn't have been released. I don't understand, I said. I told you, she said, there's no point in trying to explain it.

She stood bewildered at the doorway. Won't you sit down, I said. My break will soon be over, they'll notice I'm . . . Give them to me. I lowered my head. I'll bring them back tomorrow, I said, when the library opens. She seemed prepared to keep arguing, but then she retreated. She said, Use the bridge. You'll know which way to come.

9.

Is this what she meant, I wonder. The heat returned to the city—a furious, bitter radiation. But on the bridge—a chill, shuddering skin. Halfway across, that same itch of the left calf widens its scope. A bother with pleasure in its side. Below me is a flood, moving vehicles forget their previous being. The moving and the still have different essences, but we transfer from one to the next our entire lives. Or strive to. How do we do it.

I'm almost sure Binyamin Za'afrani's new paragraphs were speaking about this. The lines of the poems captured something too, as it changed. Not the calculations and metaphysics at their core, not an urge toward destruction and a fear of it, but evasiveness. Throughout the night I scanned both volumes, testing their spines to make sure they weren't broken.

She didn't explain it. She waited in the shadow of the columns and jumped at me from the stairs. I handed over the books unwillingly. Go away, she said. Out, out with you, dybbuk. Then she escaped, fast despite her rotundity. I chased after her, calling her name, narrow and snaky in the cold air. But she was swallowed in a charmless cluster of pink buildings, dolled-up projects whose contents I could guess.

10.

I wandered the shopping center. The men playing games. The women dragging shopping carts. Pigeons came and kissed the faces of puddles and hummed over the poinciana trees. A layer of disgust hovered over all things, as an envelope of impurity around flesh. The players looked at me with hollow, threatening eyes as I paused to watch their game. This time they didn't joke, as if the game demanded a dangerous accuracy, being on guard. No, mechanization. Mechanized things are impure in their own way. I stood there for a few minutes, pondering. Everything random, whimsical, and arbitrary about nature was revealed to me against the orderly walk of the women with their carts, the careful steps of those leaving the post office, the arm movements of customers at the spice shop. I could locate the beat, the rhythm, the beating of the big heart. I listened, *dum, dum, dum.*

I was violently shaken from my listening by the weight of a gaze. The greengrocer stood outside his shop and stared at me. There was burning rage in his eyes, black rage. I looked away, but I could still see it. A boy was standing behind him, dressed in a modern yeshiva student's outfit—a tailored suit, a white, pressed shirt. A young tenderness about him. The tightness of his eyes cleaving the shadow that enveloped him. The being of the entire place pooled inside his eyes.

11.

My building was blocked, cordoned off with police tape. The street and the facades of buildings were washed with the blue fire of sirens. Animals, said my downstairs neighbor, animals, not humans. Each time a blade of light dashed across her face, her skull stared at me from beneath the cover of skin, muscle, fat. At the edge of my father's kingdom, birds used to be girls who had sinned, and they sat on branches and chirped their pleas for grace, thousands of tongues whispering through the air at all times.

The neighbor across the hallway from me was murdered. Her body was covered in small cuts, as if she'd been in a glass room whose walls exploded. Somebody broke into her apartment last night. I didn't hear a thing, said my downstairs neighbor. Did you? Indeed, silence had filled the previous night. Her off-key singing subsided. I pitied her teeth, bitten by time. How are we going to live here now? she said. We're not like you, we have nowhere else to go.

12.

Of course, I'm awoken at night by the smell of blood. I moan somewhere in my dream, ordering my feet to move. What do we do in dreams, other than fight the paralysis that takes over our muscles. Then I choke, blood, blood, I wake up breathless. The walls pulse beneath my hands as I search through the darkness, which is broken only by the flashes of sirens outside. I can't find the light switch. My eyes quickly adjust and I no longer require the clarity of electricity. Beneath my hands the walls are meaty, warm. I listen to the soft flow inside of them.

The police officers questioned the neighbors and myself and left in their cruisers. The cruisers are patrolling almost silently around Shivtey Israel Street, only the friction of tires and the scorching of rubber sounding here and there.

I make a cup of coffee and sit at my desk. Something almost becomes clear in the depths of Za'afrani's writing, especially with regard to one short essay dealing with what he described as two levels of existence, the Beast and the Ghost. I had assumed these were developments of images from the Book of Daniel and the Book of Genesis. Maybe even something to do with Christianity's Judgment Day. But now, it seems to be something entirely different which trembles at the edge of my consciousness. What is it. A minute later I'm staring awkwardly at the computer screen. I compare scans of the book from the Tel Kabir library with the photocopies from the university library. They are the same. Same sentences, same lines. I try to memorize what I can recall, affix it in my memory. But the thought is slippery, yearning to evaporate. If I understand this new version clearly, Za'afrani was not concerned with a fracture in reality. He wrote of slow transformations into a foreign future. I once was a child, and I once knew happiness in a garden, and I once got lost in sweet oblivion, in grumbling oblivion. Just like all the other children. The signs of the past are no longer visible in me.

13.

I easily located the deserted building the greengrocer had purchased with his lottery winnings. I ascended Ben Zvi Road, flanked the neighborhood. To my left was the Tel Kabir Forensic Institute, sheltered by ficus trees, or some other kind of vulgar tree—who could even identify that heavy dullness of growth. Tel Aviv is hot. Man is destined to sweat in it, always, even after only a twenty-minute walk. A two-story building, its plaster exfoliating to reveal perforated bricks. A film of blindness like moss on the windowpanes. I walked inside. What did I expect to find. There was dirty graffiti, shit and tampons, syringes and condoms, a moist smell of dust, and stairwells on the verge of collapse.

14.

The greengrocer's daughter smiled and said, You've come for another apple. She waved her nails which were adorned with a tangle of patterns, secret codes, fake gems. Isn't it hard, I asked. She skillfully packed up a customer's shopping. Isn't what hard? she asked. With the nails, don't they break? She laughed. Why aren't you at school? I asked. What are you, the Board of Education or something? she replied. No, I said, I just think it's a shame you have to work like this. She said nothing. I mean, your brother could help out too. Her fingers, which were running across the keys of the cash register, stopped. I didn't know how to read her look. It closed off to me at once. She wore an ankle-length skirt in spite of the heat. The sleeves of her shirt covered her arms all the way to her wrist. Inside the shop an old man sorted ripe tomatoes, separating, choosing. Outside was the tumult of all the places that Tel Aviv had put out of its mind, that base urgency of life, that multiplicity of meagerness.

Yes, can I help you, friend? Her father appeared, concerned. His mustache glorious, black, his figure as thin as a cut in the skin. Just like his son. Do you have seedless grapes, I asked. I have terrific grapes, he said, like honey, but red. I followed him. I wanted to ask, I began. I looked at the plastic crates. *14.99 per kilo*, a piece of paper read. About the books you found at that building down the street. I have cheaper ones, he said, but I can't promise you they're seedless. Are you really going to make a synagogue there? Why do you ask, he asked. The books you found there. I'm a researcher at the university. I'd like . . . Oh, he said. The university. There was ridicule in his voice. I said, I'm writing about Binyamin Za'afrani. Who, he said. A poet. You gave his books to the library. Oh well, he said, secular books. Your son is a yeshiva student, isn't he, I said. His face crumpled. His Adam's apple rose and fell.

15.

Maybe it was on purpose, maybe she wanted me to see. When the greengrocer's daughter fastened the plastic bag and handed it over, her right arm was revealed. A fading but still visible red line stretched over her veins. Not a scar, a threat. She hurried to cover it up.

The clerk at the post office said, You're not from this neighborhood. No, I said, just passing through. That guy has excellent fruit, she said, and nodded at the bag I placed on the counter. Yes, I said. It's strange he didn't close up shop after winning the lottery. A modest man, she said. So modest. It must be hard, I said, being the only rich man around. He deserves it, she said, life has given him a beating. Once in a blue moon God makes up for it. For what, I asked. She lowered her voice. His wife died while giving birth to their girl. But the son, I said, the son looks younger. What son are you talking about, she asked. He wanted a son but his wife only had daughters. So what kind of envelopes do you need, regular stamped envelopes or express? A big-bodied man walked into the empty post office, a large gold ring on his finger. He fiddled with a toothpick in his mouth.

My mail is never urgent, I said, so regular envelopes are fine. I waited by the door for the man to leave. Then I came back in. I think I'll take some express envelopes as well. Sure, said the clerk. She ran a hand through her hair and tousled a bleached lock. For a moment, her beauty shone before me. Can I interest you in a cellular service, she asked. We sell airtime now, badass offer. I asked, Why did you say he doesn't have a son. I told you, she said, he prayed for a son and only had daughters. The rabbi's blessings were no good. Eventually he went to see this witch, at least that's what people around here say. How many envelopes do you need? I don't know. Three. I don't have singles, she said, I can't open a whole package just for three envelopes. How many are in a package? Ten, she said. It's ten or nothing. Okay, I said. What kind of witch? Her voice grew irritated. How should I know. That's what people are saying. She told him he would never have sons, but that one day he'd be rich. So there, she was right. She rifled through the cash register. Do me a favor, she said, go get change from one of the other stores, I'm out of coins.

16.

On the stairs leaving the shopping center, on my way home, somebody bumped into me. That same burly man with the heavy ring. He kept walking. I lost my balance and dropped the bag of grapes and the bag of envelopes. The greengrocer's daughter ran toward me from the store. The bag had opened and a few red grapes rolled over to the shade. The late-morning light melted their innards, causing them to gleam. She stood up and handed me the bag of envelopes. I don't have a brother, she said. I'm an orphan. The twin of the scratch on her right arm now peeked from beneath her left sleeve.

Back in my apartment I found one odd envelope in my envelope bag. It was a letter from the librarian. She invited me to join her, secretly, to watch a gathering that might answer some of my questions. *Come across the bridge,* she wrote. *Come tonight at so and so time, to so and so address. Find attached: a key.* And a key there was indeed, multitoothed, curved, dusky against my palm. What kind of game was she playing, the evening librarian. I called the library and was told she had quit. And the children, I asked, who will help the children with their homework. They did fine before her, and they'll do fine after her. Kids need to learn to fend for themselves, said the woman in a shrill voice before hanging up. I lay on the living room sofa and read some of Za'afrani's poems. My thoughts couldn't stick to the words and I let exhaustion gnaw on my organs.

17.

The letters on the sign on the door of apartment so and so, on street so and so, in the Tel Kabir neighborhood, as frost bit through the air, at so and so time, did not join together to form a decipherable name. I took my life in my hands and went through that meaningless cluster of letters, through that molecule-composed door. Big deal, I was inside. The tenants were out, only their furniture serving as hostile witnesses to their lives. Lace doilies and tasseled curtains and fake mahogany door frames and kitchen cabinets. Succumbing to an inane urge, I kissed the mezuzah. The engraving on the wood scratched my lips. It alleviated the irritation that spread throughout my body like a beehive as I crossed the bridge.

A telescope stood by the window. I put my eye to the viewfinder. It was pointed at the greengrocer's deserted building. Now, under the cover of night and freeze, the building was glowing. Newly renovated, it featured colorful window-panes and mosaic floors. It appeared that all the neighbors were gathered around it, going in and out in orderly groups. I shifted the telescope to better see the inside of the house. The greengrocer's son walked among the groups and paused by a few middle-aged women gathered on the first floor. He was speaking. One woman raised her finger. He nodded. He wore that same yeshiva student suit. I zoomed in. His tie featured the patterns I'd seen on the greengrocer's daughter's nails. The woman separated from the group. The greengrocer, who accompanied her, gave her a cart and she dragged it behind her as she took a few steps and then turned to walk the other way. The boy corrected her, punctuating the moves of the dance, until they turned mechanical. Then he went up to the second floor and trained a group of men to toss cards on a table, to throw dice, demonstrating the proper spring of the fingers, the appropriate bend of the elbow. A hidden signal was given and everyone disbanded, all the groups dispersing. I turned the telescope to point at the clear steel of the winter skies.

At midnight sirens screamed down Shivtey Israel Street. I was sprawled out on the sofa, reading a Za'afrani stanza and pondering. My thoughts were circling, returning to that same image, an exercise toward the automation of the human. He does not foretell this in his writing. I heard steps rushing down the stairs, beds squeaking with fear, the grating sleep of the terrorized. I followed the sounds. The outside world glowed with police beams. The lights were on at the bakery on the street corner. One of the employees discovered the dismembered body of the owner. I had no pity for him. There is a crook in every baker—for what do these fools want, other than to raise dough and command sugar.

At week's end, as if the buzzing of rumors online was not enough, a piece was published in the local paper. *The Artisan Genocide of Shivtey Israel Street,* the headline cried. The extermination of the small, growing community of independent craftsmen. The piece featured an interview with my former advisor. He said that a similar pattern of crimes appeared in a forgotten poem by eschatologist writer Binyamin Za'afrani. Charlatans rely on the ignorance of the mob, on the terror of quotations and literary references. But search Za'afrani's writing all you like, you'll never find this poem. Who knows better than I. My former advisor went on to argue that there is no point in treating this vision seriously even if reality appears to be echoing it. It's easy to write prophecy poetry. The images are all there, ready to go. Poets seeking attention climb a hill at the edge of town and prophecy its residents' wrongdoings and their imminent demise. Isaiah wannabes are a dime a dozen, my former advisor said.

My downstairs neighbor was also quick to voice her opinion. When she was asked about the artisans' community, she gently said that many of them really did move here in recent years. Prices were still low, but the original tenants were suffering. I was surprised to find that the owner of the grocery store used to work as an apprentice to an antique furniture restorer and that my bad singer of a neighbor received an education in glassblowing. There is an allegory here, I told myself, but its moral escaped me. The grapes I got in Tel Kabir were cold and delicious.

18.

I wake up. When did I fall asleep. In the early morning. And it's still before dawn. The depths of my mind conceal the enemy in the blackness behind the eyelids. The walls are meaty and do not retreat. I hear whispers. I hear scratching and grating. The smell of blood in vague veins. In my father's kingdom maladies of the body have no authority. The eyes of those who deny the beauty of celestial beings pile up in basements.

19.

I rode all the way to Bavli. All the way to Sanhedrin Street in the Bavli neighborhood from Shivtey Israel Street in Jaffa. More than an hour's ride in rush hour. I patted my shoulder. What arrogance, what courage, what glory. The northern neighborhoods are brimming with vegetation. Even in the heat wave of early November, Bavli was green, belittling the schemes of weather. I waited by a building for a resident to leave and snuck in through the opened door. I took the elevator up. How much courage is required for this everyday task, taking the elevator. I've had her address, her phone number, for over a year.

She is sixty years old and she finally, after many pleas, opens the door. I refused to back off. I sat outside her apartment, humming. After she ignored the bell, after she threatened to call the police, saying she's had enough, enough, finally she gives in. A woman alone, sixty years old, but graceful. Her body as delicate as one untouched by experience. I need help, I tell her, I have to understand.

In the fourth-floor apartment, a patterned rug adorning the living room, decorations twisting upon it aimlessly. I sit on the chair. She has a cleaning woman now, she says. What do I want. The windows are open and heat hovers in the air of the apartment. A fly buzzes in, floating over the planters. She shakes open a black, embroidered fan while I sweat. How selfish of her.

I'd love a glass of water, I say. She points toward the kitchen. On the top shelf, on the right, there are dried fruits, she says. I look at the wizened plums. It's like mocking the needy. What do you want, she says, why did you come back? Her eyes have darkened. She wears glasses. Her Hebrew is lucid, authoritative. She doesn't want to discuss Binyamin again. She's done her part. The fly hovers toward me, escaping the slashing of the fan. What answers are you looking for, anyway, she asks. He looked in places one shouldn't look. He saw things he himself couldn't understand. She says, What can I tell you that you don't already know?

I tell her the story about the bridge, about the books, about the greengrocer. What's the logic here, I ask, what's the pattern. She says, There were no houses, there was no neighborhood back then. His father, he didn't like neighborhoods. He bought some land and built them a home. He got the money, he obtained the permits. It was his passion, that house. I remember going over there. There were trees all around, not like now, with those projects of poverty. I liked playing with him. And then, when we were fifteen, they started building them, the projects. His father said it was a crime.

That deserted building the greengrocer bought, was that their house, I ask. Maybe, she says, but they left. Then Binyamin ran away for the first time. I loved him. When they found him I . . . She trails off. Then she says who knows how long she'd have kept mourning Binyamin if she hadn't met her husband shortly thereafter. It was her husband's idea, getting those books published. He thought working with Binyamin's writing would heal her. And were you healed, I ask her. She says, Why do you ask? How could you come here and ask me that? Do you know why he killed himself, I ask, why he did it that way. She said those marks appeared on his arms when he was a teenager, maybe twelve years old, red lines, like the sketches of a surgeon before picking up the scalpel. The fan beats the air, sending small shocks my way. The fly keeps buzzing. So hot, she says. In the other Tel Kabir, I tell her, the one you reach through the bridge, it's already cold. She says nothing. I ask about the greengrocer, his son, and his daughter. She says, If you want something badly enough, you find a force in the world to cut a deal with. Sometimes knowingly, sometimes not so knowingly. Sometimes you think the price is punishment; other times you believe it's fate. What kind of deal did he cut to get a son, I ask, the greengrocer. She gets up and goes to the kitchen. I remain seated for a moment longer.

20.

In the middle of the night something scratches outside the walls of my apartment, trying to get in. I wake up. Oh, do I ever. I can't breathe. I stand in the dark. One of the three moons circling my father's kingdom is always lit on one side of the heavens. I stand in the dark, completely blind. Some snaking inside the walls, and beyond them a gurgle and a groan, the scratching of claws, the tightening of jaws. The muscles taut like steel cables. I put the photocopies from Za'afrani's books in a small pouch. I have to see the final form of the house he grew up in, in the other Tel Kabir.

My body is electrified by the passage, singing itself into being. The sweat thickening on my skin from the Tel Aviv humidity freezes with the shock of chill. I cut through the stillness of the neighborhood. Lights in the windows, in the projects, turn on and off in long, planned cycles. Strings of digits and commands. I slow down as I near the Za'afrani house. The light inside is paralyzed. I peek inside. The greengrocer's son, in yeshiva clothing, sits alone in an empty living room on the ground floor. On the table before him is a book. He is pale and veiled in the aura of those immersed in study. He looks up at me as I walk toward him. He's familiar. Where have I seen him before, aside from that time at the store. So familiar. He examines me, seeming to restrain a smile of contempt that flashes across his lips. He says, Binyamin. My name is a searing skewer turning inside bowels.

21.

I've made a mistake. I must retreat. But it's too late. The greengrocer and the spice seller appear from some unknown corner and get ahold of me. They are strong, these menial laborers. One reeks of tomatoes, the other is rough like cinnamon. I don't understand you, the boy says, you people who insist on coming to a place where you are merely ghosts.

I came to see Za'afrani's home, I say. The boy smiles. There, the smile finally erupts. I ignore it. So you got what you wanted, I say, turning to the right, to the greengrocer. His mustache trembles. Are you happy with your produce? He strengthens his hold and says nothing. What are you doing here, I ask the boy. What is all this? If I could only recall where I'd seen him before. That expression, that entire face. The tightness of his eyes. He ponders for a moment and then returns to his book. The greengrocer and the spice seller pull me away. One is as stubborn as a leek, the other as earthy as cumin. I have to know. What, the boy says. What? Why, I ask. He says, Crowdsourcing. My goons stop at the doorway and I stop with them. Each group of residents executes one small routine which is a piece of the software. Its size is the size of the neighborhood, you see? No, I say, I don't see, to what end?

We deceive ourselves by believing the answer is the purpose of the question. We've found the answer, and now we're searching for a suitable mystery. And what if you've come across a version of reality in which your question is asked with urgency, in all its might? Would you not be tempted to expand it until it erased all other realities?

I've already been torn away from the door. His answer is an echo, swallowed in the noise around me. But I won't leave without a fight, I'll yell and cry, I'll scratch and kick. One day I'll whistle for the spaceship I buried beneath the mountain of garbage outside the city, and return to my father's kingdom. I cannot recall his face. His features have faded, blending with those of random strangers.

WHO'S A GOOD BOY!

BY JULIA FERMENTTO

The Opera Tower

Essy Takes a Beating

Two twenty-year-olds, best friends, take their shoes off and dip their feet in the fountain on Rothschild Boulevard.

Essy takes off her yellowish platforms, the ones with the bow. When Essy was born her parents named her Esther, but Esther is a name for old people, so she shortened it. As far as she knows, she's the only Essy in Israel. Her heels are totally black now. Sometimes when they walk together late at night, Danielle—who's always more drunk than her—stumbles behind her and steps on her heels. By accident, of course. She stains her with Tel Aviv's pitch-black dirt. And Danielle, she takes off the black ballerinas she picked up online from Urban Outfitters. You won't catch her dead in high heels, it's not her thing. She's tall enough as it is.

"Those heels," she says, "what if you need to start running?"

"Why would I need to start running?" Essy rolls her eyes, rifling through her tote bag, hoping to find a pack of cigarettes at the bottom.

"I don't know, let's say someone is chasing you."

"If someone tries to chase me, I'll look him in the eye and spit in his face."

They laugh. They know she isn't brave enough for that.

"Damn, I'm out of cigarettes." Essy frowns.

"Let's get some, there's a kiosk on Nahalat Binyamin."
Danielle pulls her feet out of the water.

"I'm out of cash. Will you buy me cigarettes, Din-din?"

"Sorry, I'm broke."

It's five in the morning, and chilly. The sun rises over
Rothschild Boulevard. You can tell that the water in the pool
is filthy. Cigarette butts float around in it, but the girls don't
care. They like sitting in the middle of the avenue with their
feet in the water.

"Did you know this is supposed to be the most expensive
street in Tel Aviv?"

They can't feel it, but at this very moment water begins
gushing with force through the subterranean steel pipes, and
in exactly thirty seconds it will burst out of the fountain, into
the air, and then land in the pool, for the entertainment of
passersby.

"Hey, excuse me, can we bum a cigarette?" Essy stands
barefoot on the sidewalk, smiling at a guy walking by. He's
around thirty years old, she figures. His jeans are nice, almost
fitted, the sneakers are good too. But what really captivates
her is his white shirt. Button-down, pressed, sleeves folded
one inch above the elbow. Is he handsome? Not a hottie, she
decides, but not bad either. Suddenly he stumbles. She grabs
him and helps him sit down beside them.

"Sorry. I've been drinking since seven. I think I polished
off a whole bottle of whiskey." He pulls a pack of Marlboro
reds from his pocket and gives each a cigarette. "Damn," he
whispers.

"I'll go get a lighter," Danielle says as she slips on her ballerinas. She would never let her feet touch the filthy sidewalk.

At the kiosk, Danielle examines the stacks of cigarette
packs. Towers of them, one on top of the other. If she could

somehow steal one for Essy—but no way. The cigarettes are behind the counter and the clerk is guarding them with his body, like some Roman soldier.

Sometimes she likes to pretend that things belong to her, things that aren't hers and things that will never be hers. All the candy in the kiosk, the books at the library, and the clothes at Zara. She walks around the kiosk with a hungry gaze, scanning the gum, the chocolate, the bottles of booze on the top shelf, and the cigarettes. Essy likes Marlboro Lights, Parliament Lights, and Winston Lights.

"Give me two packs of Noblesse, please," a man says.

The Marlboro is stuck between Danielle's lips and she lights it with the lighter attached to the cash register with a piece of string and electrical tape.

"And also—" The man turns around. Now it's his turn to scan the store as if it all belongs to him. "Do you have any Pringles?" he asks, but looks at Danielle. The clerk walks over to get the Pringles from the shelf.

Danielle moves forward, examines the expiration date on a pack of Mentos, and then quietly picks up a pack of Noblesse from the counter and exits. She doesn't run. Thinking, *I'm sorry, you must have only given him one pack. What do you want from me? You think I smoke those cheap cigarettes? I don't even smoke, maybe one cigarette here or there, and definitely not Noblesse.*

She imagines how pleased Essy will be.

As she approaches, she sees Essy and the guy still sitting on the side of the fountain. Essy is swinging her feet in the water, splashing a little. She can hear her friend giggle all the way from there. Essy tucks her hair behind her ear, maybe bites her lower lip, Danielle isn't sure. The guy moves closer, maybe he's trying to kiss her. Maybe they'll kiss in a second.

Great, now I'll have to go home alone while she makes out with this guy, stupid bitch.

Then, boom, the guy slaps Essy. Danielle blinks quickly, making sure she didn't imagine it. Essy is in shock. The guy gets up and leaves, just walks away as if nothing happened. Danielle runs and catches up with him on the corner of Na-halat Binyamin and Yehuda HaLevi.

"Hey, hang on a second!" she calls out. "Wait, are you scared? I just want to ask you something." She passes her hand along the side of the building.

"What do you want?" He turns to face her. His eyes are bloodshot.

"You just slapped my friend." Danielle is afraid. She can barely hide it. This is the bravest thing she's ever done.

"So?" he sneers.

"Why did you do that?" Danielle is impressed with her own apparent coolness.

"I'll tell you why. Because I was going to kiss her, gently, friendly-like, and she said no. And this was after she gave me the look, laughing, saying I'm cute, nice shirt, all that shit. So I say, *You're a fucking tease, and next time, don't ask a guy on the street for a cigarette, okay?*"

Danielle raises her hand, and for a moment it seems like she's going to slap *him* now. Instinctively, he covers his face, but he's also ready to take it. She comes closer and wipes her dirty hand across his chest. It looks like somebody ran over his white shirt. What a loser.

"Essy, wait up!" Danielle hurries over to her. "I got you a pack of cigarettes."

"Noblesse? Gross." Essy sighs but grabs the pack anyway. She lights one, using the remainder of Danielle's lit cigarette.

"He slapped me."

"I saw. But why?"

"*Why?* Are you serious? What, are you stupid?" Essy keeps walking away.

Danielle drags behind, stepping on her heels, staining the backs of her shoes.

"What did you say to him? Why did you run after him?"

"I asked him why he did it."

"Oh great, an anthropological study." She seems like she might cry.

Danielle wants to ask her lots of questions, but she doesn't have the courage. She feels bad for Essy, someone so pretty and cute getting slapped, just like that, in broad daylight. Somehow that kind of thing always happens to Essy. There's something about her. Even Danielle feels it sometimes—the desire to hurt her, to hit her so that she can then console her.

Essy walks quickly up Rothschild Boulevard. Her shoes are uncomfortable, you can tell with each step. She isn't trying to walk gracefully anymore. She's too tired, she has no patience left for this silly act. She stops, leans against a bench, and takes off her yellowish platforms with the bow. Then she throws one shoe at a car driving down Allenby Street. It hits the windshield.

"Bitch!" the driver yells, but she doesn't even look at him. She keeps walking. She feels like throwing the other shoe too, but there are no other cars around, only a homeless guy sleeping on a bench, wrapped in a hospital blanket. He doesn't even flinch when the shoe hits him.

"Essy, stop it, what are you doing?"

Essy bursts into tears, and Danielle can't help but hug her.

"That son of a bitch. I mean, where does this fucking loser get off, hitting me? Bitch-slapped me in broad daylight, can you believe it? So fucking humiliating, and it's even worse that I couldn't do anything, I was so shocked. I didn't say a word. And he just got up and left like nothing happened." Essy sniffles.

There's nothing Danielle can do to help. "Essy, he's just a drunk, a loser stoner. People do this kind of shit all the time."

"It doesn't matter. Next time, if anyone even gets close to me, he'll get much more than spit in the face."

Danielle walks Essy to her place on Ahad Ha'am Street. When Essy turns to say goodbye, Danielle sees that her nose is bleeding. She can't decide whether or not to tell her. Maybe it's better if she finds it on her own and cleans it in her bathroom. That way it'll feel as if nothing ever happened.

Suburban Beauty

Danielle walks home alone. She lives with her parents on Brenner Street. Just she and her parents in a pretty nice apartment, in a pretty nice building—not one of those crappy old ones. Suddenly her phone rings. She's sure it's her dad. It's kind of her thing—whenever she thinks of someone or something, they appear. This time it isn't her dad, but rather the alarm she set so she could wake up in time for her morning run. Three times a week, ten miles. She listens to Rihanna when she runs, even though she doesn't really like her. She totally doesn't appreciate how she let Chris Brown beat her up that way. She thinks of poor Essy and imagines her cuddling in bed with her cat, crying, feeling sorry for herself, knowing it'll never end. Essy cursing the whole world and swearing to hate everybody forever. And then, exhausted from repetitive thoughts, falling asleep.

Danielle enters her building. There's an envelope in her family's mailbox, but she doesn't bother to pull it out. Inside, her mother sits at the kitchen table, wearing a bathrobe and drinking green tea. It's the only thing her mother ever drinks.

She feels like telling her mom what happened. "Someone hit Essy," she says, placing her bag on the sofa.

"What do you mean?" Her mother glances up at her without letting go of her tea.

"This guy she doesn't even know slapped her on the street." The sound of her mother sipping her tea is making Danielle nauseous.

"Why?"

"*Why?* Are you serious? What, are you stupid?" She grabs her bag off the sofa and runs to her bedroom. The door slams behind her, a teenage slam. It embarrasses her. She's a bit too old for that.

But seriously, why ask why? Why? It's so ridiculous. You're almost fifty. You're supposed to have some sort of life experience. Jeez.

She lies down on the bed, kicks off her ballerinas. She pulls off her skinny black jeans and her thin, loose-knit top. It's a shame she doesn't have a little kitten she could cuddle with. But her mother doesn't like pets. Danielle is filled with self-loathing. She falls asleep.

She wakes up at two in the afternoon. Her phone won't stop ringing. It's Essy, of course. She answers. Essy's in a good mood, almost elated.

"I have a brilliant idea," Essy declares.

Usually she loves it, those firm declarations. Usually it excites Danielle, but she hates herself now even more than when she went to sleep and she just feels like killing somebody, anybody, even Essy. "What now?"

"Listen, we're super sick of Tel Aviv, right? And everything here is just so gross, right?"

"Right."

"So I say, tonight let's go out someplace different."

"What do you mean, different? Like northern Tel Aviv, with all the douches?" Danielle chuckles. Essy sounds like an overexcited teenager.

"No." Essy ignores her friend's sarcasm. "I mean a different city, outside of Tel Aviv. Brilliant, right?" She hasn't left the city in months. Every so often she goes to see her parents in Ramat Gan, just across the Yarkon River, but that doesn't really count.

"What different city, Essy? Jerusalem?"

Essy's dream is to study art at the Bezalel Academy. She says Jerusalem is the most European city in Israel. If she moved there, she could make video art and hang out with other artists and smoke hand-rolled cigarettes in the cold. "Actually, I was thinking of Zikhron Ya'akov," she says. "I went there once and it's really pretty. There's that pedestrian walkway, you know it? And I met this guy from Zikhron awhile ago and he said it's really fun to go out there, there's bars and stuff."

"And how do we get there, exactly? Isn't it, like, far?" Danielle is surprised by how easily Essy has convinced her.

"Can you ask your mom for the car?"

"Essy, you're pissing me off, and my mom's a bitch." Danielle stands up, disgusted with herself. It's two in the afternoon, her greasy hair smells of Noblesse, and her spine aches from restless sleep.

"Okay, but can you ask her anyway and text me?"

Danielle agrees and hangs up. Then the phone beeps again. This time it's her battery, but she can't be bothered to charge it. She throws the phone on the bed and it rolls off to the floor. She sighs. Everything now seems to her like a sign of despair and failure.

In the shower, she thinks that maybe she should suck up to her mother if she wants to borrow the car tonight. Then

188 // TEL AVIV NOIR

she thinks, *Fuck it, I'm an only child and my mom's a bitch and she has no choice but to give me anything I want.* She inspects herself in the mirror. At least she's hot. She's tall and fit. She has that curvy waist. And her breasts, with that perfect slit in the middle, not too small and not too heavy, and most importantly, perfectly upright. Yes, pretty perfect. Like Sophie Marceau's. Danielle studied film in high school, and she learned about the French new wave, German expressionism, and Italian neorealism, so she has a rich world of references. She tries to remember which movie showed Sophie Marceau's nude body.

"Mom, can I borrow the car tonight?" she asks her mother as she makes herself a cup of green tea.

"What for?" While Danielle was asleep, her mother went grocery shopping, had lunch with a friend, bought flowers, took a skirt to be fitted, and made a delicious low-fat broccoli quiche for dinner.

"Essy and I want to go out of town."

"Let me guess, this is Essy's idea."

"No, it's my idea, Mom."

"Fine, take the car. But drive safely and take good care of it."

"You don't want to know where we're going?" Danielle turns to face her mother, leans back against the counter, and sips her tea.

"Where are you going?"

"Jerusalem."

When she pulls over on the corner of Ahad Ha'am and Ben Zion Avenue, Essy is already waiting outside, looking amazing in her white silk minidress. Danielle knows it isn't really silk, it's satin, but it's the good kind. The sleeves are short and round, the fabric is loose, floating around her and only sporadically clinging to her body when the wind blows. When Essy gets in the car Danielle sees that the back of her dress is cut in the shape of a flower. *Damn, that's nice.* Danielle is jealous. Essy's red lipstick is also nice, and so is her thin black hair and her pale skin and her perky nose. Everything about her is pretty—pretty and annoying. Danielle only ever wears her black clothes and the same pair of ballerinas.

"Are you always a bitch or is today special?" Danielle says, lowering the hand brake.

"Why, babe? What did I do?"

"Well, for instance, right now, calling me *babe.*"

They both burst out laughing.

Essy is in charge of navigation; Danielle focuses on driving. On the way they stop at a gas station for coffee. Essy gets a pack of long Parliament Lights. They stand outside, smoking and drinking their coffee.

"How pathetic is it that lattes are like my favorite thing in the world?" Essy asks Danielle in utter seriousness.

"Pretty pathetic."

They laugh. They're such good friends. They know each other so well. All the little nuances and jokes. They both think how great it is that they have each other. Nobody understands them better than the other.

Around two a.m. they're sitting at the Mushroom Bar in Zikhron Ya'akov with three drunk twenty-six-year-old guys. At first they huddle around Essy, asking her questions, trying to make her laugh. The first to leave the game is the ugliest, a guy named Benny who works as a cook at a high-end restaurant across the street and only rarely leaves Zikhron. He quickly realizes he doesn't have the slightest chance with Essy and splits. His friends barely say goodbye. They are leaning over their beers, their bodies pulled toward Essy's without them even noticing. But Danielle can see it. She can see everything. She also knows that poor, ugly Benny will go home now, hating himself and his friends. And after smoking a joint, he'll lie in bed and imagine taking off Essy's soft white dress. It'll feel so alive in his head that he'll even hear the sound of it unzipping. He'll imagine the fabric against his cheek, running his finger down Essy's back. Her skin will feel like silk. He'll jerk off and fall asleep and wake up at eight a.m. to go to work. Saturday is a busy day in the restaurant. By the time his shift ends tomorrow, he won't even remember ever meeting a girl named Essy.

The two guys who stick around look pretty good, one better than the other. One is called Yoni, which Essy likes because she used to have a crush on a guy with that name. The other is Daniel.

"You know that my best friend is named Danielle?" Essy asks him, nodding toward her.

"Well, it's pretty much the most common name in the world, after Muhammad, isn't it?"

Everyone laughs except for Danielle. She feels like Essy dragged her all the way to Zikhron only to do some teasing and flirting with these pathetic townies, who are all excited because they've never seen a girl as pretty as her. But in Tel Aviv you can't spit without hitting a pretty girl, and Essy knows this.

It's getting chilly, and Daniel figures that the best thing that could happen to him tonight is if Essy's nipples get hard. He already noticed, looking at the cut of her dress, that she isn't wearing a bra.

"So how does it feel, sharing a name with such a large segment of the population?" he asks Danielle.

"Feels like shit," she answers honestly.

He finds this extremely funny. "Really? Why?"

"No reason, I don't know. How do you feel about it?"

"The truth is, I don't really care." He begins rolling a cigarette and offers one to Danielle.

"Want to go outside? It's kind of stuffy in here," she says. Essy and her guy are getting heated and she doesn't feel like watching. Daniel agrees and they go out to Zikhron's main drag, the beautiful avenue with the Parisian streetlamps and the white cobblestone.

"What do you do for a living?" he asks her. In the light of the avenue she notices his smooth hair, pink lips, and narrow nose. A suburban beauty.

"I work at a bookstore called Bookworm, on Maze Street. You know it?"

"Not really. Isn't it boring? I mean, what do you do there all day?"

"I read books, or I go on Facebook or IM. But it's fun to read all day long. I like it."

Daniel nods, pulls on his cigarette. His cheeks stick to the inside of his mouth. He isn't into books. "I make music," he announces.

"Really? What kind?" Danielle asks excitedly.

"Electronic music, on my computer. I mix tracks and make them my own. A friend of mine who deejays at the Mushroom sometimes plays my music. But mainly I want to work with musicians, be like a sound editor." He tells her more about himself and his career plans. He mentions the names of deejays, musicians, styles, and beats that Danielle isn't familiar with.

"Are you thinking of moving to Tel Aviv? That's where the whole music scene is, right?" For a moment she imagines him moving there and becoming her boyfriend.

He sighs. "I don't like Tel Aviv. I don't get how anyone could live there. It's so dirty, god. Besides, I'm in the process of building a home studio. I'm working really hard and saving money because I want to get the best equipment. Musicians will come all the way from Tel Aviv to record in my studio."

Danielle tosses her cigarette to the ground and steps on it. "Wow, I'm tired." She yawns.

They sit down on a bench, not saying a word. Now that they've told each other about themselves, they have nothing more to talk about. It's awkward, but also pleasant. Daniel raises his arm clumsily and puts it on Danielle's back. When he rubs her shoulder she can feel that his fingers are sweating.

"Can I kiss you?" he asks.

They kiss, mostly with their tongues and a little with their lips.

"Danielle, where are you?"

They hear Essy calling and stop kissing immediately. Danielle jumps up. Essy walks toward her, holding her purse tightly. Danielle can tell she's pissed off.

"Let's get out of here," Essy orders.

"Why? What's going on?" Danielle is annoyed.

"Come on, let's get in the car." She grabs Danielle's hand and pulls her up. Daniel stands there and watches them, saying nothing. Danielle turns back to him. He has exactly three seconds to ask for her number or her last name. But he just puts his hands in his pockets and shrugs.

They get in the car. Essy slams the door and buckles her seat belt nervously. Danielle hasn't even had a chance to get her bearings after that sweet kiss.

God, she's so jealous, she just can't handle it if not every guy wants her, going insane over her, unable to keep his hands off her. Bitch.

Essy pulls the pack of Parliament Lights from her purse, opens the window, and lights a cigarette.

"What do you think you're doing?" Danielle shouts. Essy knows she can't smoke in her mother's car. "Put that out right now, Essy!"

Her friend ignores her, blowing smoke out the window.

"Essy, come on."

Suddenly Essy turns her back to her, and Danielle sees her skin through that flower-shaped opening in the back, and the skin is scratched and bleeding. Then Essy brushes her hair from the back of her neck and Danielle sees the dress is torn. She slows down and pulls over by an open field. The road is empty and silent. The air is black. They get out of the car and sit outside, smoking, not talking. Danielle feels sick. She takes deep breaths to stop herself from throwing up. And it's not the booze.

Essy gets up, turns around. It's four in the morning. The only light comes from the moon and a few streetlamps. She breathes deeply to stop the tears, but it doesn't work. She cries and cries. Danielle is sorry for anything bad she ever thought about Essy. She takes a few steps and then throws up. Maybe it was the booze after all.

No More Mr. Nice Girl

Essy doesn't want to go home. She asks Danielle to hang out for a while. Danielle says yes. She says yes to everything. The sun is up, the streets are lit, but it's very quiet. It's Saturday and everyone is sleeping in and there are no buses. They wander the streets, barely talking. Essy chain-smokes, Danielle walks behind her, stepping on her heels. They enter a store and Essy buys a seventy-five-shekel bottle of Absolut Raspberry. Danielle doesn't even try to stop her. They will drown together.

Sweet Essy, little Essy, pretty Essy. Danielle is angry at the world. She slips a block of cheese into her bag. They'll need something substantial to absorb all the vodka they're going to drink. The supermarket employees are sleepy, they don't even notice as Danielle puts whatever she wants in her bag. Standing in front of the wine shelf, she decides to up the ante. Cheese is nothing. She slips a bottle of sauvignon blanc into her bag.

They sit down on the edge of the fountain in the square in front of the Opera Tower, by the beach, and drink, sharing the Absolut because they have no way of opening the wine bottle.

The square is empty. They can hear the water rumbling in the fountain and the waves crashing onto the beach. Essy looks at the sea, Danielle looks at Essy who drinks the Absolut in big gulps. The repulsive flavor of the vodka doesn't even make her squint as it meets her tongue.

"Let's take a stroll, I'm sick of sitting here." Essy gets up and begins walking toward Allenby.

"What do you feel like doing?"

"Nothing."

Danielle decides this time there's no way she's telling her mother what happened to Essy. Forget it. Frankly, she isn't exactly sure what happened to her friend. She only knows her back was scratched and her dress was ripped. Oh, and that Essy was bawling. She can imagine the rest.

When Danielle was outside with Daniel, Essy stayed inside the bar with Yoni. He bought her one shot after another and made her laugh. It's easy to make her laugh. He kept telling her she was pretty. It's easy to tell her she's pretty. Then Essy tucked her hair behind her ear and bit her lip and he kissed her. Essy suggested they head outside, because people were really beginning to stare. They went to the back, by the kitchen, and he grabbed her neck and kissed her hard and slipped a hand under her white satin dress and Essy liked it. Then he lifted her and pushed her against the wall and got really, really close and Essy wrapped her arms and legs around him. He tried taking off her dress. He was gentle at first, but the small, smooth buttons kept slipping between his fingers. He managed to undo one, and then discovered there were three more. Essy didn't help him or suggest doing it herself. He couldn't really bear the thought of missing out on this opportunity, so he tore the buttons open, and Essy yelled, but he had her completely pinned to the wall. She pushed herself down to get away from him and her entire back got scratched on the rough wall. When she managed to shove him off her he said, "Come on, don't be a tease."

"Have you ever been to a strip club?" Essy asks.

"No. You?"

Essy and Danielle are standing outside a strip club on Allenby. Danielle imagines walls painted with palm trees, women dancing with flowers around their necks, Spanish music playing, fruity orange cocktails, and laughter. But when they walk in, they find the club dark, empty except for a man at a corner table and one dancing stripper. She has small breasts and a glow-in-the-dark thong. This is not at all what Danielle had expected. They worry that someone will kick them out, but at the same time Danielle can feel Essy calming down, softening, going back to her normal, mellow self. Danielle takes a few long sips of vodka and returns the bottle to her bag. The last thing they need is to be caught in a place like this sneaking in their own booze.

They sit down on a black leather sofa and watch the stripper.

"Do you think she's pretty?" Danielle asks.

"Kinda. I thought she'd have bigger tits."

"Disappointing, right?"

They both laugh.

The lone guy comes over and sits beside them. Essy lurches and clings to Danielle.

He's probably eighteen. Blue eyes, strange accent, black, dandruff-sprinkled hair. "What are your names?" he asks. The way he speaks, the way his tongue swallows each word: something isn't quite right with him.

"I'm Esther, and this is Danielle," Danielle says.

Essy smiles at her. "And what's your name?" she asks.

"I'm Aviram Maoz. I live at 24 Yehuda HaMaccabi Street, on the second floor."

The girls giggle quietly. His body language is strange, with exaggerated movements.

"Is this your first time here?" Danielle asks.

"No, I come here every Friday. It's good for me to stop by. And I usually have friends here too. They aren't here now but I always sit with them. They smoke a lot. I don't like the smoking but it's fine because they're my friends." His body shifts from side to side.

"And what do you and your friends do?" Danielle asks, lighting a Noblesse for Essy and for herself.

"We look at the girls, at their boobs." He laughs.

"And do you think they're pretty?" Essy asks in her sweet, childish voice.

"Very pretty. My friend Avi always jokes about how it's too bad we can't take them home and give them hell. I know what he means. It's illegal." He laughs nervously now.

"So if it's illegal, what do you do instead?" Danielle leans toward him, waiting to trap him.

He laughs yet again, embarrassed. "I go home late at night and I lie in bed and whack off and think about the girls from the strip club."

His honest response takes her by surprise. "Are you a virgin?"

"My dad was the one who first brought me here. He said this could be a good place for me. I'm not a kid anymore but I still live with my parents, at 24 Yehuda HaMaccabi Street. You understand?"

"Would you like to lose your virginity?" Danielle blows smoke into his eyes.

He waves his hands to clear the smoke. "We're not allowed to touch here. That's what they told me. Anyone who tries to touch gets hell."

"Do you know where the bathroom is?" Danielle puts out her cigarette.

Aviram points across the room.

"Where exactly? Can you show me?"

He stands up.

"What are you doing?" asks Essy.

Danielle smiles and Essy smiles back and sticks out her tongue.

They laugh. They both think how great it is that they have each other.

Aviram leads Danielle to the bathroom. He smiles, someone actually takes him seriously for once. The girls are nice, they ask him questions. His friends only make fun of him, calling him a horny retard. The girls haven't even said anything about that. They can't even tell that he's a horny retard. "It's right here." He points at the bathroom door. "You want me to wait for you? I can wait for you."

Danielle breathes deeply and comes closer, too close.

Aviram fidgets, shifting his weight from one foot to the other. He puts his hands behind his back.

"Can I kiss you?" she asks. She can't believe she just said that, it's the bravest thing she's ever done.

"Why w-would you want to d-do that?" he stutters. His voice trembles, his upper lip is sweaty.

She grabs his face and kisses him. He doesn't move. His arms are at his sides, his tongue hidden deep inside his mouth.

Danielle follows the rules, so she begins nicely. She likes being in control. She's the one who decides where to move her tongue, what to do with her lips. She bites his lower lip and creates a puckered kissy sound.

Danielle glimpses Essy out of the corner of her eye, with her white dress now completely trampled, her hair messy, and the remnants of lipstick that weren't left on the beer glass back in the Mushroom Bar. When she sees Essy she begins kissing harder.

No more Mr. Nice Girl, baby. Too bad, you're actually a decent guy. You've probably never hurt a soul, but that doesn't matter now.

She grabs his cheeks and thrusts her tongue inside of him. It's a disgusting, aggressive kiss. Aviram feels this and hopes she goes back to kissing him like before.

"Ask if he's a virgin," Essy says, leaning now against the wall and smoking another cigarette. The pack is empty. She'll wake up tomorrow and regret all those cigarettes, but it won't help, the pain won't go away, it'll only transform into a sense of heaviness.

"Are you a virgin? I asked you before, but you never answered. So tell me, are you?" Danielle says.

"I, I don't understand." She's standing so close, he can't escape. He's nervous.

"Do you want to lose your virginity?"

He's burning inside. He dabs the sweat and moves the hair that sticks to his forehead, licks his lip. His arm is trembling. His right foot is numb. He shakes it.

Danielle leans in and gives him another painful kiss.

"Maybe you want to lose it with me?" Essy says before approaching. She kisses him now, not the way Danielle does. She's soft and slow and her big lips feel so tender. Aviram prefers this. "What's wrong? Do retards not like sex? I thought everyone did." Essy runs her hand through his oily hair. He smiles, which makes her shudder with disgust. "Gross, look." She giggles and points to Aviram's pants. He has a visible hard-on.

Danielle slaps him lightly. He snorts and the girls don't try to hide their amusement anymore. Essy bends down and unzips him. She pulls down his jeans and underwear. His entire body is shaking, his head knocking against the wall.

"Relax," she says, stroking his cheek. She feels excitement between her legs. "You've never done this, right?" Essy looks at Danielle and points at Aviram's penis.

It's not like Danielle's a virgin. She's had sex with two guys, but she's never given anyone head. She's always wanted to try it. At least that's what she told Essy.

"Come on, this is your chance."

Essy puts a hand on her shoulder. Her touch infuriates Danielle.

"Don't be scared. This is good, I can teach you now." Essy pats her back and shoots her that smile. It's the smile that drives Danielle crazy, because it makes her friend so beautiful. But right now Essy looks ugly to her.

Danielle slips her bag off her shoulder, the liquor bottle knocking against the floor. She crouches down like she's going to pee. She won't let her knees touch this filthy floor. Now her face is right in front of his penis. Her mouth is so close, but Aviram isn't trembling anymore. He's paralyzed. There's one thought that horrifies him: *Don't let me have an accident.*

Essy rubs his cheek and kisses him again, her lips fluttering against his face, his skin soft, like a child's. "You're pretty cute, you know that?"

Danielle is already convinced that this will be good practice. She opens her mouth as wide as she can. She puts his dick in her mouth and then pulls it out. She does this several times.

"Not like that. You have to kiss it. Suck in your cheeks," Essy says, making a fish face.

Danielle mimics her.

"But do that after it's already in your mouth."

She puts his dick in her mouth again, then sucks in her cheeks. She knows it's impossible, but for a moment she worries about swallowing it.

"Now roll your tongue around," Essy says sweetly, gently, and Danielle obeys.

After a moment, Danielle pulls Aviram's dick out of her mouth. She needs a breather. The sensation surprises Aviram and his entire body trembles. He tries, but he can't help it.

Then Danielle screams, touching her pee-soaked hair. "You son of a bitch, you pervert!" She starts hitting him, harder and harder.

Aviram doesn't attempt to escape. He shakes his head, his eyes glued shut.

"You sick retard!" Danielle slaps his face and his head hits the wall. "I wish you were dead!" She kicks him. He tries to pull up his pants but she won't let him. She kicks him again.

"Cut it out, he didn't mean to do it," Essy says, dragging her off him.

Aviram uses this opportunity to pull up his pants and then runs away.

Danielle continues to scream after him as her voice bounces against the club's soundproof black walls.

A strong odor of detergent envelops Essy's nostrils as they walk out. Allenby is busier now. The sun is beating down on it. The street reveals itself to the girls in all of its ugliness. Tel Aviv's fumes stain each building—the smashed windows, the crumbling structures. Only the sign outside the supermarket reveals a sparkle of cypress green, a foreign green. They walk down toward Ben Yehuda in silence.

Danielle's mind is empty. As soon as a thought pops up, she cuts it off and clears her head again.

Essy's head feels like it might burst from all the vodka she put in her small body.

"Horny retard who watches naked women and then jerks off thinking about them. Disgusting," Danielle mutters.

"I think you've traumatized him for life," Essy says, giggling.

Danielle looks her in the eye and without thinking, blurts out, "You're stupid."

Essy stares back at her without a word, but her thoughts are visible through her eyes. She thinks that Danielle is evil, that she has no compassion. Then Essy quickly bounds across the street, escaping. The 4 bus approaches. She raises her hand and waves at it. The bus stops and swallows her inside.

Danielle walks toward the Opera Tower and down to the beach. The sand is warm, but not too warm. There are people here and there. She sits down on a quiet patch of sand and folds her knees against her chest. The sun shines in her eyes. She laughs out loud.

PART III

CORPSES

THE TOUR GUIDE

BY YOAV KATZ

Neve Sha'anan

You can't tell by looking at the dead what was killing them when they were still alive. His thick body was seated, slumped to one side. His face was a bleeding steak, loose cheeks, and a shadow of stubble. My heart pounded. In his stand-up act, he used to say that back in the sixties he was as pretty as a little girl. The men who fucked him liked to run their fingers through his curly hair. What little hair he had left now clung to his forehead. The cart he took everywhere was lying at his side. He used to call it his Cadillac. I thought that was funny. I liked his Yiddish jokes too. I probably heard the story about the Nigerian diplomat with the humongous dick a hundred times, but each time he waved his hands and squealed, *"Nem de schlong avek foon meer!"* I'd crack up and translate it for those who didn't know Yiddish—Sephardic or young listeners: "Get that dick away from me!" It made me feel good, giving him a stage, bringing in an audience. I felt useful. And now he was dead.

At first the cops wouldn't let the group come through, so I knew it was serious. I decided to take an early dinner break, sent the tour group to get some food, and walked into the alley, an improvised path along a construction site's tin fence at the edge of Rothschild Boulevard.

Police cars blocked the intersection with Herzl Street, blue and red lights shining across the wet road. Cups of coffee

206 // Tel Aviv Noir

steamed below the Espresso Bar awning. Inside the café was a crowd of irritable people, denied their caffeine. A paramedic covered him with a blanket, preparing him to be hoisted onto the gurney.

I had no time to process what was happening, because just then a uniformed figure appeared behind me. Hila Farkash, one hand clad in a latex glove, placed her other hand on my shoulder, as if she hadn't begun her career as my junior employee. As if she really cared. Now she was a chief inspector. Time flies when you're out of the loop.

"You knew him," she stated the obvious. She'd never been beautiful, but in the two or three years we hadn't seen each other, she'd dried up like a rotting mushroom.

"Mordechai Weintraub. Everyone called him Mota *Sharmuta*, Mota the Whore."

"Tsk." She shook her head. "What a miserable soul."

On the contrary, I thought. He hated playing the victim. He joked about his horrid life, mixing obscenities with humor, and proved that even a gigolo could sound like Woody Allen. But instead of blabbering about neuroses, he told us how many liras he used to get for a blow job, converting the sums into shekels so that everyone could understand.

"If he were a professional miserable soul I would have stayed away," I answered.

"I meant you." Farkash smiled, pleased with her little zing.

I ignored her tease. "I thought I was done with this kind of stuff when I retired. He was used to being attacked. He knew how to handle himself, and yet this still happened."

"It's natural for you to feel angry. He was the star of your show."

"I'm more concerned with the fact that forensics isn't here."

"They're on their way," she said drily.

"The rain is going to erase the evidence, you'll have a silent crime scene on your hands."

"Once an investigator, always an investigator," she said with a cynicism she didn't have back when I was in charge.

"That's absolutely right, and this is no way to manage a murder investigation."

"I'm not certain this is a murder yet."

"Come on, Farkash, get serious."

"Did he have any enemies?" She pulled out a notepad. "Is there anyone in particular who you suspect?"

"Go figure, we all have enemies."

"I want names."

"And I want forensics," I repeated, getting irritated. "Radio them in."

"Why don't I take care of the crime scene and you take care of your tourists, and we'll each do our own jobs?"

"They aren't tourists," I said curtly. "And who said that was my job?"

In retrospect, I should have given my customers an excuse, but I felt guilty and I wasn't thinking ahead. Farkash was right. Mota was a star, comic relief, a vent to release the pressure from the tour's previous stops: the riverbank where the dead girl in the suitcase was found, the building in whose yard they finally captured the "Polite Rapist," the club where a police-officer-turned-stripper showed everybody her boobs. My target audience was the bourgeois Israeli with a full-time job, two or three children, and some free time, who came into the city for a weekend visit and happened across my flier. I also got worker union groups and retirees looking for thrills buying tickets for my moving freak show, enjoying the shock they got

208 // TEL AVIV NOIR

from the fact that things like this happened in our tiny country. Fear and sanctimoniousness are a profitable combination.

But I was still shaken up, and rather than making up some story, I gathered my participants by the kiosk in the middle of the boulevard and told them the truth. They didn't believe me. They convinced themselves it was part of the program. With my connections, I must have brought the police cars and the ambulance just for atmosphere.

I told the driver to take us to the S&M Basement. I heard text messages and whispers inside the bus all the way there. A few of my participants, who were in the know, checked out the situation, and by the time we arrived at HaSharon Street, the entire bus realized what had happened. Three couples hailed taxis and escaped. The rest gathered at the entrance to the old industrial building, suspicious and confused.

"We can end the tour here," I offered. "We'll drive you back to the meeting point."

"We only hit half of the stops," someone complained. "We deserve half our money back."

"I'm not dodging that," I dodged. "Give me a day or two, we'll figure it out."

"I'd rather get credited for another tour some other time," the man's wife intervened.

"I have everybody's contact details. I'll be in touch."

"We should have taken that other tour," one nasally woman said.

"There were no vacancies," her friend replied with frustration. "Now we know why."

Arab boys in waiter uniforms removed tablecloths and overturned chairs, preparing the floor to be mopped. The closed windows locked in the smell of meat and puff pastry. From the southern tip of the seawall boardwalk, the hotels on the beach created the illusion of a real city's skyline.

I found Little Gideonof in the kitchen, leaning on a stainless steel surface, wiping sauce with pieces of torn challah. I watched him for signs of struggle, a bloodstain. Nothing. He nodded at me with his mouth full and handed me a piece of cooked beef tongue fluttering on a fork.

"I don't eat standing up, and I certainly don't take food from the hand of someone who's fucking me over," I said.

He stopped chewing, grabbed a pitcher of water from a passing waiter, washed his food down, and let out a burp that sounded like a quick strum of a bass guitar. I didn't expect anything more from him. He was a man of few words.

"Not talking nice," said Little Gideonof. There was nothing little about him. When my old business fell through, I sadly went to see him and his brother. All the banks required collateral against loans, but my ex-wife had forgotten all of our good times and had cleaned me out in one fell swoop, like a collector cleans out a synagogue charity box: she took the house, the kids. Other shylocks wanted nothing to do with a former cop. Unluckily enough, I knew the Gideonof brothers from my days at the Clock Square Station, twenty meters away from their event hall. I made an enormous effort to give my payments on time, having seen with my own eyes what happened to people who borrowed and didn't return. Gray market, blue market, purple, brown.

"You knew the money was on the way," I reminded him. "What did you kill Mota for?"

"Who's Mota?"

"It's harder to get the entire sum without him. You've hurt yourselves too."

"Not talking nice," he repeated, this time as a threat. My

past career as a police officer was my only protection against him and his older brother. It was nothing like military protection, though. It was more like a condom.

"I want to see your brother," I demanded.

"In Eilat," he said.

"When did he go?"

"Two, three days."

That garbled my theory. He was the brute force, his brother was the brain. If his brother wasn't around, they really must not be related to the murder. Or maybe it was just an alibi.

"When will he be back?" I asked.

He pointed at the window. Outside I saw an Arkia airplane descending toward Dov Airport, its body illuminated by the city's lights. Little Gideonof returned to his sauce. It was funny to see a Bukharan who liked Ashkenazi food. It made me pity him.

"You need to watch what you eat," I said. "All that food, it's a shame."

"Talk nice," he growled at me through a mouthful of dough. "And bring money or we find you."

She was standing by a bulletin board covered in posters for deejays and rabbis, bent down, sleeves covering the holes in her arms. I hung my helmet on the handlebars of my moped and gave her an apologetic hug. She was as thin as the ribbon you hang a medal on. Whenever I touched her, I wanted to stand at the threshold of the moment when her body grew accustomed to the beatings and the humiliation and stop the apathy from seeping into her soul. The veteran Eritrean refugees on Har Zion Avenue were used to seeing us together. If someone watched us with wonder, it meant they only recently crossed over illegally. I left the infiltrators and the shelter-seekers for the bleeding hearts. Charity begins at home.

"I'm sorry, I should have told you we weren't going to make it to you on the tour last night. Have you been waiting long?"

"No matter," she said with a slight accent, pulling a cigarette from the pocket of her sweatpants. "I heard Mota dead."

"What else have you heard?"

"Bus get scared, run away on you."

Hinges creaked. A door along the peeling plaster wall opened with effort, like a swollen eye. Her little pimp peeked out. He reminded me of my Iraqi neighbor from HaZiyonut Avenue, back when I still had money and a home. I'd return from the station or the precinct at dawn and find him waiting for the paper delivery guy. He never answered my "Good morning," and made me wonder what it meant to be a normal person.

Now I noticed her glazed eyes. She was high.

"Go home to your mother," I said. "Only for a week, until we can figure this out."

A thin smile and shaking teeth—that's how she laughed. What I said really was ridiculous. What mother and what home? What would they do for a whole week up in Karmiel, besides fighting over the vodka bottle? There wasn't enough heroin for her in the entire Galilee region. The urge would begin on the way to the train station, and before she was even past Tel Aviv University, she'd be dope sick.

"No need," she said.

"It's getting dangerous here. Not for you specifically, but I'm still worried."

She chuckled again. So alone and so vaporous. Every day of her life was more dangerous than anything I'd experienced on the police force. A client could decide to cut her up instead of paying. She could overdose, contract AIDS, syphilis, get pregnant. The people I brought to see her on the tour were sorry for her for a moment, felt guilty for their apathy, begged her to go to rehab. I understood them. She made me feel better about myself too. I used to think the tour was a break from her shitty life, until she told me it was nothing more than a chance to speak some Hebrew. I pulled out my wad of cash and counted four hundred shekels. She stuck the bills between her jeans and her boot. Soon she'd buy another hit, connecting with her heart once more.

"Have you eaten anything today?" I asked.

The door squeaked again. I glanced over for just a moment, but when I looked back she was gone, and I was left alone with the stench of ammonia from the urinary tracts of Tel Aviv.

The first phone call woke me at eleven. I thought it was that blonde from the radio again, a crime reporter who wanted me to discuss the murder on the air.

"Izzy Schuster?" a woman asked. She sounded like a teacher from the countryside.

Fucking Google. We appeared one after the other in the search results, and people never paid attention to what they clicked. Twice a week I received phone calls intended for my competition.

"Huh?" I blinked into the light, surprised to find it was already another day. Then I lied, "Yes, that's me."

"It's my husband's birthday on Friday. Are there any seats left? Two people."

"Let me check." I pretended to leaf through a datebook. "No problem. Meet me at five thirty at the edge of the Nokia Arena parking lot, in Yad Eliyahu."

She repeated what I said slowly. I heard the call waiting beep and switched lines.

This time it was really for me, not for Izzy.

"How did you hear about me?" I asked.

"You were mentioned on the morning news, and I also saw your name in the paper."

"What was it in reference to?"

"A man who was part of your tour has been murdered. I assume you already know this."

"I was sure people would be nervous and stop calling," I admitted.

"Not necessarily." He sounded like a putz. "We're actually pretty excited about it." He continued babbling until I interrupted him.

"All right, I have you down for six people. Meet me at the Nokia Arena parking lot, Friday, five thirty."

"Thanks—and good luck."

"With what?" I asked.

"You're a former police officer. I imagine you must be conducting your own investigation."

"Oh yeah, sure, sure."

"Do you have any leads?" He seemed pleased with himself.

"The problem with leads is that they can lead you nowhere."

But he was right. I needed to find the maniac who did it. I wasn't concerned with justice. Nobody was. But my people could be in danger, and so could I. I needed investigational materials and could only rely on connections. I hated relying on connections. The last time I did that, I ended up on the streets, depressed, waiting for happy days that rarely came. I called Hila Farkash.

"What the hell do you want?" she said.

"Whatever you're willing to give me."

"I was willing to give you a lot, but you wouldn't be serious."

"Holy shit!" I finally got it. "Don't tell me you're still into me."

"Eh," she snorted, "I'm not that desperate."

"I'm sorry to say, but yes, yes, you are."

"And what about you? Your life is garbage."

"You know, being insulted is a choice."

"And what's being insulting, a necessity?"

A moment after I burned yet one more bridge, I got another booking. And fifteen minutes later, another two calls came in. I was fully booked by the afternoon, and had to stop myself from getting overbooked. I called the driver and reserved a bus for Friday night. He was surprised. We'd never had anything like this. I took a shower, jerked off, and drove to the funeral.

The Aztecs landed a pyramid in the Kiryat Shaul Cemetery. That's what it looked like from a distance, anyway. Inside were three floors of concrete domes with hives of graves. Mota had bought a low alcove in advance, considerate of the undertakers who would have to carry him. They sealed him in with a few bricks, apologized to the deceased, and dispersed. Two drag queens wiped tears behind rhinestone sunglasses. I gave them my phone number and two hundred shekels. They opened umbrellas and wobbled away on high heels, ignoring the Orthodox Jews who watched them from the burial home.

I bent down and placed a stone on the small ledge. Then I took off my yarmulke and turned to leave into the rain.

Izzy Schuster appeared right then at the edge of the dome, folding his arms across the suspenders that held up jeans from the Stone Age. His ever-present bag hung off his shoulder. "You're wasting your money." He shook my hand. "They don't know anything."

"It's not for information," I said.

"Sure, it's so they say the Kaddish prayer for Mota in a synagogue."

"Nobody came besides the four of us," I observed with surprise.

"What did you expect, the philharmonic to play a requiem for the *sharmuta*?" he said in his hoarse voice. Izzy still displayed the kind of energy that had made him the most furious and relentless crime reporter, until he was finally fired under coercion of the police commander and the minister. At least that's what he says. We were afraid of him on the force. He mocked us and brought us down. He knew more criminals than I did, understood the inner workings of both the police and organized crime. He knew what was going on way before we did. People loved giving him intel, wanted to appear in his column, even anonymously. My tour of the city's sewers had actually been inspired by his original crime tours.

"I wish I'd called you right after it happened," I said.

"Why?" He searched around, then walked to the burial alcove and tapped the gray bricks, as if expecting Mota to open up.

"Because if there are any rumors about who did it, they'd reach you."

"Who says they haven't?"

"Really? Who is it, then?"

"You."

"What's wrong with you?" That's all I managed, working hard to keep calm, ignoring the chill that ran down my back. "Why would I do a thing like that?"

"You were mad with envy," he said without hesitation.

"Envy for what? You and I split the city and the nights between us."

"And that helped you at first, but then it went to your head."

"It helped both of us, and the people we work with. This way there's enough work for everybody."

"You stole my creation. You took it down, word for word."

"Those stories and events are no less a part of my life than they are a part of yours."

"You let other people do all the hard work and then came in to collect."

"If that's how it is, you should have kept Mota rather than give him away."

"Everyone knows your head is messed up. That's why they kicked you off the force."

"Whatever," I sighed. "At least nobody takes you seriously."

He nodded and pulled a camera from his bag. A police car drove quietly up the road to the cemetery. It stopped and Farkash emerged. I still didn't get it, even as she stood beside me and grabbed my arm.

"Come on, let's go," she said, dragging me off as if I were a drunk driver.

"You're kidding," I said when it finally clicked. "You're arresting *me*?"

"Ronny, let's not do this."

"You're enjoying this," I said angrily. "I can tell, don't think I can't."

"Watch your head," she said, placing a hand on top of my head as I bent down and slipped into the car. The flash in Izzy Schuster's camera blinked like the police car's flashing lights.

The city's least experienced attorney sat across from me. He worked for a criminal attorney who owed me a favor and promised to send over an ace. Instead, he sent an arrogant kid who was more concerned with the fit of his jacket than with my arrest.

"What do they have on me?" I whispered into the phone. Not that my whispering mattered. The basement of the Tel Aviv precinct had a meeting booth like in the movies, with a window separating the person in custody from the visitor. We spoke on a closed-circuit phone which I knew was tapped.

"Meaning?" He looked at me with confusion.

"Meaning, what's the police's version?"

"I don't know."

"I know you don't know. That's why I want you to go see Farkash, make eyes at her, remind her that I like her and she likes me, get her to talk."

"Dude, that's not my style," Preppy Boy announced.

I sighed. "Then go to my apartment and get the list of people who participated in my last tour."

"That's the kind of thing the firm's secretary does."

"You're afraid to go to Jaffa, worried someone's going to steal your Breitling."

"I don't understand how that list is going to help you," he said, tickling his iPhone.

"Forty-plus people who can testify to having been with me at the time of the murder. Trust me, that's crucial evidence in a custody extension hearing."

"But the police would need to question them separately," he said. Then I knew I was in bad shape: he wasn't only shallow and inexperienced, he was a pessimist.

"More power to them. Let them question them. And I want a gag order."

"There's no point," he said. He turned his iPhone screen to me. Through the bulletproof glass, I saw a picture of me being pushed into the police car on Izzy Schuster's website.

"He's still grieving. He's now in the anger phase. He's taking it out on me. Eventually he'll get to bargaining, then depression, and, finally, acceptance."

"They told me you speak like a social worker."

"I try to consider other people's feelings. Do you find that pointless too?"

"It's completely unnecessary," he said, and for the first time I caught a twinkle in his eye. "You're a celebrity now."

I walked between the mopeds driving freely on sidewalks and crossed Salame Street toward Bugsy Café off Washington Avenue. I silently wished the judge a long and happy life. The questioning of my tour participants led him to decide there was no reason to prolong my custody. He saved me a few nights in solitary—it's forbidden to place an ex-cop with other arrestees.

It was almost Sabbath, but the place was still full. Izzy Schuster sat on a barstool by the window. When I walked in, he glanced up from the *Haaretz* culture and literature supplement. I didn't expect that. People stared at me. For a moment, I really did feel like a celebrity. He ordered me a double espresso with warm milk and club soda on the side. He knew where I liked to sit and what I liked to order and what time I was getting released. He really did know everything.

"So who killed Mota?" I asked.

"A man who's well known in the fertilizer industry. Mota had blackmailed him for years."

"You don't say."

"One of his former clients. The whole thing is documented, including photos. Want to see?"

"No thanks. So that guy killed Mota himself?"

"God forbid. It was only supposed to be a warning, but it got out of hand."

"And you knew that even before I was arrested."

"Oh, of course." He smiled smugly.

"So what was the arrest about?"

"I was trying to send you a message, but you've been slow to catch on."

"That might be true. What was the message?"

"That you're to cease and desist with your tours, effective immediately."

I froze for a long moment before I was able to speak again. "What?"

He didn't answer, only watched me with his watery eyes. I suspected he was enjoying this, punishing me for something that wasn't my fault. I should have left right then.

"What's wrong, not enough clients?" I tried hard to sound tough. "If you're having problems, I'm happy to accommodate you and—"

"You partnered up with me like some minor-league mafioso." He leaned closer. "You simply *informed* me you were going to split everything with me. I've had enough of your audacity."

"Listen, people in the field are going to get screwed. They rely on us for their livelihood, for some warmth."

"They rely on no one," he said. "And if you're such a saint, get up and go, because anyone who cooperates with you is going to be removed."

"What do you mean, *removed?*"

"Removed from my tour. What did you think I meant?"

"I won't budge," I said and stood up. "Do what you want."

"No problem, smart-ass, you'll have your own pigheadedness on your conscience."

"Section 428 of the criminal code calls this extortion under threat."

"They can call it Moses for all I care." He sat back comfortably.

"I see you've learned some things from writing about Israeli outlaws."

"Only the good stuff," he said.

I thought of crossing Salame Street back to the precinct, going into Farkash's office, and reporting what happened. But I guessed that before I even left her office, Izzy would tell the whole town how I ran to cry to Mommy. I dropped it. I wanted to walk, to think about how to handle his threats, but it was getting late. I hailed a cab. I checked my messages. There were no cancellations. There were so many voice mail bookings that I lost count. There was also a reminder from the Gideonof brothers, my shylocks. Big brother was back in town and I'd better make my payment on time. And there was a text from Shishko about that night. I was glad to hear from him and texted back.

Meeting as usual. I'll let you know when we're close.
Is Izzy cool with this?
Totally. I met him.
Seriously?
He's a little crazed but it's all good.
Okay. I'm sad about Mota.
God save him.

The purple bus was at its usual spot at the edge of the parking lot, illuminated by the stadium's limelights. There were two minibuses behind it, and about eighty people standing around. Almost twice as many as usual. I pulled my regular driver aside.

"People couldn't get ahold of you, so they called the transportation company," he said. His eyes sparkled and his mustache jumped. "I took some initiative and ordered two more vehicles."

"That's crazy. It means I can only speak to some of them on the way."

"So you'll only speak to some of them on the way."

"I won't be able to tell anecdotes between stops."

"Nobody knows that's part of the program."

"This doesn't look professional."

"*I'm not like him*," he mocked.

"What's that?"

"All year long I hear you complain about being compared to Schuster, wanting to be original. Here's your chance."

I looked at the enormous crowd. My spirits were low. I felt that nothing good could come of this, that I was betraying a commitment, but I couldn't say what commitment this was. And, as I said, it was late.

Toward the end of Nordau Boulevard was an old, squat juice stand. Shishko finished telling my participants about a jewelry store he'd robbed in the late '70s and placed his hands against the wall, revealing his muscles beneath a formfitting Tel Aviv Marathon T-shirt. The audience was riveted. They were cooked to perfection. Earlier in the evening I realized that the effect was actually stronger with this many participants. I couldn't figure out how they stayed so fascinated without Mota, or while riding in silence, without me telling stories between stops. But the facts spoke for themselves.

Shishko hugged the concrete and leaped to the roof of the juice stand in two quick movements. His silhouette stood out against the clouds. The audience roared with amazement and I put the mic to my mouth and called out like a circus announcer: "Shishko the Spider! Sixty years old! Broke into thousands of homes and businesses, never caught in the act. The only robber in the world who trains Special Forces and elite military teams. Let's give him a round of applause!"

Cheers echoed from the Bauhaus buildings, both the crumbling and the renovated. I waited for Shishko to come down so that I could interview him about his childhood in boarding school, how he began stealing, and how he finally returned to the straight and narrow. He took a bow. I smiled. He didn't normally bow. Then his sharp face became distorted, and he folded up and fell down on the roof, moaning. People stepped back with alarm, hands covering their mouths.

Somebody called out, "I'm a medic!" A few others helped raise him up to the roof. The first guy took his shirt off and improvised a tourniquet around Shishko's leg. Shishko was finished. No more training or running. My stomach turned over with fear and helplessness, but my head was clear. I got up on a bench and searched the roofs, windows, and balconies. I thought I'd recognize something. Nothing. I heard no shots, and a bullet could have come from anywhere, even a moving vehicle.

Police cars pulled up and with them was Hila Farkash, exhausted. Shootings don't fill cops with adrenaline. On the contrary: wounds mean more work than death. We watched the firefighters lowering Shisko, the Bulgarian Tarzan, a man's man. Spent every day of his life at the beach, fell asleep every night with a cold glass of arak. I couldn't go near him. I felt very guilty.

"Your hair looks good like that," Farkash said, in an effort to say something positive and unrelated.

"I expected him to screw with me," I replied with concern. "But I never thought it'd come to this."

"Who is he?" she asked, but I could tell by her voice she already knew.

"Izzy Schuster is blackmailing me. He's pressuring me to back off or else."

"He told me that's what you'd say."

I looked at her with amazement. My driver came by to ask what was going on. I didn't know what to say. I asked him to take everyone over to Dizengoff Street and wait for me there. He walked around and called everybody back on the bus. I returned to Farkash.

"What did Izzy tell you I'd say?" I felt fear approaching, but not of Izzy's cunning or the potential for violence. A fear of empty and meaningless days.

"He called me and said you'd try to blame something heavy on him, and then you'd accuse him of extortion and threats."

"And you believe him?"

She shrugged. Her eyes were prettier than I remembered. "Why don't you cut it out?" she offered.

"You're suggesting I close up shop?"

"I'm worried about you. He isn't playing games."

"We'll see," I said. "Just promise me you won't leak anything."

"Only if you promise to take care of yourself."

"If you promise to interrogate him—that's a bare minimum."

"If you promise not to cut your hair," she countered, touching my head as if she was blessing me.

The Gideonof brothers were waiting outside my building, pressing the finicky buzzer over and over. I hesitated before taking off my helmet. They looked calm, though.

"You not home," Little Gideonof said as I approached.

"Not right now, no," I responded.

Big Gideonof—who was smaller and older—observed me with a protruding bottom lip and red blotches on his nose, cheeks, and forehead.

"You got sunburned in Eilat," I pointed out.

"Huh?" he growled.

"Your brother said you'd gone away."

"Yes, strong-strong sun."

"I have a part of the sum to pay you," I said. "It's up in my apartment."

They followed me into the stairwell which smelled of *hreime* and *mafrum*. When I began climbing they stopped with expressions of misery.

"Seventh floor," I said.

"We wait here," they said in unison.

What a ruse, I thought. A broken elevator as protection from thugs. During the five minutes I spent in the apartment, I received four calls from people wanting to book a tour. They wanted to see blood, that was the only explanation. I asked them to call back in the morning. When I went downstairs, Big Gideonof counted the money, pocketed it, and that was that.

"Okay?" I asked. "So goodbye for now."

"Bye-bye," they answered, but stayed put.

"Nothing to celebrate at the event hall tonight? A Bukharan song festival, maybe?"

"Protecting you," said Little Gideonof. "More important than songs."

"Huh?" I said suspiciously.

"You our asset," the big one explained. "Something happen to you, money is gone."

"What could happen to me?"

"Shishko survive is a miracle. You need also be scared."

"We protecting you, no worry about anything."

"Okay," I said. It worked for me, after all. "If you need anything, let me know."

I walked upstairs. I wanted very badly to go to sleep, but first I tried to salvage what was left of my life. I called the stripper, the ex-cop, to find out if she was on my side. She didn't pick up. At this hour the club was packed and she was dancing on a pole and collecting bills, I told myself. I called Perla, the shopping mall pickpocket.

"I'm not supposed to talk to you, bye," she said.

"Did Izzy threaten you?"

"I'm not supposed to talk to you," she repeated. "Love you, Ronny baby, bye."

"How much is he paying you? I'll give you double."

"Money isn't everything in life," the pickpocket preached. Then she hung up.

On Saturday morning the streets around the Old Central Bus Station were deserted and derelict, like books thrown out of a scholar's house. I saw her leaving the twenty-four-hour supermarket on Salomon Street with a can of Red Bull, a pack of Marlboro reds, and a small purse, raising a sleeved arm to hail a cab. It was hard to believe, but she looked even thinner than usual. I pulled my moped over next to her. Little Gideonof was behind me in his Mazda 5, perusing the pastries in a nearby bakery from a distance.

"Where are you going?" I asked her after we hugged.

"To the marina," she said. "My friend is taking care of a yacht."

"Take a rain check, okay?"

"Low profile is best right now."

"I'm starting something big, I have about a million bookings, I could pay you a lot more."

"Izzy doesn't want me to talk to you."

"This has nothing to do with him. It's all new people with new stories, but I could never find another gem like you."

"One of your gems almost die last night," she said with a thin smile.

"No one will harm you." I pointed at Little Gideonof. "We're being protected until we can regain our footing, until everybody remembers their lines. After that, if we have any problems, you can go back to him."

"I'm scared."

"I'm asking you. I'm begging you."

"I ask him about working for both of you. He loves me too."

"He doesn't love you enough to let you go. And he doesn't love you like I do. How many times did I visit you? How much money have I given you?"

"I know, I know."

"Give me a chance," I begged, my head hung, desperate. "Give me a chance."

In a moment of quiet I could hear an airplane descending toward Ben Gurion Airport, a car driving on HaRakevet Street, Dudu Aharon's voice floating from Gideonof's car, and her raging heart yearning for the drug.

"Then don't ask me to talk to people," she said.

"Because you hate it when they pity you."

"I hate it when they looking at my teeth."

"Just come by, say hello, I'll say a few words, and that's it."

"And don't leave me to the end of the tour."

"No problem," I said. "Starting tonight, you're the first stop. Thank you, honey, thank you."

All Saturday long I ran around, tying up loose ends, rehearsing, reserving buses. My driver made sure people on other buses would be able to hear me too. One hundred and fifty people. It was too many, but I couldn't resist the temptation. At five thirty I reported to the parking lot. A television camera crew was there interviewing the drivers. When I came near, they turned the camera on me, illuminating me with a tiny spotlight.

"A few questions about you and what's going to happen tonight," one reporter asked.

"After the tour," I promised.

"People are expecting some action."

"I'll be a lot more communicative at the end of the night."

Right then, as if they'd been waiting in line at a pay phone, the criminals I'd recruited the previous day began calling, one by one: a South Lebanon Army man who dealt drugs, a lawyer who smuggled prostitutes through Egypt, a robber who specialized in post offices, and all the others. Some of them had lame excuses. The others didn't even explain why they were canceling on me. Rather, they expected my gratitude for letting me know.

We drove for two minutes on LaGuardia Road, then turned onto Rosh Pina and over to Vilna Gaon Street, where I let everyone off the buses, trying—and failing—to make an alternate plan. I turned on a small police light I'd bought off a crooked cop. The blue flashes sent the Eritrean refugees running and put my audience in nervous focus. Gideonof's Mazda protected me from afar. I began by speaking about the failure of governmental control in Southern Tel Aviv. Then I saw her, a waif floating toward me down Bnei Brak Street, just like we planned. When she was next to me I hugged her shoulder, and when she put her mouth to my ear, I could smell cinnamon gum.

"Izzy Schuster bought your debt from the Gideonof brothers," she whispered.

"You don't say," I replied, trying to maintain a poker face.

"They not guarding you. Big Gideonof beat Mota and shot Shishko."

My expression must have revealed something after all, because just then the two brothers got out of their car and lumbered over.

"Everybody go home," she said. "Now, Ronny, fast."

"I can't. I have to give them something."

Her stoned eyes gaped for a moment with realization, with amazement, and then extinguished. Little Gideonof closed his fingers around her arm. It was so thin that he could have held onto two more of them. They exchanged a few words, mostly Russian curses. The audience watched with terrorized, compassionate silence. It looked staged. It looked great, actually. Classic. Then they dragged her, kicking at first, but not for long. A door in the wall opened and the three of them were swallowed inside.

I signaled to everyone that I'd be right back, and walked in after them. I was greeted by the smell of grease and bits of metal and old mufflers, cartons full of spare parts. She stood there, her arms folded, her head wobbling in tiny motions, trapped between the Gideonof brothers. Izzy Schuster turned around in a ragged office chair to face me. Next to his desk, a model was hugging some sort of machine in a calendar. Both of them were lit by a fluorescent lamp that buzzed in the kitchen.

"What do you want?" I asked.

"You've known the answer to that since yesterday."

"First of all, let her go," I said.

"You've known since yesterday, but you've been doing the exact opposite."

"Let her go," I repeated.

"And then what?"

"You tell me. Or maybe you'll kill me, like you did Mota."

"As I said, it was only meant to be a warning for him to stop working with you." Izzy folded his arms across his chest and Big Gideonof lowered his eyes. "Mota fought like a man and things got out of control. Believe me, it's eating me up."

"I'll believe you if you let her go right now."

"And then what?"

"We'll talk this through, we'll work it out."

"Ah, we'll talk. That's the most you're willing to do to get her out of here?"

"Don't test me, Izzy. I'll call Farkash right now."

"Don't make me laugh. The Gideonofs will kill both of you before you even finish dialing."

"There are 150 witnesses outside. You may be a maniac, but you're no idiot."

"Now you're testing me."

"What do you want, a chunk of the profits? Copyrights? No problem. Whatever you want, that's fine."

"Just cut it out, Ronny," said Izzy, as if he was only being kind. "Bygones."

I looked into his eyes, and then into hers. I knew it was all lost. They knew it too. Perhaps, I thought, it had all been lost from the day it started.

"Nothing's good enough for you," I blurted angrily at him. "Nothing but winning, being a boss."

"This is supposed to be light entertainment," he said. "You're taking this too hard, you're being dramatic."

"*Capo di tutti capi*, that's what you are," I said.

"Fine," replied Izzy. "Go outside and tell them to get back on the buses. I'll take it from here."

* * *

Worried and defeated, I walked down HaAliya Street. A police car, shining with rain that had poured elsewhere, pulled over, and Farkash smiled at me through the open window.

"You need a ride to your moped?"

I leaned down to her. "I was just on my way to your office."

"I was just on my way home," she said.

"You know, I've never been to your place."

"That's your loss."

"What does that mean?" I asked hopefully.

DEATH IN PAJAMAS

BY ALEX EPSTEIN

Masarik Square

D eath wore a leather jacket over blue pajamas. He opened the door and came in. Without a word, he sat at the counter facing King George Street.

It was 7:24 in the morning. I'd just opened up shop and made myself an espresso. To really wake up, you have to blow on a mirror. That's exactly what I was about to do when Death came in.

I pulled my mirror from my purse, kissed it for good luck, and turned to Death. "Is it true what they say? That you sleep in fresh graves? That your favorite season is spring? That you have a twin you've never met and who when you finally meet you'll spit in his face and hug him, not necessarily in that order?"

Death didn't answer.

An elegant woman in terrible high heels then entered, greeting me. A draft snuck in behind her. The tall woman asked about the coffee blends we used, and when I answered her—Magic Noir—she said, "Large latte, extra foam." She asked if I could hold onto her lilacs. I shrugged politely.

As I foamed the milk, the radio announced a missile attack near Hadera.

"So," I tried again, "is it true what they say? That you don't like Venice? Because in your dreams it's always crowded there? That you were seen wiping sweat from your brow on the Bridge of San Luis Rey in Peru? Playing chess at the Samarkand train station? Smoking a cigarette during the Battle of Stalingrad? That your epitaph is going to be . . ." I paused for dramatic effect, cleared my throat, thought for a moment, and said, "*Here lies Death . . . killed in action?* Is it true?"

Death didn't even turn to face me.

A third customer, a stocky man with a goatee, came in and sat to the right of Death. He removed his glasses and blew on them. Death volunteered to wipe them off with his blue pajama sleeve, peeking from beneath his leather jacket.

It was 7:27.

The third customer put his glasses back on, picked up a copy of *Haaretz* newspaper, flipped through it, found what he was looking for, and began mumbling: "It's very interesting what they say. Very interesting. Listen: *Color only rarely appears in dreams.* That's a pretty surprising absence, considering how extreme the rest of a dream's attributes are."

"Those who sow a storm," I said, serving him a glass of orange juice, "will reap a typhoon."

Death couldn't resist the urge to look my way. In his eyes I saw the glint of melancholy surprise. The radio said there was a shooting near Elkana.

The third customer downed his orange juice in one gulp. "In one of my dreams," he continued, leafing through the open newspaper, "I met a strange fellow with a pipe. He asked me for the quickest route to a legendary volcano that spews . . . breast milk. I pointed him in the right direction, east, secretly hoping that the volcano would drown him in tar-tasting lava. Very good, this juice."

He paid and left.

Another moment and I'd have solved one of the greatest secrets of creation: who has more of a soul, the coffeemaker or the juicer? But then Death pulled a pack of Lucky Strikes from his pocket and began coughing, drawing my attention. I was growing sick of him.

"Tell me," I said, "do you mind if I read your palm?" I grabbed his hand before he could respond. "Open your fingers. Yes, that's it. Hmm . . ."

He didn't say a word. He coughed one last time but obeyed. His hand was simple, quite smooth. Few remarkable lines, definitely not an old man's hand.

"Look," I said, "your destiny line is broken. That usually signifies insecurity. In your case . . ."

Death neither confirmed nor denied my claim.

Twenty minutes later, the coffee shop was swarming with wounded people, medics, police officers, sappers, and a sweet old lady who wanted to know if we served chocolate milk. Beautiful smoke wafted all around.

It was 7:45. The radio announced a double car bomb attack in Jerusalem. I drank red grapefruit juice and played checkers with Death, quickly licking my lips. He was as silent as a fish and didn't even laugh when I told him the only joke I remembered about him. (In the joke, he, Death, stands at the foot of a married couple's bed. He tells the husband: "I've come for your soul," and the husband wakes up his wife: "My soul, get up, someone's here for you.")

Another customer emerged from the bathroom, her broken high heels in her hand. A flame burst out of the room behind her. Death blew in that direction, extinguishing the fire with ease.

She whispered, "I'm all right, nothing happened to me in there."

"To me neither," I said. I captured Death's last checker piece. Before I folded the board, I remembered to place a lilac in its center.

Death scratched his head. The headline in the paper the juice-drinking customer left on the counter said, *Explosive Car in the Heart of Tel Aviv.*

Many more interesting things happened in the coffee shop before and after everything blew up outside along King George Street: A girl whose doll had a missing right arm came in and asked for carrot juice. A giant man wept because his cell phone stopped working. A beautiful naked woman riding a snow-white horse appeared from a cloud of smoke and cried, "Follow me!" and someone whose T-shirt said *Shady Shade* was about to step outside, but I grabbed her shoulders at the last moment and told her to sit down, that she was way ahead of schedule.

It was 7:50. I whispered, "One, two, three," leaped over the counter and onto Death, and before he could even blink I held up his arm and sniffed his armpit. Neutral scent. He tried mumbling something but his lips failed him. Instead, he whimpered and then went silent.

"I don't like you very much, friend," I finally told Death. "I think I'd like you to leave."

Death seemed deeply insulted. He examined the passersby on King George Street and then turned to me.

A beggar with a Juventus scarf walked in and asked if I wanted to buy a music box that played three tunes. I said yes. Death and I sat together, fascinated by the sweet sounds that emerged from the box and rose to the ceiling like rings of smoke pulled by spiderwebs.

To really wake up, you have to blow on a mirror.

I went to the bathroom, and when I came back I smiled at Death and said, "You're an introvert, huh? Look, I'm sorry for what I said earlier. I didn't mean to insult you. You know, I have my own problems. Is it true what they say? That you're an orphan?"

The radio announced eight dead soldiers stationed along the Egyptian border, a Palestinian woman who had a miscarriage and lost her twins because she was delayed at a checkpoint that was bombed last night, and a neighborhood in Beirut that disappeared from an atlas in a university library, or something like that.

"You're confusing me, Death." I laughed.

I think I saw a little smile form on his lips.

And many other interesting things happened at the coffee shop before everything exploded outside: A couple came in, embracing each other, and mumbled, "You'd think we were in a hurry. One croissant!" and I answered, "You'd think I was a waitress. You want butter on that?" and the second hand on the clock began moving counterclockwise, and a truck driver parked by the window facing King George argued with a police officer who wrote him a ticket and then they came in together and ordered a croissant. The radio announcer lamented, "Moon beating on my chest, half is bright, dark is the rest. From myself I try to run. Happy tune? A bitter one." A chair by the counter walked outside all by itself and fell apart in front of our stunned eyes. Et cetera.

Death said nothing. He was silent from the moment he entered, he was silent as people came in and went back out, he was silent as he observed them, some with compassion and others with despair, he was silent as the bomb began to tick, he was silent that first moment, when the windows shattered into large and small shards, like blood drops and hearts and fists. He was silent as he opened his arms so that nothing happened to me, and only after the first ambulance siren sounded (to really wake up, you have to blow on a mirror, a window, on a hospital monitor where the jumpy horizontal line will stretch from left to right for one last instant and then disappear), only then did he take my hand in his.

He put my hand on his chest. My heart skipped a beat. I closed my eyes, paralyzed. I tried not to breathe.

And then, finally, Death whispered: "If you don't mind, I'd like a glass of mineral water. I don't like tap."

THE EXPENDABLES
BY GAI AD

Ben Zion Boulevard

Margalit Bloch was a successful woman.
She was fifty-one years old, good-looking, smart, and intriguing. She lived in a rent-controlled apartment on Borochov Street in central Tel Aviv, which meant that everything was walking distance, and she knew the city like the back of her hand—art exhibitions, the theater, a farmers' market here, a flea market there, designer sales, shoes, bags, the works. She had a job in television as a props person, but quit two years ago when Channel 1 implemented its reform plan and offered terrific severance to longtime employees. Her retirement might have seemed like a greater success had her husband, Nathan, not discovered the cancer within him exactly two months later. But that is what happened, and instead of going on a long trip abroad to meet up with their only son, Ari, who'd been traveling the world for a year, they were sucked into the tedious yearlong labor of dying.

After her retirement and her husband's death, Margalit felt hollow as a flute. She knew she needed a new source of income. Nathan was an artist. He taught art, painted custom portraits, but ultimately left her nothing but an ugly plastic storage container filled with all his equipment and the pieces he could never sell. He'd tried, had held a couple of exhibitions, but they were always of the community center genre and were met with reservations. Not to mention that the paintings were what one of her friends in the know termed "too simple," lacking the necessary depth.

They never managed to buy an apartment either, and her current rent-controlled place used to be her parents'. Nathan and Margalit had moved in after her father died. A year later, Margalit's mother died as well, and the apartment was effectively forfeited to them.

She blamed their borderline finances on Nathan. He was afraid. She was more daring, but for some reason rarely recognized opportunities in time. By the time she did, and tried to convince Nathan to take a chance, they had already become less attractive. Like that apartment on Shalom Aleichem Street, the closest they ever came to buying property. It belonged to two people who'd inherited it from their grandmother. One of them was in the process of building his own home and was in dire need of money. Margalit heard about them from a friend who lived in the building, and spotted the opportunity, but Nathan hesitated. The grandson changed his mind at the last minute and his sister moved in with the daughter of one of Margalit's friends.

At least she had the rent-controlled apartment. At least, she knew, she would always have a place to live.

Yoel Guttman, an acquaintance of Nathan's, entered her life during the week of the shivah. She knew him vaguely, knew of him. Now he came to console her, having seen the obituary in the newspaper. He told her he and Nathan had taken sketching lessons together. He had realized he was not talented enough and decided to go to law school instead. He'd tried to convince Nathan to study law as well because of his excellent attention to detail. Was he implying that's what Nathan should have done? Studied a real profession rather than some nonsense? Margalit was on edge. She said that they made do with what they had, and something about her expression, the way she pursed her lips in defense of her husband, impressed Yoel immensely. He thought about her for some days afterward and then came back for another visit. This time, he suggested she open a small secondhand shop. He was the legal counsel for the administrator general and had access to apartments whose owners had passed away. She could get her hands on possessions left by people without families whose apartments had to be cleared out, he said, and her background in prop work would help her choose well.

The idea appealed to her. This was the kind of initiative she'd never taken, the unfulfilled potential that was hidden within her all these years. It flattered her that Yoel recognized this side of her.

For Yoel, this was an excellent way to get closer to her. He'd lived alone all these years, single. Maybe his moment had finally come.

The first time Margalit came to one of these apartments, she wore a blue tracksuit, had her hair pulled back in a ponytail, and looked to Yoel like a curious schoolgirl. She began sorting through things without any unnecessary niceties. She was surprised with herself, she told him. She had always been clean and organized, and now here she was, burrowing into other people's smells, pulling out anything she liked with a kind of passion. He took with him any money and Jewish artifacts, and explained that they were to be donated to different institutions around the country. She brought a shopping cart to the next apartments she visited, into which she packed the anonymous lives of strangers.

Yoel did some rummaging as well, but his style was more focused. He only looked for documents that had to do with the apartment and the bank accounts of its owners.

"What happens to all these assets?" Margalit asked him.

He smiled knowingly. "That's where I come in."

There was something twisted about that answer, but Margalit smiled back. Though not a fan of guns, she was happy to be beside an accomplished hunter.

"These people have completed their roles in life," he told her. "And so far, no next of kin has come forward." He explained that he would sell these apartments on behalf of the state, and once in a while he'd sell an apartment to himself, on "special terms."

Yoel Guttman had accumulated quite a few walls in his capacity as caretaker for the expendables.

Three months and four apartments later, she found a tiny, inexpensive shop on Dizengoff Street. Ari, her son, who'd returned to Israel right before Nathan died, helped her renovate the store, and rather quickly, maybe because of the high quality of the items, or perhaps because of her good taste—like the small armchair which gave each customer the sense of being the center of Margalit's life—the shop gained some regular customers, and drew quite a few enthusiastic tourists, and things were looking up. On the wall hung one of Nathan's paintings, removed from the ugly balcony in their apartment, and she promised herself that each time she sold one of his works she'd hang another one in its place. She didn't think Nathan's paintings were appropriate for an exhibition, not because they were too simple, but because they weakened each other when shown together. This worked better. She sold two right away. Then the paintings stopped selling.

Yoel's interest in Margalit had so far been satisfied by spending time with her, sniffing her hair as she walked past him, and rubbing against her here and there. He scouted as many apartments as he could, had never worked as hard as during those months, and Margalit accepted all of his invitations.

She liked the strange apartments, the quiet, the conversations with Yoel, which contained a secret promise to keep this greedy aspect of their lives to themselves. Within a few hours she'd leave the apartment with a cart filled with valuables whose importance to the deceased she couldn't possibly guess: books, pictures, jewelry, clothes. The clothes were immediately wrapped in large trash bags and sent to the dry cleaner's, and only later sifted through. Her crawl space was filled with skillfully packed boxes of Nathan's things that she couldn't bring herself to even sort through, let alone throw out.

She felt that Yoel wanted her, wanted her body, and it gave her confidence. She was more aware of herself when she was around him, but each time he looked at her lustily, she closed her eyes. Her husband, still plaguing her mind, was only half the trouble. Mainly, she couldn't bear herself. Her relationship with Nathan was the one pure thing in her life. Her and Nathan, a couple, with one child. Not a perfect life, but clean. They had never crossed any red lines. They had neither debts nor indiscretions. And in Yoel, on the other hand, there was something lowly. Those apartments, that look in his eyes. And damn it, she was attracted to that.

Days went by. Margalit didn't like to leave herself a lot of free time. She was an energetic and busy woman who fell asleep easily each night, naturally tired, no sleeping pills required, and got up early, raring to begin her day.

It was almost good. She was doing well, but she still missed the smell of paint in her apartment, Nathan's serenity, the purity of a man who was sure of the path he'd chosen. There was something lost about her actions now. And if that wasn't enough, Ari couldn't find his place. He had returned to Israel after a long time abroad. Working on fishing boats in Australia, selling posters in Japan, jewelry in America, clothing in Europe—all the popular jobs for young Israelis abroad. Since returning to Israel, he hadn't been able to achieve anything meaningful. Margalit pushed him in different directions. She got him a job as a cook in a restaurant by their house because she believed he'd internalized her home cooking more than he'd thought, and had all the ingredients at home to practice, so why not? After he was fired from the restaurant, she said he always had a cinematic eye and proposed video editing. That didn't take, either. He even tried learning tai chi, because Margalit recalled that he'd stayed longest with martial arts as a child. But that, like the other attempts, began with a shot of energy and then withered away, without even a sense of desperation. There were always reasons for the failure, and they were always external. When Ari listed them to his mother, she was easily convinced. It wasn't *him*. She paid for all the classes he took, because they were educational. She even bought him a moped so he could get quickly from one place to the next. Her doubts about him were suspended, and as she signed checks, she argued out loud with the ghost of Nathan. "You see, he's doing well, he's making do, not everyone has to go to university." And Nathan never answered, which just made her more confident.

But then there were those quiet hours in her shop, when she arranged the items she'd gotten that week, wiping dust off the shelves or just staring out onto Dizengoff Street, which had recently regained much of its former traffic. People missed being out on the street, walking simply forward rather than twisting in the labyrinths of shopping malls. In those quiet hours she thought of her son, who lived without passion, without real introspection, without purpose. People always said the next generation was going to be more advanced, that only children were more talented. In the one conversation she ever had about Ari with a neighbor whose son was a genius violinist who performed all over the world, the woman said, "It's better to have a son like yours. Mine is strange." And Margalit was consoled by that, especially after that neighbor's son killed himself. She sustained herself with this notion for years, but now, when Ari was twenty-six, living in his child-hood bedroom, never finding his place in the world—a leaf, not a tree trunk—she worried about him, and realized that somewhere along the way, she'd gone wrong.

And to think how she insisted on calling him Ari, stress-ing the second syllable. A lion. Nathan had wanted to call him Mordi after his own father, Mordechai, but he couldn't convince her. She wouldn't give in. She had such a difficult pregnancy with him and decided that the name would be her call. She was so insistent. Now she admitted to herself that her only child was nothing but a Mordi, Mordi Bloch.

But there was a kindness in Ari that touched her heart. With what little money he had, he always bought her flowers or took her out to a movie or a nice restaurant. It was as if the moment he had a little cash he wanted to show her that he was all right, that he wasn't such a terrible disappointment. And those gestures melted her heart every time.

One night, as she was about to close shop and head out, Ari appeared. Though they lived together, she didn't see very much of him. They lived by different schedules. She kissed him, happy and surprised.

"How are you?" she asked. He smelled nice, and she felt proud.

"I'm going into real estate entrepreneurship, this time it's final." There was an enthusiasm in his voice she wasn't familiar with. Entrepreneurship, a term that had spread through the city ever since interest rates were lowered and asset sales blew up. The concept buzzed across Tel Aviv.

"It's booming. I thought that boyfriend of yours might be able to help me out a little with estates." Ari Bloch, Margalit Bloch's only son, felt that he finally had a chance at success.

"He isn't my boyfriend," Margalit corrected immediately. "And his name is Yoel."

"Yoel, fine. I thought he might be able to toss me a bone." Margalit didn't answer.

"A friend of mine has an agency that's doing well. I need some money to buy in. He guarantees I can make a profit from a deal he's closing this month. Something big. An apartment with building permits on the roof."

"That all sounds great, but why do you have to become a partner? What does he need a partner for? Work for him for a while, get to know the business."

"Enough, Mom, I can't play games anymore. I have to get a life. This is my chance."

Margalit was ready to lock up and go home. She rolled out the small shopping cart she always took home with her.

"You keep asking me what I want to do. So there, I want to buy and sell."

She crouched down to lock the door. "Real estate is a serious business. Maybe you should study it first, go back to school?"

"Why school? I want to buy and sell. I'll learn on the job."

She turned the bottom lock and stood back up. "How much money are we talking about?"

"A hundred thousand shekels."

"That's a lot of money."

"Yeah, it's an investment. But it's worth it. This isn't like all those stupid classes I took. I'm going to get a fifth of it back by the end of the month."

"If that sale he's talking about goes through."

"It will. It's practically a done deal."

"Why don't you wait for it to close?"

They were now walking south toward Borochov Street. Ari stopped. "I knew I shouldn't have told you. I knew you didn't trust me. You're just like Dad, you only pretend to be different."

"Ari, it's not that I don't trust you, I just don't see what the rush is. Let's have Yoel over for dinner. Talk to him, get his opinion. I'm sure he'll have something to say about this."

"Mom, I need the money this week." He glared at her. "I finally want to do something, something of my own, not something *you* made happen. I want to do this."

"Ari, sweetie, we're in the middle of the street. I've had a long day. Let's talk about this quietly, at home. Can you calm down for a minute?"

"Forget it, Mom, I'll figure it out." He walked away from her and returned to the moped he'd parked outside the shop.

"Ari, wait," she called.

He waved her off and drove away.

She was restless that night. What if this really was his breakthrough? What if this was a calculated risk? She should support him, back him up—that would be the only way for him to continue with confidence. And maybe that was the problem all those years, that they always doubted him and never demanded that he truly deal with anything. Maybe that's why he could never catch a break. Maybe that's what Nathan meant when he once told her that their solutions couldn't solve the kid's problems.

Then she remembered what she had almost been able to forget.

When he was in Europe, right before he returned to Israel, Ari spent a week in a German prison and was banished from Germany forever for holding and using hashish. In another time, being banished from that very Germany would have been considered an achievement.

She remembered a poor phone connection, tears, and fear, but she had been so preoccupied with Nathan's illness and never went to visit Ari. She told him that his behavior was his way of dealing with his father's impending death. She asked him to hold on. She didn't breathe a word to Nathan about it. Her silence had been her parting gift to him.

But the event, though never discussed again, remained in her consciousness. Now it bloomed in her—the fear that he might try to get the money in other, crooked ways that might hurt him. She had to help her son, had to make sure it worked out. She didn't wait till morning. She called his cell phone at midnight. He was with friends. She told him she'd loan him the money and fell asleep happy.

It was worth it. The deal came through, and so did another smaller one, and it seemed that Ari was doing well. And as always, like any other time he had money, he rewarded his mother, and himself. He bought new clothes. He took a shower every morning and left for the office. Soon after the deals were closed, he rented a small studio apartment with a sea view.

When he moved out, Margalit's loneliness was solidified. Now she was completely alone, but she knew it was for the best. Ari working and living his own life gave her a sense of normalcy and that was good enough for her. Her relationship with Yoel didn't rise above functionality. Maybe now, when she had the apartment all to herself, something would happen. She'd finally be able to say nice things about her son. So far she'd always avoided the topic, but now her son had an office, he was in real estate, everything about him cleared up overnight. It was time to have Yoel over for dinner. They could talk over food and wine, maybe they would get closer, maybe Yoel would be able to help Ari with his business.

But Ari's success quickly began looking like a single stroke of luck. The next time he came to visit her at the shop he told her he was in debt, that he hadn't told her the truth because he thought things would work out and he didn't want to upset her, but that it was all done now and he was going to move back home.

Two days later, Yoel told Margalit about a vacant apartment, which she looked forward to checking out. Maybe she'd tell him about Ari. She showered, put on a tracksuit, pulled her hair up, and looked in the mirror. She took special care of her appearance that morning, half-aware of what she was doing.

"The deceased was a foreign citizen," Yoel said when he opened the door. "He came to Israel a few times a year. It's mostly clothes."

Margalit took a quick tour of the apartment. It was mostly empty and she thought for a moment that she'd have nothing to take to the shop. The kitchen seemed as if it belonged in a hotel room—nothing but a coffee machine, espresso beans, and small packets of sugar—but there was a nice bar in the living room and she thought about having a drink. She was nervous. She offered Yoel a glass of Campari with soda that she found in the fridge. She looked at him innocently and handed him a glass. They toasted and laughed. Then they put the glasses in the living room and went into the bedroom, which contained a closet and a file cabinet, the things they had come for.

Yoel began sifting through documents and Margalit opened the closet. They worked quietly for a while. The dead man's clothes were clean and fresh. A plastic bag in the closet contained some dry-cleaned shirts. The clothes were new. She transferred most of them into her shopping cart, but didn't touch the towels or linens. She found two summer suits hanging in garment bags and put them in the cart, then noticed that they were heavier than she'd expected. She glanced at Yoel, checking to see if he'd seen, but he was busy reading. She peeked into one of the bags and saw a stack of dollars at the bottom. She zipped up the bag and folded it carefully into the cart. Then she looked into the other bag and saw more foreign bills. She glanced at Yoel again, but he didn't seem to be aware of any of it. Her heart was pounding, she was pumped up with adrenaline. She couldn't believe this was happening, the closest she could ever get to winning the lottery.

She closed the cart. Suddenly, she felt an urgent need to live. Watching Yoel, her body burned. She walked over and touched his face. He was concentrating on some paper and jumped when she did it, confused by the gesture. He put the paper down and she kissed him. The touch of his lips was strange and foreign to her, but that seemed natural—she hadn't been with anyone but Nathan in so long. Yoel pulled away and met her eyes. Then he gave in. He peeled the track-suit off her, pulled off her thin T-shirt. He didn't say a word and never stopped kissing her, except for when he hurried to the closet, pulled out a large towel, and spread it on the bed. He laid Margalit down. He pulled off his pants quickly; he seemed to be following a protocol. He caressed her and slipped a finger into her. Margalit was completely aroused, as

if her mind was ordering her body to stop her from thinking. She heard herself whisper, "I want you inside me." He
groaned, abandoned his plan, and penetrated her.

She felt good. That friction, his excitement—which she
created. That joy, the togetherness of man and woman, a joy
that used to be part of her everyday life. He came so hard that
all his limbs went limp at once. He rolled over on the bed and
caught his breath. He didn't notice her tears.

Pretty soon he sat up on the bed and put on his pants.
His face was glistening with the euphoria of a satisfied man.
He smiled at her. Within a few minutes Margalit sat up too
and began getting dressed. Yoel went back to his documents,
now whistling pleasantly. That relaxed her. She removed the
towel from the bed and shoved it into her cart. She smoothed
out the bedspread and went to the bathroom. She wiped his
sperm away and washed her hands and face. Then she fixed
her hair. It was as if nothing had happened.

She returned to the living room for another round of
Campari. Normally she wasn't much of a drinker, but the bitter sweetness of the drink gave her strength. She brought the
bottle into the bedroom and filled Yoel's glass. Everything
seemed simple all of a sudden.

She walked over to the large window and gazed out at
Tel Aviv. She tried not to think about her theft, as if it were
an intimate, feminine act, like changing a tampon. Since the
apartment was on a high floor, facing west, she could catch a
glimpse of the sea. The small streets and rooftops lay beneath
her, a blossoming urban field. She loved the city. She shut the
window and smiled to herself. Last night she couldn't sleep,
thinking of her son, and today she had a way to help him, and
a chance with a good man. Limits exist only in our minds. We
can always cross them.

Yoel downed his drink and went over to the cart. "How are the suits?" he asked. "Should I try one on?"

Margalit held her breath. Yoel had never shown any interest in the clothing before.

He opened the cart and pulled out the towel. "Why don't you always bring it, from now on? What do you think? It could be our towel."

Margalit's eyes filled with terror.

"We don't have to, we don't, I was just kidding." He took out one of the garment bags, pulled the zipper, and examined the suit. "Like new," he said, impressed, and pulled it out. He said nothing about the weight and didn't search the bottom. He put the jacket on.

Margalit knew she had to act natural. She walked over to smooth a wrinkle on his shoulder but bumped into the cart. The garment bag fell off and its contents spread over the floor. Bundles of what she now identified as British pounds were revealed in the mess. Yoel stared at the money for a moment. Then he kicked over the cart and the second garment bag fell out. He grabbed it, unzipped it, and turned it over. Bundles of dollars fell on the floor next to the pounds. He stared at her with more sadness than she could imagine. He began collecting the money into his briefcase, one bundle after another. The dead man's jacket still hung off his body.

Margalit turned to him. "I need the money," she said.

Yoel laughed. "You don't say." He continued to gather the money, not looking her way.

"My son's in trouble."

Yoel stood up and met her gaze. "How long have you been stealing from me?"

"I never stole from you, Yoel, this was the first time. I swear."

He poured himself another drink and made a face. It was clear he didn't actually like to drink. "I like you so much. I've never felt this way before. All these years."

Margalit hurried to answer: "I never—"

But Yoel hushed her. "I've been trying to get close to you for months. I keep telling myself to give you time, to be patient. And now you've ruined it all, because of your loser son."

"He's not a—"

"Quiet!" he shouted. "Don't interrupt me."

Margalit collapsed onto the bed.

"I met Nathan once, years ago. Your son had just been born and Nathan showed me a picture of him with you. I was so jealous." He finished packing the money and zipped his briefcase. "I thought you'd never have me. I was ready to settle for spending time with you in these apartments. And today it finally happened, you kissed me." A bitter smile stretched on his face. "I thought I was delirious. I was suspicious for a second, because women haven't been good to me. They always wanted me for my money. And I have money, Margalit. But I felt your body melt, I felt you giving yourself to me. As if you really wanted it." He closed his eyes. "You slept with me for that." He pointed to his briefcase. "You wanted to distract me."

Margalit shook her head and raised her hands despairingly. She got up to leave. She turned her cart upright and began to gather her belongings. How did everything become so tainted?

Yoel pushed her onto the bed. "You're not going anywhere."

Margalit sat there, paralyzed. It can't be. Everything was so right just moments ago. Why does the goddamn truth always show its face in the worst possible moment? She could have left here with money, and she would have improved her method in the next apartment, taking only some of the money, maybe some jewelry. Yoel would never have known, and she would have grown used to him, made him whistle more and more. Ari would have been saved.

"I want you inside me," Yoel said, doing a bad impression of her. He unzipped his pants and crawled over to her on the bed. "I want you inside me. Go on, say it."

"Yoel, please, don't do this."

He slapped her, hard. "Don't do what? No one's ever been in these apartments with me before, you know that? It was a secret. A professional risk. I brought you into this palace, I was generous, I invited you to share my treasure."

She tried to get away, but he was stronger than her.

He ripped off her pants and underwear. "And what do you give me in return?"

She whimpered. "Yoel, don't."

"Say it already!" he screamed, and slapped her again. "I want you." Now he was trying to enter her. "Inside me."

"Stop it!" she yelled.

But Yoel wouldn't listen. He put a sweaty palm over her mouth and kept going.

She was gripped with horror. What would she do with all the anger he was going to release inside of her? She moved her hand around and found the bottle of Campari by the bed. She grabbed it and slammed it into Yoel's head. It made a terrible crashing sound.

And then another.

The bottle didn't break, but Yoel collapsed. She pulled herself from beneath him and he slipped to the floor. She got dressed and stared at him from above. His eyes were slightly open, his lips slightly parted. Nothing special. She leaned down and zipped his pants. Yoel didn't move. Then she smoothed the bedspread. She went over to the shopping cart and pulled out the towel she'd shoved in there only moments earlier. She wiped the blood from the floor. Not a lot of blood, but enough to get noticed. She smoothed her clothes and hair and sipped the pink remains from the bottom of the glass. She put the towel and the empty glass in her cart, grabbed the briefcase, and left.

ALLERGIES

BY Etgar Keret

Florentin

The dog was actually my idea. We were on our way back from the gynecologist's office. Rakefet was crying, and the cab driver, who was, for once, nice, dropped us off on the corner of Arlozorov Street, because Ibn Gabirol Street was closed for a demonstration. We started walking home. The street was crowded and humid and people around us shouted into loudspeakers. A giant scarecrow with the treasury minister's face was planted on a traffic island. People were stacking bills around it. Right when we walked past, someone set fire to the bills and the scarecrow began burning.

"I don't want us to adopt," Rakefet said. "It's hard enough to raise a child of your own. I don't want someone else's." She paused. Around us people were screaming, but she only looked at me, waiting for my answer.

I didn't know what to tell her. I didn't really have a say in the matter, and even if I had, this wouldn't have been the time to give it. I could see how upset she was. "Why don't we go buy a dog tomorrow?" I finally said, just to say something.

The scarecrow was glowing bright red now. I could hear a police or television chopper circling above us.

"We won't buy," Rakefet shouted over the noise. "We'll get a dog. There are plenty of stray dogs who need a home."

And that's how we got Seffi.

We picked Seffi up at the Tel Aviv SPCA. He wasn't a

puppy, but hadn't finished growing yet. The caretaker said he'd been abused and that nobody wanted him. I tried to find out why, because he was actually a handsome dog, looked like a purebred, but Rakefet didn't really care. When we came up to him he flinched like we were going to hurt him. He trembled and howled the whole way home.

But Seffi quickly got used to us. He loved us, and he cried whenever one of us left the apartment. If both of us left at the same time he barked like mad and scratched the door. The first time it happened we decided to wait downstairs until he stopped, but he never did. After a few attempts we just never left him alone. Rakefet mainly worked from home anyway, so it wasn't too complicated.

As much as Seffi liked us, he hated everybody else, especially children. After he bit the neighbor's daughter, we always had him wear a leash and a muzzle. The neighbor made a big scene, wrote letters to city hall, and called our landlord, who didn't even know we had gotten a dog. We received a letter from his lawyer, demanding we move out of the apartment immediately.

It was hard to find another place in our neighborhood, especially one that accepted dogs. So we moved a little south. We found a place on Yona HaNavi Street. A very large but very dark apartment. Seffi liked it. He couldn't stand the light, and now he had a bigger space to run around in. It was funny. Rakefet and I sat on the sofa and talked or watched television and he ran around us in circles for hours, never getting tired. "If he were a kid we'd have given him Ritalin ages ago," I once said. I was only joking, but Rakefet answered seriously, saying that we wouldn't have, because Ritalin wasn't invented for kids, but for lazy parents who couldn't handle their children's energy.

In the meantime, Seffi developed a strange allergy. He got

a scary red rash all over his body. The vet said he was probably allergic to dog food and suggested we give him fresh meat instead. I asked if the rash could have something to do with the missile attack on Tel Aviv, because although Seffi had no reaction to the actual explosions, he was very nervous when the siren sounded, and the rash only broke out after that first alarm. But the vet insisted that the siren had nothing to do with it, and asked again that we give him fresh meat, but only beef, since chicken would be bad for him.

Seffi liked the beef and the rash disappeared. But he soon began reacting violently toward anyone who came to the apartment. After he bit the supermarket delivery guy we decided not to have people over anymore. We were very lucky with the delivery guy. Seffi tore his bicep. The guy didn't want to go to the hospital because he was an illegal Eritrean refugee. Rakefet cleaned and dressed his wound and I gave him a thousand shekels in 200-shekel notes and apologized. He tried to smile, said in a heavy accent that he'd be fine, and limped out the door.

Three months later the rash came back. The vet said Seffi's body had grown used to the new food and that we had to make a change again. We tried feeding him pork, but he couldn't digest it. The vet recommended camel meat and gave us the number of a bedouin who sold it. The bedouin was suspicious, because he didn't have ministry of health permits to sell the meat. He'd make appointments with me on different intersections, always a couple of hours' drive south. I paid him cash and he'd fill my icebox with meat. Seffi loved it. When I cooked the meat he stood in the kitchen and barked pleadingly at the pot. His barks sounded almost human, like a mother trying to convince her little boy to get off the tree he was climbing. It cracked us up.

One day when I took Seffi out for a walk, he attacked the old Russian man from the second floor. He didn't bite him, because he had his muzzle on, but he did jump up on him and pushed him down on his back. The old man received a serious blow to the head and had to be taken to the hospital. He was unconscious when the ambulance arrived. Rakefet told the paramedic he'd stumbled. We became really depressed, knowing that when he regained consciousness we'd have to move again. Actually, I was depressed. Rakefet was mainly worried that Seffi would be taken away from us and put down. I tried telling her maybe that was the right thing to do. He was a good dog, but a dangerous one. When I said it Rakefet started crying and turned cold. She wouldn't let me touch her. Then she said I was only saying that because I wanted to get rid of the dog, because he was giving us a hard time with his special food, and not being able to have people over or leave him home alone, and that she was disappointed, because she thought I was stronger, less selfish than that.

She wouldn't sleep with me for weeks afterward, speaking to me only when she had to. I tried telling her that it had nothing to do with selfishness. I'd happily endure all the difficulties if I thought the situation could be solved, but Seffi was just too strong and scared, and no matter how closely we watched him, he'd continue hurting people. Rakefet asked if I'd have our child put down too. And when I said that Seffi wasn't a child, he was a dog, and that she had to accept that, it just ended in another fight. She cried in the bedroom. Seffi went over and started howling too, and I could do nothing but apologize. Not that it helped.

A month later, the Russian man's son came over and started asking questions. His father had died in the hospital. Not from the blow to the head, but from an infection he caught there.

The guy wanted details on what happened, because he was suing social security. He said there were deep animal scratches on his body, but the emergency services' report said his father had just stumbled. He wanted to know if there was anything we hadn't told the paramedics.

We didn't let him in the apartment, but as we spoke in the stairwell Seffi began barking and the guy asked questions about the dog and wanted to see him. We told him he couldn't come in, that the dog was new, we only got him ten days ago, long after his father had the fall. He insisted on seeing him anyway, and when we refused again he threatened to come back with the police.

That very night we packed up our things and went to stay with Rakefet's parents for a few days. I met some realtors and found an apartment in the Florentin neighborhood. It was small and noisy, but the landlord didn't mind the dog. Rakefet and I went back to sleeping together. She was still a bit cold, but the drama with the Russian's son brought us closer together again. She also saw that I was standing up for Seffi, and that softened her.

Then Seffi's rash returned again.

Our old vet was no longer available. It turned out he was a high-up in the military and had been killed on reserve duty, carrying out a retaliation attack in Syria. Rakefet refused to try to find a new vet, scared he would tell us to put Seffi down. We didn't want to keep giving him camel meat. We tried fish and meat substitutes instead, but he wouldn't touch anything, and after he didn't eat for two days Rakefet said we had to find a different kind of meat, before he starved to death.

She crushed some sleeping pills her mother had given her a long time ago, when we flew to New York for our honeymoon, and put them in a bowl of milk. From our balcony we saw some cats in the yard approach the bowl and sniff the milk. None of them touched it, except for one thin, red-haired cat. Rakefet told me to go downstairs and follow it, but the cat wasn't going anywhere. It lay down by the bowl. It didn't even move when I approached it. It looked at me with almost human eyes, giving me a sad but accepting expression, like he knew just what was going to happen and simply had to accept it, because the world was shit. When it fell asleep I picked it up, but couldn't take it upstairs. I felt it breathing in my arms, and I couldn't do it. I sat on the steps, crying. A few minutes later I felt a hand on my shoulder. It was Rakefet. I never even heard her coming down the stairs. "Leave it," she told me. "Leave the cat here and come upstairs. We'll find another way."

We decided to try pigeons. On Washington Avenue, right by our house, there were a ton of fat pigeons that the old neighborhood residents liked to feed. We searched the Internet for ways to hunt them. There were plenty of methods, but they all seemed pretty complicated. Finally, I bought a professional marble-shooting slingshot at a military equipment store in the Central Bus Station. After a few days of studying and practicing, I was quite the marksman. When Seffi ate one pigeon and seemed to respond well, Rakefet and I drank two bottles of wine and fucked all night long. Happy fucking. We felt very, very good, and we felt that we'd earned all that goodness, fair and square.

Rakefet suggested I hunt the pigeons at dawn, when the streets were empty, to avoid any eyewitnesses. Ever since then, twice a week I set the alarm for four thirty a.m., head out while the whole street is still asleep, scatter bread crumbs, and hide in the bushes. I'm addicted to these hours, to the gentle cold air of the morning—not freezing cold, but cold enough to wake you up. I lie in the bushes, listening to music on my earphones. It's my quality time. All alone, just me, my thoughts, my music, and occasionally a pigeon in my sights. First I only hunted two or three at a time, but now I'm starting to get more. It's fun, coming home to my wife with my game, like some sort of caveman. It's really improving our relationship, or at least helping us fix whatever broke back then, when Seffi jumped on the old man.

When we Googled hunting methods, Rakefet found a great French pigeon recipe: pigeons in wine, stuffed with rice. It's the most delicious thing in the world, and Seffi loves it when we eat the same food as him. Sometimes, just for kicks, I sit next to him on the kitchen floor and we both howl at Rakefet as she cooks our pigeons.

"Get up," she always says, laughing. "Get up, or I'll think I married a dog."

But I tilt my head back, close my eyes, and keep howling, and I only stop when Seffi comes closer and lovingly licks my face.

CENTER

BY Assaf Gavron

Dizengoff Center

We sat inside the villa, sipping black coffee and staring out the window: it never stopped raining. The sky was low, the garden wet and green. Piles of floor tiles, sacks of cement, and tubs of paint crowded beneath a plastic sheet that blew in the wind by the pool. I was about to ask Srulik if he thought we could head home after we finished our coffee—we weren't going to get any work done in this rain—when an unfamiliar ringtone sounded. It wasn't my phone or Srulik's, and it wasn't the villa's landline either. I shot Srulik a quick look and saw deep grooves between his large eyebrows. "It's the other phone," he said. "Get it from the jacket by the door."

The other phone? What phone? I wondered, putting down the small glass and walking toward the coat rack by the front door. I found the phone ringing in the coat pocket and hurried back, handing it to the boss.

"Hello?" The wrinkles grew deeper. "Yes," he said into the phone. "Yes, this is actually a good time. I just had a cancellation because of the rain. Hold on, I'm writing it down." He covered the mouthpiece and whispered to me, "Write." He removed his hand and said, "Yes, go on." On the edge of an old *Haaretz* I wrote in pencil: *Dizengoff Center. Apartment tower. 11th floor. Monbaz.* "We'll be there in fifteen minutes, man." He hung up, turned to me, and said, "Let's go, doctor, we have a job."

We were silent the first few minutes of the drive from the northern Tzahala neighborhood to Dizengoff. The rain on the roof of the car and the monotonous dance of the windshield wipers silenced a conversation the radio announcer was having with a meteorologist. Finally, stopped at a red light, without even the moving landscape to break the silence, I asked Srulik, "What's the story with that other phone?"

His fingers drummed on the steering wheel through his woolen gloves. He whistled and looked at me sideways. Then he faced forward again and said, "It used to be Cindy's phone. When we broke up and she went back to Canada, I was left with it."

Strange, I thought. Why walk around with an ex-wife's phone? But before I even had a chance to ask, Srulik said, "I know what you're thinking. You're thinking, why would the person calling on that phone talk to me about a job and not ask to speak with Cindy?"

"Um . . ."

"I know, I know that's what you were thinking. Come on, I'm always two steps ahead. So it's like this: One day I got a call from the yellow pages, on my normal phone, not this one. They offered to print an ad for the renovation business. They gave me a good rate, explained the target audience, *ana aref*, that kind of stuff. Then they said, two for one. Meaning, I can print a second ad and only pay for one . . . I still know what you must be thinking."

I wasn't thinking anything.

"You're thinking, what would I need two ads for? The renovation ad will go on the renovation page—what's the other one for? And then the lady on the phone asks me, *Don't you have anything else to advertise?* I thought about it. I had another line, another phone, why not advertise something else?

So I thought, there's this dream I've had for years, of opening an investigation firm. Why not? What's the worst thing that could happen? I have a phone. I have an ad in the yellow pages. I have a brain that thinks two steps ahead. Someone calls, I'll try to help them. Seemed interesting, a bit of a change of pace."

I stared at him blankly. I didn't know what to say. A detective? Srulik? He's not even that good of a handyman.

"Don't look at me that way," Srulik said. "Renovations and investigations are very similar. What do we do? We take things apart and then we put them back together, layer after layer. Revealing and covering up. Investigating is exactly the same thing."

I said nothing. At that point we entered Ibn Gabirol Street and were about to turn right on Nordau and then left on Dizengoff. The rain seemed softer in central Tel Aviv than in the northern neighborhoods, but it didn't stop. The radio announcer read out an unending list of traffic jams all over the country. "Two questions you're asking yourself. One, if I have a private investigator's diploma. And two, what I wrote in my ad. So, one, no, I don't have a diploma. And, two: *Private investigator with diplomas and recommendations. One hundred percent service. One hundred percent reliability. One hundred percent responsibility. Seventeen years of experience.* That's what the lady recommended I write. And she said, *Don't call it AAA Private Investigations or anything like that. People know you only do that to be the first on the list.* So I called it Srulik Lasry, Special Investigation Services."

I didn't know what to say. I've been doing renovations with Srulik for six months and I've never heard about this. Not about the ad, not about the investigations. I've never even heard that other phone ring. I also couldn't figure out what my job was, and how much I'd get paid.

"I know exactly what's going through your mind," Srulik said as we drove below Dizengoff Square, and for seven sudden seconds the rain stopped banging on the roof of the car. "You're wondering if I'd gotten any investigation work since posting the ad. So let's just say . . . let's say not really. Nothing serious. I found a lost cat once for a student." He swallowed and slid the truck down the steep concrete ramp into the guts of the Dizengoff Center parking lot.

"Come on," he added as he pressed the button to lock the car, which bade us farewell with beeps and blinking lights, "let's go see what this Monbaz guy has for us."

Apartment Tower, 11th Floor

The city looked wet and dark through the windows in Monbaz's apartment, and Dizengoff Street resembled a tired bus to the Bnei Brak neighborhood. Monbaz served us espressos and lit a thin cigar. He wore rimless glasses and shiny leather shoes.

We sat in a spacious living room. A giant flat screen hovered black before us. A fuzzy white carpet caressed our socks from below. We were asked to take off our muddy work boots when we came in. After a bit of small talk about the weather and the view and the name Monbaz, which signifies descendants of Queen Helena of Adiabene, Srulik leaned back and asked, "How can we help you?"

Something flickered in Monbaz's eyes as he observed Srulik. "I want you to find out what happened to a guy who disappeared a few days ago."

"Name?" asked Srulik.

"Lior Posen."

"Relationship?"

"Partner. Business partner."

"When was he last seen?"

I was surprised by Srulik. He asked his questions in a level, professional tone. If I hadn't known him, I'd have thought he was a real detective.

"I don't know. I last saw him on Friday, around two p.m."

Srulik checked his cell phone. "Three days ago," he said.

I cleared my throat. "Should I be writing this down?"

"No, no," Monbaz and Srulik said in unison. They looked at each other and chuckled. Then their expressions turned serious again.

"Where did you see him?"

"In the pool on the roof of this building."

"Does he live here too?"

"No. But he goes to the gym here."

"Why do you think he disappeared?"

"He isn't answering his phone or returning calls. He isn't answering e-mails. He never came home on Friday. He's married and he has a child."

"Has his wife called the police?"

"I asked her to keep the police out of this. I told her we'd find him."

Srulik turned away from Monbaz's eyes for the first time and fixed his gaze on the ceiling light. He reached over to pick up his coffee cup. He sipped and put the cup down, then relaxed his nervous posture. "So what's the story, Monbaz?" he finally asked.

Monbaz hesitated. I now noticed he was wearing a thick gray sweater, dark slacks, and socks with a diamond pattern. He seemed put together. So did his place. He said, "I need you to give me your word that this stays between us. I don't want the police getting involved. I didn't contact them for a reason, and it's the same reason I didn't call a well-known investigation firm. I opened the yellow pages and saw your ad. I don't want anyone knowing I contacted you." It was clear Srulik had passed some sort of test. He got the job.

"You have our word," Srulik said.

"Posen and I are partners in a start-up company. We got an offer from a large American firm. They want to buy us out. $163.5 million dollars. We need to give them our answer by the end of the year, which is four days from now, on Friday. Because of expenses and tax issues, if we miss the end of the year, the deal is in jeopardy. Even if it doesn't fall through, the price would drop significantly—"

"Google?" Srulik intervened.

"No, not Google."

"Yahoo?"

Monbaz squirmed in his seat and adjusted his glasses. "That doesn't matter right now," he said. "Anyway, our partner contract defines that the decision to sell must be unanimous. I'm for it. So is another partner, Sharon Reich. Posen was against it, and now he's gone."

"How many partners own the firm?" Srulik glanced at me, still reflecting the height of professionalism.

"Three."

"And you suspect Sharon."

"Did I say that?"

"Have you spoken to Sharon since Friday?"

"Of course I have."

Srulik turned to me again, then put two fingers to his lips and blew. "Where are your offices?"

Monbaz pointed out the window at the building next door. "There, the twenty-fourth floor. I can see from here which rooms still have the light on at night." He smiled.

"What do you do?"

Monbaz got up and asked, "Anyone want a soda? Another coffee?"

We both shook our heads.

He walked to the kitchen that opened into the living room, and while he poured he said, "Something cool. An application that helps you find misplaced things. You take a picture of something with your cell phone. Say your keys, or your wallet, and the app remembers the exact coordinates. Then, when you search for it, the app tells you where it is. It's going to be a hit."

Srulik half smiled. He seemed impressed. Then he frowned slightly. "Why did Lior Posen object to the sale?"

Queen Helena's descendant dropped his arms to his sides and said, "He thought we could sell it for more money within a year. He didn't want us to get too excited."

Apartment Tower, Swimming Pool

It was only early afternoon, but the light outside reminded me of twilight. The rain had stopped, leaving its dark and heavy clouds as backup. Two old men and a young woman swam in the pool on the roof, and on the floor beneath, at the gym, a handful of people pumped the pedals of exercise bikes.

We walked around the men's dressing room. Srulik lowered his big black mane of hair and sniffed the air around the sinks, as if trying to capture remnants of the cologne Lior Posen had sprayed himself with before disappearing three days earlier. Then he saw a scale in the corner and mounted it. "Wow, ninety-eight kilos, I can't believe it." He looked crestfallen. He went to the rows of lockers that covered one of the walls and fluttered his fingers over them. He stopped at locker 99. "Look," he said. A transparent sticker was attached to the locker, printed with Lior's name. I pointed out that the adjacent locker had Monbaz's name. "Nice work, doctor!" He smiled at me. He scanned the ceiling and walls. "No cameras. Let's get our tools from the car."

Twelve minutes later, Srulik stood in front of the broken-into locker. "Look at this. Condoms, a twelve-pack. Only . . . seven left. Deodorant, cologne, bodywash, goggles, jogging pants. And in Monbaz's locker . . ." He fiddled with the lock. "Even more boring. Come on, let's get out of here."

Office Tower, 24th Floor

It continued raining all night, and the weather report said it was going to keep going all week. Roads became rivers, gigantic puddles pooled at intersections. Srulik said he told the client in Tzahala that we'd return next week, when it dried out. We wouldn't be working on her pool renovations this week. He picked me up and we drove back to Dizengoff Center, for a company meeting.

On the way, Srulik said, "You must be asking yourself, why would a married man keep a pack of condoms in his gym locker? And you're right to be asking that. At this meeting, take a good look at the women. But I'll do you one better, doctor. That Monbaz guy, something about him doesn't add up. He said nothing about the lockers. When I asked for Posen's wife's number, he squirmed. Something stinks here."

I didn't know what to say. I hadn't noticed any of that.

"I know exactly what you're thinking," Srulik said. "You're thinking, if he's the one who made Posen disappear—because Monbaz wants to sell the company by the end of the week and Posen objected—why would he book a PI? And that question, doctor, is one I can't answer just yet."

The windshield wipers swooshed from side to side, moving water from the center of the glass to its edges. A swarm of red lights stood ahead of us in the lane. Gusty winds shook traffic lights and trees.

"Look at that," Srulik said, but I couldn't tell what he was motioning to. "Now, don't think I just stopped there. I did call Posen's wife. I got her number. I told her I was looking into her husband's disappearance on behalf of the company, that the investigation was in good hands, and that, due to the sensitivity of the business deal, we prefer not to involve the police at this point. She confirmed what Monbaz said about the time of disappearance."

The center appeared before us like goalposts: two towers on opposite sides of the street, and the bridges connecting them on top. We parked in the underground lot and went up to the company offices. The view was more impressive than the one from Monbaz's apartment. We could see the entire shoreline from the conference room. White foam scratched the surface of the wild gray sea.

Eighteen people were convened around a large table. Monbaz introduced Srulik and me. I watched the women, as Srulik instructed. There was one well-kept blonde who sat by Monbaz at the head of the table and spoke. She was sexy. Another woman, very beautiful, with pale skin and smooth black hair, whispered to a curly haired man next to her who, for some reason, was wearing sunglasses on his forehead. The third looked like a lesbian—cropped hair, square forehead, brown eyes, broad shoulders, and big breasts. In the middle of the meeting someone came in and said, "Sorry, I need Olga," and the lesbian got up and went with him. After that everybody started chattering and Monbaz scolded the pretty woman with the black hair: "Tamar! Quiet. I want to continue." So I knew two names now. Was one of them Lior Posen's lover?

The one who stretched those five missing condoms over him? Five minutes later, Olga came back.

I turned to Srulik, but he was concentrating on the meeting. I didn't know how he was going to save himself from embarrassment and hide the fact that he was a complete novice. On the other hand, sitting at the offices of a high-tech company with a view of the sea was better than doing renovation work in the rain. I hoped the missing person would just reappear and solve all of our problems.

Monbaz spoke through most of the meeting, mainly discussing the sale. I waited for him to mention Posen, and when he did, with a nervous cough, the room turned silent. "The truth is, right now the sale is in jeopardy, because Lior isn't answering calls and hasn't been seen by anyone since Friday."

I looked carefully at the women, but saw no visible reactions.

"We hoped he would turn up somewhere, but there are only three days before the year ends, and this is becoming an issue. Have any of you seen him or heard from him since Friday?" He peered around the room and I tried to notice if he was lingering on anyone in particular. From the corner of my eye I saw Srulik examining everyone as well.

"What does that mean, the sale is in jeopardy?" a firm-bodied bald man asked in a deep voice. "If he doesn't show up for the shareholder vote he loses his voting rights, no? And then the call is yours and Sharon's to make, right?"

"No, Vladi," said Monbaz. "Our lawyers discussed this at length yesterday. To approve the sale, all three shareholders, Sharon, Lior, and I, have to vote unanimously. If one of us objects, for whatever reason, the sale won't be approved."

A murmur began around the table. Beautiful, pale Tamar shot Vladi a quick look.

"Unless . . . quiet . . . unless," Monbaz continued, "something happens to one of the shareholders. Meaning, some-thing that hasn't . . . something—"

"Unless he's dead," the blonde sitting next to him inter-vened. "God forbid. But if we find that he's . . . I mean, as long as he's missing, as long as there's no unequivocal evidence—" She moved her eyes over everyone around the table. "We can't close the deal."

Monbaz nodded along.

From this point on, the atmosphere in the room was tu-multuous. A few minutes later, Monbaz brought the meeting to a close and we joined him in his office. The blonde came in with us.

"You were a little harsh," Monbaz told her.

"You know he isn't dead," she said. "But what I said is true, it's what the lawyers said."

"How do you know he isn't dead?"

"He made himself disappear, it's pretty obvious. This way he doesn't have to make a decision."

"But what difference does it make? It would have been the same had he stayed and objected. The sale wouldn't have gone through. Why disappear?"

"You'll see. A couple days into the new year he'll turn up with some excuse. He doesn't have the balls to stand up to us and all the employees and pull the rug out from under us. Son of a bitch." Bitter wrinkles appeared in the corners of her eyes. She wore a cream-colored silk blouse and a skirt, beneath which peeked dark panty hose. Her blond hair was shoulder length and her pleasant scent filled the office. She was tall. A woman who knew she was attractive. "Monbaz, are you going to introduce me to our guests?"

He introduced us and then said, "This is Sharon Reich, my partner."

When she shook my hand her collar moved and I saw a tattoo, some Latin phrase, swirling down her shoulder toward her chest. As she turned back to Monbaz I saw another one, a small turtle, on her neck. She said she had to run out to a meeting, added, "I hope you find out where that bastard is hiding," and left. The phone on Monbaz's desk rang.

Srulik came up to me and was about to say something when Monbaz spoke into the phone: "What? Who is this? Where? Hello?"

Elephant Bridge, Shopping Center, 3rd Floor

The large plastic-and-fiberglass elephant opened its giant mouth and spit out sliding children. Monbaz led us, on his face a bewildered expression he hadn't been able to hide since receiving that phone call. In the elevator, he said the voice on the line was distorted and never identified itself. "He said, *You have a memento from Lior Posen in the dumpster near the elephant.*"

"What's the dumpster near the elephant?" Srulik asked.

"It's a dumpster for electronic waste. We use it sometimes for screens, cables, that kind of stuff. Here it is."

We approached carefully. Among some Styrofoam, a toaster oven, and a DVD player, a thick red sheet of plastic emerged.

Srulik was the first one to speak: "It's a leg."

Monbaz said, "Don't touch it."

I stood there, staring. I could see a toe, the outline of a foot, an ankle, and a muscular, manly calf. The rest was covered by garbage. The leg was wrapped in a thick layer of polyethylene, the insides of the wrapping smeared with blood. I pushed down the urge to vomit.

Monbaz said, "If I take this out, I have to call the police.

I'm going up to the office. Check this out, take pictures, and then put it back. Then come up to the office and we'll consider our next step."

Srulik told me, "Go to the pharmacy and buy a pack of sterile plastic gloves. Ask them to put it in the largest bag they have. On your way, check for footsteps, blood trails, anything."

When I returned he put on a pair of gloves, told me to keep watch, and reached in for the leg. I stood with my back to him, listening to the whispers of the Styrofoam and to Srulik's heavy breathing by my ear. He cursed quietly, but a moment later whispered, "Let's go," removed the gloves, and began walking. The pharmacy bag was in his hand. "Only a leg," he whispered, "not an entire body." He walked down the spiral ramp strewn with stores, bypassing baby strollers, goth girls, and European-looking grandmas absorbed in cellular conversations.

Parking Lot, Level -2

Behind a concrete pole, in a deserted corner of the parking lot, Srulik donned another pair of gloves, removed the limb from the polyethylene, and shone a flashlight on it: a man's leg, dismembered below the knee with a sharp object. Clean work. The leg was quite hairy and a Latin phrase was tattooed vertically along the shin bone. Srulik took pictures of the leg from several angles, repacked it, and put it back in the bag. We dropped the leg in the electronic-waste dumpster and went back to Monbaz's office.

Office Tower, 24th Floor

Sharon Reich's shock seemed authentic to me. We stood in her office, the door closed behind us, Srulik's cell phone presenting the pictures of the leg on her desk, her eyes red and puffy, her head shaking from side to side. Monbaz said nothing. In fact, no one had said anything since Monbaz saw the pictures in his office, got up and told us to follow him, went into his partner's office, and placed the phone on her desk.

"Is he dead?" she finally asked.

"Who knows?" said Srulik. "Are you sure it's his leg?"

She responded by pulling her sexy silk blouse off her shoulder. A red patterned bra strap adorned the shoulder, and beside it was a tattoo like the one in the photo: a phrase made up of Latin letters.

"What does it mean?"

"It's a quote from Nietzsche. One half of the quote is written on his skin, and the other on mine. The full phrase is: *There is always some madness in love. But there is also always some reason in madness.*"

"Yours is longer," I said. Srulik looked at me, but Monbaz and Sharon didn't react. I realized those were the first words out of my mouth all day. I took a step back.

"What does it mean?" Srulik asked again.

Sharon broke into tears.

Monbaz said, "Stay here and take it easy. I'll get you a Valium and some tissues. I'll talk to these guys in my office and we'll decide what to do."

Once the door to Monbaz's office closed behind us, Srulik took two assertive steps toward him and said, "Monbaz, if you want us to work together, you have to be honest with me. What we did with the leg is against the law. We should have reported it to the police. This will cost you."

"You'll get paid, we had a deal—"

"All right, never mind that. But what's the story? What's with the tattoos? Why did she call him a son of a bitch? If you want our help, you have to tell us everything you know."

"Lior and Sharon used to be a couple, but that was a long time ago. I don't think it has anything to do with what's going on. That's why I didn't mention it. They were together years ago. Now he's married, and has a child—"

"Yes, I know. And Sharon? Is she married?"

"No."

"Was she angry with him after the breakup?"

"Maybe, I'm not sure. I didn't know them well enough—"

"And that phrase, in the tattoo, *the madness in love, the reason in madness.* What's the story there? Did they have something special?"

"I don't know. Anybody who falls in love thinks they're crazy, that they have something special, don't they? Srulik, I really don't think that's the right direction."

"Okay." Srulik walked over to the window and gazed out at the sea. "Let's put a pin in that. I want you to tell me now who exactly is going to make a profit from selling the company. Meaning, who will make a profit once Lior Posen's body is found and the sale can be closed."

"Everybody." Monbaz seemed calmer. Discussing his two partners' relationship clearly made him nervous.

"How much?"

"It varies. The partners would make more than ten million dollars each. And there's a group of about ten veteran employees who would make between half a million and two million, depending on experience and position."

Srulik whistled and looked at me. "You hear that, doctor? We're in the wrong profession." He turned back to Monbaz. "I want a full list of employees and the amounts they would make from this deal, and anyone else who might cut a profit. Doctor, go down to the center and walk around. Look for places the body might be hidden. Parking lots, stores, alleys,

I don't know. Then come back up and get a computer from Monbaz and read all you can about the center. Go on, get out of here. Come on, Monbaz, let's make that list."

The Electric Cave, Level -2

The huge underground space in the depths of Dizengoff Center echoed Srulik's loud voice. Trucks entered, loaded garbage, and left. Fruit bats hung silently off the ceiling. The cold penetrated our bones. "I know what you were thinking, doctor," he said, rubbing his gloved hands. "You were thinking, what's that Srulik doing sending me on online searches? What's he doing sending me to look for a body in the center? But I had to show Monbaz we're pros, you see? Investigations are like renovations: you have to prove you know what you're doing. That's half the work."

I nodded glumly, though I'd already forgotten about his unnecessary tasks from the previous day. "This electric cave used to be a dance club or something," I said.

"Let's wait here for a while. I asked Monbaz to tell the employees about Lior Posen's leg at the meeting, but to explain that it doesn't prove he's dead, and that as long as he isn't dead, the sale can't go through. There are lots of people in this company who would make millions from this sale. You get it, doctor? It would take care of them for life. What do they care about a boss they didn't even like?"

"What about the woman? The tattoos? The fact that he dumped her?"

"Unrelated. The way she talked about him, she couldn't have killed him. But Posen was fucking somebody else with those condoms. I think it's someone else from the company. Maybe if we find her she can help us, but who knows? I don't see a motive for murder right now."

My head was spinning. It was all very theoretical and cyclical and there was no unequivocal evidence, and we were getting nowhere. "So what are you saying, really?" I finally asked. "Do you have any idea where he might be?"

Srulik said nothing for a few moments, dipping the tip of his shoe in a small puddle. "No," he finally answered. "Let's see if Monbaz's bait gets anything. Whoever cut his leg off must not be too sophisticated. It didn't actually change anything. We'll see, there are two days left before the sale deadline."

Cafe Neto, Shopping Center, Level 2

The beeping of an incoming message made me jump in the middle of eating my croissant. Srulik furrowed his brow at the screen. "Monbaz got another phone call. There's another 'surprise' in the large trash bins behind the center, on Bugrashov Street."

This time it was a hand.

Sharon Reich recognized the ring on the finger as belonging to Lior Posen.

Srulik said, "Is he crazy? This still doesn't prove death." He went to buy a fingerprint kit and checked the fingers on the dismembered hand and the mouse on Lior Posen's computer—there was a match.

Monbaz, looking more scared than ever, asked, "Shouldn't we call the police now? What am I going to tell his wife?"

Srulik said, "Let me try one or two more ideas."

Before we returned the arm to the trash bin, he cut a square off the polyethylene cover and told me, "Doctor, check out stationary stores or something like that, stores where you could buy this kind of thing. And ask Sharon where they got their matching tattoos."

Psycho Tattoos, Shopping Center, Level 2

Sharon said they'd gotten them at one of the stores in the center. "What difference does it make?" she asked.

I didn't know what to say. Really, what difference *did* it make? "We're checking all possible angles," I said.

As I was leaving her office, she said, "I know he fucked Tamar. Obviously it made me crazy, of course it did. First he leaves me, then he marries some bimbo, and then he goes and fucks around with someone else from the company?"

I turned around, my hand still on the doorknob. She peered out the window. She didn't have a view of the sea, but rather of the apartment tower where Monbaz lived. Ugly roofs, covered in puddles, flecked the landscape with white squares.

"Like a threefold betrayal," she said, not waiting for me to respond. "Every time he turned the screw just a little more." She stared at me intensely. "But that's no reason to kill him. The fact is, we continued to work together after he left me, right? You think I would do a thing like that?"

I shook my head quickly. "No," I said. I didn't know what else to say, so I left the room.

Tribal Tattoos and Piercing is located in a small hallway that forks by Agvania Pizza. It's one of the emptiest, sleaziest hallways in the center, a few feet yet light-years away from the shiny ground floor, filled with coffee shops and appliance stores. Planet Tattoos and Psycho Tattoos are right next door to Tribal Tattoos. I walked past all those stores but didn't go in. What for? At the end of the hallway was a stationary and art supply store called My Art.

I showed the clerk the polyethylene.

"Yes," she said. "We have that. You need some?"

"No." I shook my head.

"Then why do you ask?"

"Just checking."

She had a bleached streak in her hair and wore too much makeup. She looked at me with a quizzical half-smile.

I asked, "Did anyone buy one of these in the past few days?"

She kept her quizzical half-smile on, but then something flickered in her eyes and she asked quietly, "You want me to take a look at the receipts and check who bought this recently?"

I said yes, and she flipped through the invoice book and found one in the name of Olga Kozushko. She made a copy for me.

"Nice," Srulik said when I showed him the copy. "I like the way your mind works, doctor."

We questioned Tamar about Posen and she admitted to having been his lover for the past year.

We questioned Olga. She admitted to buying the polyethylene at My Art. She claimed to have used it to wrap up things in her private storage space in Bat Yam, to protect them from the unending rain.

The rain really was unending.

"Bat Yam?" Srulik asked, rubbing his eyes. "What do you think, doctor, should we go check out Olga's storage space?"

I didn't know what to say. We found lots of stuff, but we still had no idea how it was all connected to Lior Posen's dismembered limbs.

Maccabi Boxing Club, Parking Lot, Level -2

"What did you say Olga's last name was?" Srulik asked.

"Kozushko."

"Pssssh, what a name."

We were sitting inside his car in the parking lot. It was a quarter to seven in the evening. Srulik held on to the wheel with his gloved hands, but we weren't moving anywhere. It was two days before the end of the year. Monbaz and Sharon Reich were hysterical. They'd just finished yelling at us earlier. Srulik had told them everything was under control, that we were closing in on the killer, but now, all he could say was "Pssssh" about Olga's last name.

That afternoon we had questioned Tamar again. "I already told you we were together," she raised her voice at Srulik. "What happened, did that jealous bitch send you over again? Do I look like a killer? Who are you, anyway? Two losers!"

She was the closest one so far to calling our bluff.

They had twenty-four hours to approve the deal. They needed Posen—dead, alive, or missing a couple of limbs, it didn't matter.

The lights of a moving car shone over us in the parking lot. "Do you believe Sharon? Maybe it really was her. Maybe it was revenge."

"That doesn't make sense," said Srulik. "It goes against her current interest. If it was important for her to kill him because he betrayed her three times, she could have waited another week and done it as a millionaire."

"And Tamar?"

He closed his eyes and rubbed them again. He was insulted by her attitude. We had done a background check on her. There was a group of friends she had lunch with, there was her department, Quality Assurance. But it brought us nowhere.

That morning we visited Olga's storage space in Bat Yam. Nada.

Srulik's regular phone rang. He looked at the screen and answered. "Yes," he said tiredly. Then again, "Yes." Finally, after a long silence, watching a woman with grocery bags through his window and nodding quietly, he said a final "Yes," after which he hung up. "It was the pool lady. The weather report says the rain will stop tonight. It hasn't rained like this for seventeen years, she said, with the sun not even peeking out for a whole week. She wants us back at work the day after tomorrow."

I nodded and said nothing.

Srulik had been wearing a long overcoat these past two days. And a top hat. He went back to holding the steering wheel with his gloves after putting the phone back in his coat pocket. "Got any plans for tomorrow night? New Year's?"

I didn't. I didn't even like going out on the weekends, so why would I go out on New Year's Eve?

"What's with you?" he asked.

"Nothing. It sucks that we can't solve this."

"Don't take it to heart. Hey, did you hear about the tunnel that leads from the Kirya military base to Dizengoff Center? They dug it so that the bigwigs can escape into the center in case of a nuclear attack or something."

"Really? Have you seen it?"

"No, I think it's just an urban legend . . . Give me some of that stuffed cauliflower."

I passed him the tinfoil container we got at the Tunisian stall at the center's food fair. He poked his fork through it, jabbed a few pieces, and chewed them patiently. While he concentrated on the food, I glanced up and saw Vladi, the company's bald system operator. He was walking by the bare concrete wall right in front of us and then disappeared into a fold in the wall. I opened the car door and got out.

"Where're you going?" Srulik mumbled, still focused on the food.

"Follow me," I said. I heard the door and his footsteps behind me. The fold in the wall that Vladi disappeared into was the doorway to a bomb shelter. I stepped inside carefully, followed by Srulik. The hallway behind the doorway was dark and smelled of urine. We turned a corner and found ourselves in a large, lit room. On the floor was a blue mattress and there were air conditioners installed on the walls, alongside some martial arts posters. Along two of the walls there were heavy punching bags and boxing pears. A trophy cabinet was attached to the wall by the door.

"Can we help you?"

We turned around. The voice came from a near corner, where a man in a sweat suit sat on a bench. A few younger guys sat next to him, dressing up for a workout. One of them was Vladi.

"What is this place?" Srulik asked.

Vladi must have recognized his voice, and looked up with obvious alarm.

"A boxing club. Can we help you?" the older guy asked again.

"We're here to see him," Srulik said, walking toward Vladi.

But Vladi didn't have much to tell us. He practiced boxing here three evenings a week, after work. Once he'd given us this information, he put on a mouth guard, wrapped bandages around his hands, and pulled boxing gloves over them. Practice was about to begin.

We took another long look around—the punching bags, the pears, the trophy cabinet, the bare concrete walls—and headed back to the car.

Srulik drummed on the steering wheel.

Something was bothering me. Vladi's nervous face. The boxing ring. I recalled the company meeting where he discussed the sale. Something . . . something had to . . .

"Hold on a minute," I told Srulik. I got out of the car and hurried back to the boxing club.

"I have to check something," I told the trainer, who stared at me with surprise. I walked over to the punching bags and felt them. There was something about the bags in the deeper, darker, less frequently used part of the ring that had seemed strange to me before. Only when we got to the car and I tried to interpret Vladi's alarmed look did it hit me: there was an odd protrusion in the third sack. I unzipped it.

Office Tower, 24th Floor

No one was sitting in Monbaz's office. Monbaz and Sharon Reich, Tamar and Olga, Srulik and me—everyone was standing up.

Tamar told us everything. She'd made an appointment with Posen in his office for Friday afternoon, after he went to the gym. It was a regular date they had at a time when the offices were empty. They got almost completely naked and were about to have sex on the sofa in his office when Vladi walked in and hit Posen over the head. It had been Tamar's idea, and she'd recruited Vladi and Olga to the mission. It wasn't about the money, she said, not *only* about the money. He had promised to leave his wife. Not only did he not leave her, but Tamar found out that he was still fucking Sharon. So Vladi hit him over the head and Olga walked in with the plastic sheet. Vladi had the key to the boxing club and they scattered the body in three different punching bags and planned to quickly get rid of it. True, looking back it was a bad idea, because of the elbow that was bulging from one of the bags, but Vladi thought the boxers at the club wouldn't notice. On the contrary, a punching bag filled with body parts is a better simulation of an opponent than one filled with sand, rice, cloth, or whatever is normally stuffed in them.

Srulik was the one who'd gotten the confession out of Vladi. He told him Tamar had explained everything to us, so Vladi told Srulik the whole story. He said Tamar got them on board, he didn't even know how. I understood it perfectly. Tamar had such intense charisma. It wouldn't surprise me if Vladi had a little crush on her and she knew and used it. Olga had a crush on her too. She used that fact to get her carried away with the idea. Plus, let's not forget, all three of them were in for two million dollars if the sale went through. Then Srulik had Monbaz call Tamar and Olga in separately and told each of them that Vladi had spilled the beans. We cross-referenced the three testimonies and got the entire story.

Dizengoff Street

We stood outside. It was close to ten p.m. Late December. The air was cold and sharp, but the sky was completely clear. "There's the moon," said Srulik. "I haven't seen that son of a bitch in a week."

Monbaz and I gazed up.

"Did you see how our doctor solved the mystery?" Srulik asked Monbaz proudly. "I told you it would be all right, didn't I?" He seemed pleased, though Monbaz was pale and I was nauseous. "But between you and me, Monbaz," he went on, "I know exactly what you're thinking. You're asking yourself, do Srulik and the doctor know who the real brain behind the murder was, the guy those three are protecting? Isn't that so, Monbaz? Isn't it?"

Monbaz glanced up and said, "What?" He eyed Srulik nervously, then opened his mouth and began mumbling something.

"Just joking, man!" Srulik rumbled with laughter and gave

Monbaz's thin shoulder a hard slap. He chuckled loudly for a few more seconds, his large palm never leaving the company man's shoulder.

ABOUT THE CONTRIBUTORS

Danny Schück

GAI AD was born in Beersheba and at the age of seventeen, following her father's death, moved to Tel Aviv, where she still lives with her family today. She is a graduate of life sciences at Tel Aviv University. In the 1990s she lived in New York and worked with Alzheimer's patients, which was the basis for her novel *7 Harimon St.*, winner of Israel's Prime Minister's Prize. She has published four books and the latest one, *The Gauchmans*, was long-listed for the Sapir Prize.

Ronen Lalena

SHIMON ADAF was born in Sderot, Israel, in 1972 to parents of Moroccan origin. He has published three collections of poetry and six novels. His third collection of poetry, *Aviva-No*, won the Yehuda Amichai prize in 2010, and his novel *Mox Nox* won the Sapir Prize for Literature in 2013. He resides in Tel Aviv and teaches creative writing and literature at Ben Gurion University.

Goni Riskin

GON BEN ARI is an Israeli writer, screenwriter, musician, and journalist. He was born in 1985 and has published two Hebrew novels—the second of which, *The Sequoia Children*, is now being translated into the English. Ben Ari won a 2013 grant from the Jerusalem Film Fund for development of his script for the Yiddish-language Western *Der Mensch*, directed by Vania Heymann, which is now in preproduction.

SILJE BEKENG, born in 1984, is a journalist and critic for the Norwegian literary journal *Bokmagasinet Klassekampen*. She has worked as a freelance writer and critic in New York and Jerusalem, and currently lives in Oslo, Norway.

Thomas Langdon

ALEX EPSTEIN was born in St. Petersburg, Russia, in 1971 and moved to Israel when he was eight. He is the author of six story collections and three novels, which have been translated into English, Russian, and Portuguese. In 2003 he was awarded Israel's Prime Minister's Prize for Literature, and in 2007 participated in the International Writing Program at the University of Iowa. Epstein was a writer in residence at the University of Denver in 2010. He teaches creative writing in Tel Aviv.

JULIA FERMENTTO was born in 1984 and published her provocative debut novel, *Safari*, in 2011. The book garnered immediate critical and popular success, and Fermentto was hailed by *Haaretz* as "the voice of her generation." Since then she has published short stories and opinion pieces in the Israeli press. She is at work on her second novel and is studying for an MA in literature at Tel Aviv University.

ASSAF GAVRON is the author of five novels and a story collection. His fiction has been translated into ten languages and adapted to the stage and cinema. He is the winner of the Israeli Prime Minister's Creative Award for Authors, Buch für die Stadt in Germany, and Prix Courrier International in France. His latest novel is *The Hilltop*, published in the US by Scribner in fall 2014.

YARDENNE GREENSPAN (translator) earned an MFA in fiction and translation from Columbia University. In 2011 she received the American Literary Translators Association Fellowship. Her translation of *Some Day* by Shemi Zarhin was chosen for *World Literature Today's* 2013 list of notable translations. Greenspan's translations include works by Rana Werbin, Gon Ben Ari, Nahum Werbin, Vered Schnabel, Kobi Ovadia, Yirmi Pinkus, Ron Dahan, Alex Epstein, and Yaakov Shabtai.

MATAN HERMONI, born in 1969, is an Israeli novelist, translator, and literary scholar. He published a series of translations into Hebrew of Yiddish poetry and prose, among them works of Isaac Bashevis Singer and Moyshe-Leyb Halpern. His novel *Hebrew Publishing Company* was awarded the Bernstein Award, and was short-listed in 2011 for the Sapir Prize. Hermoni's latest novel, published in 2014, is *Second Time Around*.

YOAV KATZ has written screenplays for film and TV. He is a two-time winner of the *Haaretz* short story contest; won the 1999 Moses Fund literary prize for his book *Multisystem*; and is author of the best-selling novel *Home Run at Ben-Gurion Airport*. He has also translated to Hebrew novels by prominent authors such as Ernest Hemingway, Graham Greene, Ian Fleming, and others. He lives in Giv'atayim with his wife Dinat and children Mili and Tamar.

ETGAR KERET, born in Tel Aviv in 1967, is the author of five story collections, three children's books, and three graphic novels. His writing has appeared in the *New Yorker, Zoetrope*, and the *Paris Review*. His books have been translated into many languages and published in over thirty-five countries. In 2007, Keret and Shira Geffen won the Cannes Film Festival's Caméra d'Or Award for their movie *Jellyfish*. In 2010, Keret received the Chevalier Medallion of France's Ordre des Arts et des Lettres.

Yehiel Yanay

DEAKLA KEYDAR was born in New York in 1975, grew up in Israel, and currently lives in Tel Aviv. She has published a book of short stories, two best-selling novels for teens, two children's books that were translated into Greek and German, and several short stories that appeared in Israeli and foreign anthologies. Her most recent novel was published in September 2014. Keydar studied screenwriting at the Sam Spiegel Film and Television School, and gives creative writing workshops.

Jonathan Shaul

GADI TAUB is author of the best-selling novel *Allenby Street* (adapted to a prime-time drama series on Israeli TV), as well as other best-selling works of fiction and nonfiction. He is also an op-ed contributor to the Israeli and international press, including the *New York Times* and the *New Republic*. He Holds a PhD in American history from Rutgers University, and teaches at the Hebrew University of Jerusalem. His book *The Settlers* was published by Yale University Press.

Inbar Zaafrani

LAVIE TIDHAR is the World Fantasy Award–winning author of *Osama, The Violent Century* and the forthcoming *A Man Lies Dreaming*. His novella *Gorel & the Pot-Bellied God* won a British Fantasy Award, and he is also the author of the graphic novel *Adolf Hitler's I Dream of Ants* and the forthcoming comics miniseries *Adler*. He grew up on a kibbutz in Israel, and has spent much of his adult life traveling around the world.

Jim Katsis

ANTONIO UNGAR was born in Bogotá, Colombia, in 1974. He has written two short story collections, *De ciertos animales tristes* (2002) and *Trece circos y otros cuentos comunes* (2003), as well as two novels, *Las orejas del lobo* (2006) and *Tres ataúdes blancos* (2010). The latter won the prestigious Herralde Prize in 2010, and in 2011 was short-listed for the Rómulo Gallegos Prize for the best Spanish book published in 2009–2010. His books have been translated into ten languages.

Vasco Szinetar